# Walking Through Hell

# Rex Inverness

## Praise for Rex Inverness:

"Like Melville and Conrad, Inverness can graphically capture the passion and danger of the sea and bring the heart pounding experience to his readers in the safety of their living rooms."

J.P.
Novato, Ca
\*\*\*

"Inverness is a remarkable writer and storyteller. His knowledge and firsthand experience at sea pours out in every word."

S.P.
Glen Cove, NY
\*\*\*

"The first time in years the reader can experience life at sea without the fear of getting sick and drowning."

M.S.
Middletown, RI
\*\*\*

# WALKING THROUGH HELL

Other Books by Rex Inverness:

Drawn to the Sea
Torn Between Destiny and Desire
Gentleman Pirate
Two Warriors Collide
Bonnie Mae
The Cursed Seven
Lobstah
Leviathan and Death of a Liberian Seaman
Delivery Captain
Longboard Mike
Unlikely Mariner
Accidental Heir
Built to Withstand the Devil
You'll Never Get Out

## MV2

Maritime Fiction Novels
Bristol, Rhode Island
02809
www.rex-inverness.com

## Dedication

To my wife… with incredible patience and understanding she selflessly encouraged me to write this story and pursue a dream.

## Acknowledgments

Memories of the camping trip my brother, Brad, and I made through the high sierras helped set the stage and years later lots of Balashi beers, the warm Caribbean, the Aruba sunshine and good friends helped inspire this story.

# *Chapter One*

Jamie stood atop a massive granite mountain – one of many in the Sierras. His boots were rust colored from the light red dust covering them. The last four hours spent climbing to the summit he'd kicked, climbed and clawed himself up Tell's Peak. His lungs worked hard to draw the oxygen his body craved from the thin air at 8872-foot elevation. His shoulders ached from the backpack straps which felt like they'd permanently dug into his flesh and would leave scars and disfiguring indentations. He began to regret having packed so much weight.

Suddenly, he felt a numbing coldness run down his spine, he became lightheaded and fell, first to his knees then onto his butt. Feeling solidly connected to the ground gave him the stability and security he needed until the dizziness faded.

At first, he hoped the sensation he felt was the thrill of adventure and the physical manifestation of courage – but he knew better. It was abject fear. He accepted it and knew his desire to overcome his lack of self-confidence and courage was the reason he stood alone, high in the rugged mountains where he could struggle to overcome his all-to-familiar condition of living in fear – living his life as a passive observer and waiting for people or circumstances to exploit him as he helplessly accepted his destiny. "Damn that's going to change. I'll grow a set of balls and become a man or die trying," he crowed out over the ridge until he heard his echo return.

He slipped his pack off his shoulders and the discomfort of the weight subsided. He reached for his canteen and swallowed the cool water and gathered the courage to look around him. *Jamie, this was the adventure you wanted – to be in the wilderness alone and prove yourself worthy,* he thought. He remembered a story he'd recently read about a Native American boy who was sent into the wilderness by the tribe elders, and he returned to the tribe a man. Jamie smiled and thought, *Okay if he can do it so can I.*

From his vantage point, he gathered the courage to look off into the distance over the desolate valley below. Near the limits of his sight, he saw a large blue body of water, "That must be Lake Tahoe," he said.

Cautiously, he leaned forward and looked over the edge. The sheer cliff dropped vertically nearly two hundred feet. Below, a large collection of giant boulders were scattered about like massive marbles. They were in many shapes and sizes however uniform in their color and texture. Each rock had a rough surface and were pale grey with white and black specks of color.

# WALKING THROUGH HELL

He opened his topographical map clinched in his left hand. Jamie looked at it then off in the distance. First he looked East, then West, North finally South finding landmarks which he located on the paper spread out on the ground in front of him.

A moment later he fixed his position, "Confirmed, I'm at Tells Peak just as planned. No wonder it's hard to catch my breath, I'm at nearly nine thousand feet elevation. I don't think I've ever been so high in my life," he spoke to himself, and it didn't seem weird to him. It had long ago been a tool he used to calm himself when he was scared or afraid.

Satisfied with his orienteering, he remained on his butt soaking in the commanding view he had all to himself. Loon Lake and Devil's Peak were to the North. Lake Tahoe was off to the East and Robbs Peak was to the West.

The sun was still hanging high in the clear sky and the dry air was hot and carried many complimentary aromas – then there were other competing smells that fought for his attention. He recognized rag weed, pine needles, thistles and the unmistakable fragrance of the fine red powdered dirt whose odor changed distinctly with fluctuations in humidity and temperature.

Jamie's backpack was up against a rock in a sliver of shade provided by a rugged tortured tree. He leaned against it to rest for a few minutes, drank more water and ate an energy bar before continuing down into Desolation Wilderness.

He thought about the personal dare he'd committed too and his goal to push himself out of his dull comfort zone, survive the ordeal and hope to come out the other side reborn a man with genuine courage and confidence. *All I want to be is like the men I admire – not the person I've been my entire life. No longer will I be that guy who is weak, timid, afraid and relegated to the shadows where he lives unnoticed, unrecognized and exploited by others.*

He was tired and determined to remake himself and start over as an 'Alpha Male'.

# *Chapter Two*

Jamie Taylor Davis was born in 1990 and the third and final child in a dysfunctional family. His father was a simple man of marginal education who worked long hours as a laborer to provide for his family. He was married to a woman who he had nothing in common with or had any attraction for.

Jamie's mother was a hippy, free spirit. His parents met during the summer following high school. She got pregnant and shortly after they married in a union based on obligation and responsibility. Regardless, the father's frustration and misery finally drove him out the door one evening before Jamie was born. He disappeared and was never seen or heard from by the family again.

Jamie grew up in a home that was filthy, dirty, loud and temporary occupied by his mother's friends who stayed for a few hours, maybe a day or even a month or two – but it always ended the same. There was a fight, and the guy grabbed his bag and slammed the door.

Jamie had learned early to become invisible. He became very good at it and would go days on end without his sibling or mother even acknowledging him. He avoided his hippy mother who smoked pot,

11

partied and rode an emotional roller coaster of depression and anxiety.

His two sisters escaped their surroundings by marrying the first man who showed interest and their lives soon resembled the misery they'd known all so well.

By the time Jamie started school, he'd been routinely conditioned to avoid contact and confrontation. He wouldn't step forward, lead or take charge. Although his teachers tried to encourage him to engage with his classmates, he refused. Frustrated, one by one the teachers gave up and his classmates chose one of two paths – they either tuned Jamie out or simply ignored him while others chose to bully and viciously harass him.

It was a senseless pursuit, Jamie never fought back or got angry he simply curled up and waited for the punishment to stop.

His passiveness and timid behavior continued through high school. Soon after he graduated he found employment at a large manufacturing firm in the accounting department. Eight years ago he started as an Accounting Clerk and his duties and job description hadn't changed in all that time.

It wasn't that he wasn't a good employee or reliable, honest or trustworthy. He was all that but he was Jamie. He came to work on time, kept his head down and worked to exactly 11:30am, took fifteen minutes to eat at his desk and precisely at 11:45am he closed his lunch box, set it under his desk and returned to his work until 5:00pm when he closed his computer, stowed away his pens and the papers on his desk, clocked out of the building at 5:20pm and walked to the bus stop for the short ride to his simple apartment across town.

He had no friends and never dated. His only contact outside of work was his weekly visit to his mother and the occasional interactions with the local grocer and other neighborhood merchants.

This was his life day-in-and-day-out. Coworkers and neighbors tried to engage him and encourage him to join them – but he politely declined and moved away from the sense of danger, adventure, risk and uncertainty which accompanies interaction with people. He shrunk up into his shell and like a hermit crab isolated himself from the activities and life surrounding him.

Not able to understand his reluctance to engage with them one by one they gave up and as they walked away wondered, *what's wrong with that guy?*

## Chapter Three

Jamie's life was so structured and routine, his daily repetition of events were carried out with minute by minute precision. He climbed out of bed at 7:00am each morning, the bed made by 7:03am and then he moved to the bathroom. By 7:30am he'd completed shaving, showering and had combed his hair, applied deodorant and brushed his teeth.

The clothing he wore was laid out the night before and was rather plain but always clean and pressed.

He was at the bus station at 7:48am to easily catch the 7:58am bus which dropped him off a block from his office. He made his way to his desk by 8:10am – twenty minutes early. Occasionally he'd get a coffee from the employee lounge but most days he opened his computer and began work long before his coworkers were seated.

The remainder of the day was precisely predictable, except for Friday night when he stopped for a bouquet of flowers and a short bus ride to his mother's home for dinner and the weekly interrogation, "Jamie, do you have a girlfriend yet? Jamie do you even know any eligible women? You are twenty-five years old…. Hell do you even like women? Are you gay? You can tell me," she'd persist.

He'd listen to her silently eating a poorly prepared meal and he'd look pitifully at her blood shot eyes and the unmistakable aroma of marijuana and wished he hadn't come.

A week later, month after month and year after year on Friday evening he'd arrive at her home with a bouquet of flowers and ready for two hours of bad food and verbal abuse. He hated the Friday night ritual but then again it was his life. Always the punching bag and never the boxer.

*\*\**

Jamie was raised in a town outside of Sacramento called Lodi. It was a strange town with historical ties to cattle and early hydro mining operations where land locked barges and high pressure water pumps were used during the California Gold Rush to mine dry river beds by barge and millions of gallons of water used to create a pond. The barge floated in the landlocked pond and its high pressure pump tore away the dirt moving the pond in the direction the nozzle was aimed. The spoils were dredged and sifted by eager men in search of gold nuggets.

It was a poor town and Jamie was lucky to have found an office job. Most worked as laborers or in manufacturing. There was a constant sense of desperation in the town's people with little hope to get ahead or to leave the chains holding them in place. The broken down town offered little opportunity or hope for property, security or wealth for most of its occupants.

For Jamie it was just another reality which he'd resolved himself too. By the time he was a young man, he'd accepted his fate. He would be unseen, quiet, vulnerable, exploited – simply one of the unremarkable masses. The other people.

# *Chapter Four*

Jamie watched television, during a mindless cop show he saw a victim buy a gun. It caught his attention and he leaned in towards the screen and watched as the victim became confident and gathered strength and resolve to face the man who had victimized her.

Jamie felt a strange sense of confidence as he watched and began to wonder how he could kindle those feelings within himself.

Jamie began to think what it would be like to own a gun and better yet to use it to defend himself. He thought, *to be the center of attention and to command respect like the alphas do…* Then he sighed and said, "Why do you need a gun to do that?" His eyes teared and he yelled at the television, "Why are you such a coward?"

Later that evening he sat at his computer and found a gun range with rental pistols in Sacramento and arranged a time to shoot a pistol. The next morning he looked at the bus schedule and calculated the time and route he'd need to get to the range and back.

The out of character activity put him behind his schedule and he missed the 7:58am bus. The

17

driver, so accustomed to seeing Jamie at the stop waited for a minute hoping he'd show. Reluctantly he drove away with his passengers complaining in his ear. He tuned them out and wondered, *what happened to Jamie?*

Jamie caught the next bus and was at his desk before 8:00am. His coworkers noticed and among themselves whispered, "Jamie must finally have a girlfriend – thank God."

*\*\*\**

When Saturday came Jamie was up early and shattering his weekend routine, he prepared to go to the range and fire a gun for the first time in his life. He knew it was more than the experience of firing a gun, it might offer him a sense of confidence and control instead of his life of fear and victimization.

He caught the city bus and located the range. Not to disturb or annoy anyone, he patiently waited until it was 10:00am before he walked into the store.

As he stepped into the shop, he immediately knew he wasn't in a place he should be. He forced himself to take deep breaths and looked around the store. There were long guns hanging from the wall and stacked along one another in a rack behind the counter.

Inside the glass counter, two dozen pistols of different sizes and shapes were on display. Against the walls were neatly stacked boxes of ammunition. Around the room were various accessories, he surmised, were used for hunting and shooting. He was overwhelmed. He'd never seen anything like it before. He began to rethink whether he'd made a mistake coming when a burly man with a pistol on his hip and massive beard moved in front of him. In a booming voice the man said, "Can I help you?"

Jamie looked at the large man and his flight instinct screamed, *Run for your life.* But he stood still and meekly said, "Sir, I am here for my first shooting lesson."

The man's face softened and he replied, "Good, come with me to the counter." He turned and moved in a heavy ambling way like a Grizzly Bear and stopped behind the glass display case. Jamie followed him and faced the big man.

"My name is Jamie Davis and I have…" and the man looking at his counter finished the sentence, "a shooting lesson at 10:00am."

Jamie's heart sank. Once again an alpha male had run over him and he was powerless to stop it. Jamie looked down at the counter, finally holding on to the counter timidly replied, "Yes."

The gun store owner looked at Jamie and knew he'd crushed his timid customer. He softened his voice and eased his bearing and in a kind voice, "Welcome to Lodi Gun Sales and Range. May I ask you a few questions before we start to help me make your time here optimal?" The whole time he wondered why a milk toast guy like the man in front of him was in a gun store. He thought, *Maybe you're here to get a gun yourself but who cares. Your money is as good as anyone's money,* and he grinned.

"Mr. Davis, have you ever fired a gun before?"

"No," Jamie gazed up at the man.

"May I ask why you want to shoot a gun today?" He stopped and looked at Jamie and said, "Honestly, I don't care. This is one of the questions our new socialist ass-wipe government officials require we ask."

Before Jamie answered, the store owner began to type on the computer keyboard as he said, "None of your business." He smiled at Jamie with a sense of defiance and Jamie smiled back.

The gun store owner came from behind the counter satisfied he had fulfilled the state required Bullshit and said with a grin, "Jamie what would you like to try today? We have 22's, 32's, 380's, 357's, 9mm, 40 cal and 45 cal." Before Jamie could consider his response the owner continued, "I'd recommend we start small for your first time. How about a 380?"

Jamie, relieved said, "Okay, I trust your recommendation."

The burly man shook his head and lumbered like a pregnant bear back behind the display case and faced the wall, reaching for a smaller pistol hanging there with a number of hand guns similarly displayed under a neon sign that read 'Rentals'.

With his right hand he grabbed the Glock model 42 and pulled it from the display. Gripping it by the handle, he pointed the pistol toward the floor and with his left hand pulled the slide back until the chamber was visible. He looked inside to ensure the gun was empty then released the slide which slammed closed with a loud metallic sound. He pulled the trigger and Jamie heard a metallic sound when the firing pin snapped forward and the gun was silent.

Again, the gun man pulled the slide back until it locked in the open position and he set the weapon down in front to Jamie. "Jamie, this is a Glock model 42 semi-automatic 380 caliber pistol. We will be firing it today in the range." He smiled as if he was sharing a secret with a kid at Christmas.

He pushed the unloaded weapon towards Jamie and said, "Respect it but don't be afraid. Go ahead and pick it up and hold it in your hands." His eyes softened, "Go ahead pick it up."

Jamie reached for the object. It was the first time he'd held a real gun. His hands trembled and he felt the familiar chill of fear run down his spine.

"Don't be afraid, it's perfectly safe and I'll stay with you until you're comfortable and can operate it safely." The man said, "Now let me show you how to operate it. This is the slide release." He pointed to a latch on the side of the gun. "Push the release down with your thumb – keep your fingers clear of the chamber," he warned.

Jamie pushed down the release and the slide accelerated forward closing the breech and struck the barrel with a loud metallic sound. The gun jumped a little in his hands and he jerked.

"Don't be afraid," said the trainer and he continued. "Here is the safety." He pointed to a lever on the side of the pistol. "When the safety is on the gun will not fire. Release the safety and if the trigger is pulled the gun will fire."

Next Jamie was shown how to load a magazine into the gun.

Last he was shown how to aim with the aid of the gun mounted sight. The trainer, satisfied his student was ready, walked him to the range, handed him ear muffs and safety glasses, put his eye and ear protection on, stapled the target onto the cardboard backing and set the target down range at 7 yards.

"Okay Jamie here we go. Let's dry fire a few times before you shoot."

He showed him how and Jamie practiced pointing the gun at the target and squeezing the trigger, 'click', 'click'.

Again, satisfied the range officer placed a loaded magazine into the pistol and handed it to Jamie. He cautioned, "Jamie, the gun is now loaded and dangerous. Keep the muzzle pointed away from yourself and anyone else." The instructor stepped back behind Jamie and said, "Fire when ready."

Jamie aimed the gun at the target as he'd been taught and squeezed the trigger, 'BANG'. The gun sounded and kicked in recoil. Jamie jumped and the bullet missed the target completely.

The range master stifled a laugh and in an encouraging voice said, "That's okay, everyone misses the first time." He had Jamie shift his stance a little and squared his shoulders perpendicular to the target and said, "Try again."

Jamie found the target with the sight on the tip of the pistol and squeezed the trigger… and BANG. This time he didn't recoil from the sound and the bullet flew true and found the target.

His coach leaned over, "Nice shooting for a beginner."

The lesson continued and two things began to change that morning. First, Jamie began to sense, for the first time in his life, he might be good at something, and a sense of calm and self-pride filled him – he guessed it was the feeling of confidence and it felt good.

Secondly, his aim improved.

## *Chapter Five*

Jamie returned home. The new feeling of self-confidence grew quickly and he momentarily basked in a feeling he'd rarely felt before – and it felt good. "Hell it felt great," he said to himself.

The further he traveled from the ground zero of the water shed event, his feeling became weaker until it was only a memory.

He laid on his bed and forced himself to remember every aspect – large and small of the feeling – he mumbled, "That was like a drug and I could easily become addicted to it."

He rolled over on his side and wondered what his life could have been like had he'd been born with self-confidence and had learned to stand up for himself. He thought, *I could have changed so many things. I could have had a better job, made more money and even – just maybe had a girlfriend a time or two along the way.*

H punched his pillow and rolled over onto his other shoulder and thought, *Naw, and even if, I can't change the past.*

He shifted onto his back and stared at the ceiling and for a moment felt anger erupt inside him and he said to the ceiling fan, "But I can control the future." As the self-directed anger consuming him began to subside, he kept the thought alive, *I can control the future* and he felt the ever-so-faint feeling of self-confidence reemerge. He forced himself to concentrate on the faint signal trying to penetrate his brain. He struggled to feel like he'd felt at the range. He focused with all his energy until finally his mind was so exhausted, he gave up and dozed off.

As he fell asleep, he thought, over and over again, *I want, no I need the feeling of self-confidence. I want to fully enjoy the rest of my life.*

# *Chapter Six*

The following Monday, Jamie found himself going through the same routine as he prepared for work. With minute by minute precision he accomplished the tasks as he'd done for nearly his entire life.

His bus ride to the office was routine and he was at his desk, his usual time twenty minutes early. As he organized his desk his mind kept coming back to the elusive feeling he'd experienced the day before. He'd begun to call the feeling a 'Twanger'.

Jamie walked into the employee lounge to pour himself a cup of coffee. As he entered the lounge he saw his long-time co-worker, Maggie Rose Petty. In the last eight years, they'd worked together, she had hardly said a word to him – as if he were invisible.

She turned as he entered the room – this had happened many times before and she would say, "Hi," pour her coffee and walk out of the room without another word.

Jamie, expecting her to act like all the other accidental meetings in the office, nearly fell over when she turned, looked at him carefully and uncharacteristically smiled and in a soft and relaxed voice said, "Jamie, there is something different about you today. You look really nice." She blushed and slipped around him and moved to her desk.

Jamie stood there silently with his coffee mug dangling from his finger. His mind screamed, *what just happened? She never seems to see me when we're in a room together and she never has spoken to me before.* The fear of her having talked to him morphed into curiosity, then into excitement, then into something wonderful – he surmised it was a 'Twanger'.

He filled his mug and this time couldn't help himself and he walked the long way to his desk so he could pass by Maggie Rose's desk.

Her back was to him as she looked at her computer screen. He cleared his throat, "Hummm." She looked over her shoulder and swung her chair around.

"Oh hi Jamie, what's up?"

He stood there for several seconds struggling with a weak cowardly feeling which by instinct and reflex had popped up, as they had his entire life. The 'Twanger' deep inside him emerged and gradually over shadowed his fear. He smiled and said, "I just wanted to say hello and thank you for the compliment this morning."

She smiled and looked into his eyes. It took every ounce of courage he could muster to not look away – he was glad he did. She leaned back in her chair and said, "Jamie you're welcome. You really do look very nice today. I meant it."

She looked up at the clock on the wall and said, "I need to get back to work – its 8:30am and you know, as well as I do that Mr. Crabapple will be walking through the cubicles to make bed checks and will get upset if he sees us chatting."

She spun her chair around and said, "Bye, Jamie, I enjoyed our chat." Jamie backed away and before he turned towards his desk said, "Thank you Maggie Rose – you always look very nice."

He moved down the narrow walkway, ahead was his desk. He fell into his chair with a sigh. His heartbeat quickened with excitement. He smiled to himself convinced he felt another 'Twanger'.

# *Chapter Seven*

Jamie began the daily tasks of an accounting clerk. It was half an hour after the official start of the day he felt someone flick his ear lobe, he turned around and felt vomit come up into his mouth. He swallowed hard and standing over him was Chad Mann.

Chad was younger than Jamie. He was handsome, with blue eyes and a charismatic smile. He was lazy, always late to work and the office bully.

Chad looked down at Jamie and reached over and drove his knuckles into Jamie's head. It hurt and the assault made him winch in pain. "Knuggy," Chad chuckled and began to laugh.

"What do you want," Jamie asked. He felt like he'd always felt around Chad and other alpha males – small, weak, afraid and intimidated.

"Hey shit for brains, I woke up this morning with this hot chick lying beside me. But you wouldn't know how that feels." He smirked.

"Butt stain, I feel great today and I'm going to make it my business to see if I can't get you to soil your trousers again." Jamie blanched. Chad was referring to several months ago when he bullied him so badly Jamie had an accident. Chad, in the middle of a third round of belittling and painful verbal and physical taunts smelled what he'd caused and in the cubicles where they worked surrounded by co-workers who'd come to watch Jamie being tortured yelled, "Haw shit, the loser shit himself," and laughed. The crowd roared.

Devastated, humiliated and embarrassed Jamie went to the bathroom to minimize the damage, cleaned himself and his clothes the best he could then returned to his desk, shutdown his computer and went home for the day.

For weeks after, the office dwellers whispered and giggled when they saw Jamie. Chad called him, "Skid Mark and Butt Stain."

Needless to say, Jamie had already endured years of bullying and torment and the incident was yet another he'd added to the long list.

Not today, however. As Chad stood over Jamie intentionally intruding into his personal space to intimidate. Jamie felt the fear fade and the 'Twanger' as he called it, fill him with courage.

Jamie looked into Chad's face and said, "Leave me alone Chad. I have work to do."

Chad stuck his face right up into Jamie's and growled, "What are you going to do about it? I've just started to ruin your day Butt Boy."

By then a small crowd was watching from their cubicles, some had begun to migrate around Chad.

"Chad, leave me alone," Jamie spoke in an unaccustomedly powerful voice.

Chad slapped Jamie's face and said "Shit yourself Skid Mark," then what happened surprised everyone in the office.

Jamie jumped to his feet and in the process kneed Chad in the groan with the strength he didn't know he possessed. Jamie's clinched fist struck Chad in the face. The blow broke Chad's nose and blood exploded over his face. His neck snapped back and he fell unconscious on the floor.

Everyone froze then gradually began to clap and cheer Jamie for decisively ending years of Chad's reign of terror.

Mr. Crabapple came out of his office and stormed towards the commotion, "What the hell is going on," he bellowed and the crowd immediately disbursed until it was just Jamie standing over Chad who was still lying unconscious and profusely bleeding. "What the fuck, Jamie? What have you done to my nephew?"

Crabapple knelt near Chad growing more angry and concerned by the second. The fat man was perspiring and breathing heavily as he fretted over how he'd explain to his wicked and caustic sister that her son had gotten the shit beat out of him in the office.

He looked up at Jamie and nearly screaming said, "Get your personal stuff and leave immediately. You're fired!"

The dumpy manager was consumed in worry about how his sister would react. Her pretty son would never look the same. Crabapple looked at the shattered nose and shook his head, *Nope, you'll never be a looker again,* he thought then yelled, "Somebody call 911 for an ambulance."

# *Chapter Eight*

Jamie gathered up his belongings; surprised after eight years at Crabapple, Weiner and Pyle, the box he held was only half full. He walked past Chad, who by then was sitting up holding a towel over his nose. His uncle coddling over him like a mother hen.

Once the office bully, Chad coward and looked away as Jamie walked by, "See you later Chad. Goodbye Mr. Crabtree," Jamie said and moved to the elevator. He walked by the cubicles lined up on either side eight feet apart, he heard his co-workers offer whispered words of encouragement. "He deserved it, Good for you Jamie, Thanks and good luck…" were discreetly whispered strategically just out of ear shot of Crabapple.

Jamie waited for the elevator to arrive and felt reasonably calm and comfortable. He thought, *and I thought I'd be an emotional wreck if I ever got fired.*

*Ding,* the elevator door opened, he stepped in and looked back to the habi-trail he'd spent much of his life in dull misery. He pushed the button for the first floor and the doors began to close on the memory.

Just before the doors closed, Maggie Rose slipped in between them, "Hi Jamie. I hope you weren't going to leave without goodbye."

She handed him a piece of paper with her name and phone number on it, "Here, call me sometime and we can go out," she said and smiled. The doors opened on the first floor and he began to leave.

He turned facing her and said, "Thank you for everything."

Maggie Rose stepped off the elevator kissed Jamie then stepped back into the car and said, "Call me Jamie and by the way, nice work on Chad. He needed to be brought down a few pegs." The doors closed and Maggie Rose was gone. Jamie left the building and walked to the bus stop.

He felt the sun on his face – it was unusual because he was normally at his desk during mid-day. *The sun feels good*, he thought and decided, "I need a vacation."

The bus pulled up, the doors opened and Jamie felt his new friend, 'Twanger'. Together they climbed aboard for the last trip to or from Crabapple, Weiner and Pyle. He smiled and thought of Maggie Rose and a brighter future thanks to 'Twanger'. Now he needed to figure out how to keep the feeling of confidence and courage alive in him.

# *Chapter Nine*

Jamie returned to his small apartment and set the box of personal belongings on the kitchen table.

He couldn't explain it but the 'Twanger' albeit at that moment the fleeting sense of strength and confidence quickly evaporated and was replaced with the all too familiar feeling of self-humiliation and fear which seemed to control his life. He felt hollow, empty and afraid.

Jamie looked around the small room and his eyes examined each item and picture on the wall. Each had a memory and significance to him. He concentrated and let his memory dredge up every detail.

The watercolor next to the refrigerator he'd purchased at a flea market in Fresno in February 2012. He'd paid five dollars for it.

His focus shifted to a miniature sleeping black cat made of clay. It sat on the counter in the corner next to the back splash and the refrigerator, *my mother gave me that as a house warming gift when I moved in the summer of 2011,* he thought.

He moved to the next item and on and on …, the room began to close in around him and his mind ached with fear and a sense of hollowness caused by his feeling of failure and paranoia. His modest home and surroundings reinforced his complete failure and all the horrible fragility and emotionalism which defined and haunted him every day of his life.

Moving to his bedroom his heart raced out of control and his face and armpits became moist with perspiration.

Jamie fell face down onto his twin sized bed and began to cry. He felt crushed by the familiar feelings of helplessness, failure and fear – as if the walls were closing in and he would soon suffocate.

*\*\*\**

The next morning the sun penetrated his bedroom and he awakened to the cheerful sound of birds singing for one another. His eyes were scratchy and his head hurt. He sat up and shifted to the edge of the bed, the sharp discomfort of muscle pain shot hot daggers of protest through his shoulders, back and abdomen. He winced in pain.

A thought flashed through his exhausted brain, *Wait a minute, you didn't take the beating yesterday, Chad did. Why are you feeling like shit? So what if you lost a lousy two-bit job and in the process, gained respect from your coworkers and took Chad, the bully, down a few pegs.* He smiled, *in front of the entire office so he can't deny it.*

For a moment the pain lessened and he felt stronger. Then it began to gradually slip away. He cried out, "Come back 'Twanger' I want to feel this way all the time."

The warm sense of confidence moved away becoming less and less until he felt it disappear and once again, he was left in a prison of weakness, fear and self-pity.

Without thinking, he stood up tightened his bed and began mindlessly carrying out his morning routine like he'd done for most of his life.

It wasn't until he was dressed, finished his breakfast, made his usual lunch of baloney, white cheese and mustard on Wonder Bread and placed it into a paper sack next to his satchel, he realized, "I've got nowhere to go." He looked at his reflection in the mirror, "Where do you think you're going? You don't have a job."

Jamie fell heavily into the chair and leaned his elbows on the table and storm clouds of dark and painful emotions surrounded him. He began to worry as he thought, *How will I pay the bills? How will I find another job? How will I tell my mother I was fired from my job?*

He felt himself spiral down an emotional toilet when the phone rang. He snapped out of his panic attack and focused on the wall mounted phone beside the refrigerator. Jamie listened to it ring several times before he reached for it and placed it against his ear – "Hello."

Maggie Rose said, "Oh hello Jamie. I called to make sure you're okay and ask if you needed anything?"

He smile and replied, "Thank you for caring enough to call. I'm okay. I guess I will need to find another job soon though."

She looked around the office to ensure no one was listening to her talking to the 'hero/villain' who beat down the boss's nephew. *The coast is clear,* she thought. "Jamie, my father has an auto parts store and he's looking for some help. I told him about how you stood up to Chad and got fired – he offered you a job – on the spot."

She waited a second or two and said, "Don't say anything right this second. Meet me for dinner tonight at 7:00pm at Joe's Pizza and Pub on Market Street." She paused and said, "I really can't talk now Crabapple will be walking in the office any second. See you at seven, bye," she whispered.

"See you there," Jamie spoke into the dead phone. He felt a 'Twanger', and smiled.

# *Chapter Ten*

He arrived at Joe's twenty minutes early and patiently waited out front for Maggie Rose Petty.

He glanced inside to see if there were tables or if he should put his name on the waiting list. The frequent glances through the large window assured him there were enough tables. He felt the money he'd placed in his front pocket after carefully folding the bills he'd withdrawn from the ATM an hour before.

Jamie began to worry that this was another cruel joke being played on him when he looked at his Timex wrist watch and it read 7:05pm and a crushing sense of disappointment began to fester in his gut. When he looked up he saw Maggie Rose walking quickly across the street waving at him. She continued in a hurried gait until she faced him. The ambers of disappointment deep inside him vanished the instant he saw her and were replaced with joy and excitement.

In a series of choppy sentences, the result of her struggling to catch her breath she said, "Oh Jamie, I'm sorry I'm late. Crabapple kept us late to lecture us on company loyalty. What a crock of sh ...," she clipped the last word with her teeth and blushed.

Jamie smiled and said, "It's okay, shall we go in and have dinner and talk?"

"Okay," and she grabbed his arm, slide up beside him and together they walked inside. They found an empty table and sat across from each other. The plastic table cloth was red and white checker board and felt damp and slightly sticky. Laminated menus were stacked between the condiments and the metal paper napkin dispenser.

Jamie looked around the restaurant. A large brightly lit menu above the kitchen caught his eye. He shifted his gaze to the counter where several customers were sitting on stools eating pizza and drinking beer by the pitcher. Jamie felt like he should have insisted they meet at a nicer place – after all, this was his first date of sorts. The thought rushed like a lightning bolt in his mind and he began to tremble.

Maggie Rose pulled several napkins from the dispenser and handed them to Jamie, then grabbed a few more for herself. Then with excitement in her bright blue eyes and attractive smile she exclaimed, "Jamie, I hope you're hungry – I'm starving." She looked at his face and said, "I really love their Pepperoni Pizza and how about we split a pitcher of Bud?"

Jamie felt a 'Twanger' growing in his heart and he smiled at Maggie Rose, "That sounds wonderful. I love pizza and beer too."

Quietly they looked at each other and Maggie Rose could sense she was watching Jamie's budding transformation into a confident and self-assured man. She thought, *you're a work in progress but I can see a butterfly is trying to emerge from the cocoon. I hope I'm right, you're such a nice guy.*

Together their focus was directed to the sound of a woman clearing her throat followed by an emotionless, near robotic spiel, "Welcome to Joe's Pizza and Pub. My name is Margie and I'll be your server. The menus are there," she pointed to the laminated papers on the table, "May I bring you something to drink while you look over the menus?"

Maggie Rose smiled at Jamie, "May I?" she asked. He nodded. Maggie Rose cocked her head to one side and looked at the disinterested woman hovering over her and said, "We'd like a pitcher of Bud and a large Pepperoni Pizza."

Margie's eyebrows lifted for a second or two and she scribbled down the order into her note pad then squinted at her chicken scratch. "That'll be a pitcher of Bud and a large..." Maggie interrupted.

"Make that an extra-large."

Margie huffed and scribbled and said, "and an extra-large Pepperoni Pizza."

Maggie Rose, giddy with excitement said, "Yes that's right. We're celebrating tonight."

The waitress looked up at the young woman and thought, *to be young again and in love.*

41

"Congratulation," she said, turned and headed to the kitchen to place the order for the pizza in the queue. Reached behind the counter, she retrieved a plastic pitcher and placed it under the Budweiser tap while wishing she was anywhere except waitressing at Joe's. She watched the pitcher fill until the foam began to flow over the rim of the vessel.

Margie straightened her apron subconsciously as she let the foam subside and settle towards the beer surface. She carried the pitcher in one hand and two, not entirely clear plastic glasses, in the fingers of her other hand. She approached the table where Jamie and Maggie Rose were talking.

Quietly, the middle aged waitress stood beside the table for a moment; jealousy flashed thru her mind. She watched the two people talking while sparks of interest electrified the air around them. She dropped the pitcher on the table with a thump and the glasses rattled the way plastic sounds when it strikes a hard object.

"Your pizza should be done in ten minutes," she announced and then retreated back to the counter. Margie wondered why she just acted out that way, *They didn't do anything to deserve that,* she thought.

The two diners poured beer and continued to talk. The entire time Jamie felt the new and exciting feelings of having someone to talk too and it was remarkably easy and comfortable for him. He thought, *another first, dining and talking to a woman who seems to genuinely enjoy talking and sharing stories with me. It's a 'Twanger'.* He smiled and felt warm and relaxed.

Maggie Rose did all the talking and that was fine with Jamie. He was content to watch her and listen to her voice as much as the stories she told. She spoke with passion, confidence, ease and intelligence.

"Jamie, it was so brave of you to stand up to that bully Chad. You know you weren't the only one he pushed around. All of us have been abused or harassed by him and he always gets away with it because he is Crabapple's nephew. Damn him. I hate him and for one, I'm so glad you kicked him in the nuts and broke his weasel looking nose."

Maggie Rose laughed and threw her head back, "You should have seen that jerk today. He's wearing a big white bandage over his swollen nose and both eyes are black and blue and swollen nearly shut. He looks like a damn raccoon."

She leaned in and with a twinkle in her eyes and in a conspiratorial whisper said, "And for the pleasure of seeing you beat his ass and then get to see him looking like a clown, we all were subjected to Loyalty Training by the 'Crab-man'. It was absolutely worth it." She giggled.

Margie delivered the pizza without a word. The two giggled as she waddled away then dove into the piping hot pie and ate silently for several minutes.

Between slices Maggie Rose asked, "So what do you like to do for fun?"

Jamie's face froze and his eyes fell to his plate as he silently set the piece of pizza down. He shifted in his seat for several seconds and looked uncomfortable.

Maggie Rose saw the transformation and reached for his hand and said, "Jamie, what's wrong? I'm sorry if I was prying. I was just curious. I was hoping we may have similar interests that we could do together." She reached over with her other hand and held his hands and offered, "Would you like me to share mine with you?"

"Isn't this pizza wonderful?" She said trying frantically to change the subject as she searched his eyes for a clue of what he was thinking.

Jamie looked up at her face and commanded a 'Twanger' of courage and his recently found feeling of confidence and ease to blossom within him – and it did. It started with a distant glow deep inside him and the ambers began to burn more brightly and radiate within. Soon his courage and confidence returned.

He looked down at their hands entwined together and said, "Maggie Rose, you are the first person to ever ask me that. To be honest, I've never had a hobby or interests that I did for fun. I guess I'm just a loser." His eyes fell upon the table again. "I'd like to have hobbies and interests," their eyes connected in an emotional stare.

She smiled, "That's great. Let's eat some more of this delicious pizza and stop the interrogation." She smiled and lifted another piece of pizza and folded it in half and shoved it into her mouth. "Yummmm," he heard her say.

Jamie felt his 'Twanger' burning brightly within him and knew it was because he was so comfortable with the woman across the table. He grabbed his pizza but before he took a bite said, "Maggie Rose, thank you for your understanding and kindness."

Her mouth was full but she managed to say, "You're welcome," in a muffled voice through the crust cheese, tomato sauce and pepperoni; temporarily occupying her mouth.

## *Chapter Eleven*

The next morning Jamie's routine was much different. By 9:00am he stood in front of a store with mufflers, exhaust pipes, fan belts and hoses hanging in the windows. Inside there were aisles of auto parts and accessories, he figured everything necessary to fix a car was there.

He looked at the piece of paper Maggie Rose had given him the evening before and then up at the large sign above the window *Petty Auto Parts and Accessories*. In smaller print below it said, *We've Got Everything You'll Need to Keep Your Vehicle on the Road*.

Jamie opened the door and entered the store. The lights were bright and made it easy to see the neatly stacked contents on the shelves.

His nose registered a number of aromas he was unfamiliar with but assumed they were associated with the parts, tools and cans, bottles and containers of liquids for detailing, maintenance and repair.

In the background he heard country music, then he noticed a large man behind the counter. He was nearly bald with thick dark eyebrows. He was heavy – nearly as big around as he was tall; but then again, he wasn't that tall either.

Jamie approached the counter facing the man wearing a blue work shirt with the name Artie Petty in red thread over a white patch. The man looked up from an impressive stack of invoices and set down his pen. Jamie could see he was frustrated and he mumbled, "Damn paperwork." He took a long look at Jamie and thought, *You don't look like the typical gearhead or mechanic type I usually see in here. Sonny, you don't look like you would know how to fix anything… probably don't know the difference between an end wrench and a box wrench.*

He placed his massive hands on the counter and asked, "What can I help you with young man?"

Jamie fought the urge to cower or fly out the door and desperately searched inside for the confidence he needed.

He swallowed hard as Artie looked on silently. "Sir, my name is Jamie Davis. I am…" he corrected himself, "was a coworker of your daughter Maggie Rose."

Artie cut him off, "Marie? Why she uses that stage name I'll never know. Her mother and I spent a lot of time choosing Marie and I think it's a much nicer name than Maggie Rose." He ranted then smiled. "So you're the one." His faced softened and his smile turned into a mischievous grin.

"Marie told me you stood up to that Chad character in the office and put him down like a rabid animal. She told me you broke his nose and kneed him in the balls."

Artie reached over the counter and extended his hand – Jamie reached over and they shook hands.

Artie continued, "Over the years, Marie has complained about that jerk and the way he tormented and bullied the guys and harassed the women and always got away with it because of his uncle. More than once I was ready to show up in that office and disassemble that punk myself. Thanks, you saved me the trouble."

Artie studied the man in front of him and thought, *You don't seem like the kind of guy who'd have the guts to stand up to a bully. You're kind of small. Bet you never lifted anything heavy or been to the gym either. Your eyes hold a spark of confidence but your body language is quiet and timid – my customers will eat you alive. I bet you don't know shit about cars, parts and working on engines. Oh well, I promised Marie, or Maggie Rose I'd give you a job since you lost the last one standing up to that office asshole.*

Artie came around the counter and stood in front of Jamie. "Marie tells me you need a job since you lost that shitty job at Crabapple's shithole. He thought, *I wish Marie would leave that shithole too. Anything would be better than that.* Artie sized up

Jamie once again and thought, *Here we go.* "Sonny, I could use a hand around here." He let that sink in.

Jamie looked around the store and didn't recognize much of the inventory except the quart containers of motor oil and a few basic parts and tools. *How can I do this job I don't know anything about cars and so on*, he thought as he looked up at Artie and was about to say no thank you.

Artie preempted Jamie and said, "I know this is all very foreign to you Jamie. I get it. What I'd like you to do is keep the books and do the paperwork, order inventory and manage receipts. That will be a great help." He cocked his head to the side and smiled, "You see, I like working with customers and helping them fix their cars and I hate paperwork. I hear you're really good at paperwork and above all an honest man I can trust. I think together we'd make a good team – by the way so does Marie." He winked and Jamie blushed.

Artie was on a roll and continued, "You can start as soon as you'd like. I don't know what you were making at Crabby's place but I can start you at $12.50 an hour and we'll see how it goes."

He stuck his hand out and Jamie grabbed it with all the strength he could muster and said, "Thank you, sir. I would like to accept your offer and start immediately."

Artie grinned and put his strong arm around Jamie's neck and led him to the back of the store.

"First we need to get you some work clothes. What's your shirt and trouser size?"

Jamie told him while Artie pulled several blue shirts, like he was wearing, from the rack on the back wall near the office and pulled two pairs of trousers from the shelf below the rack. "Here you go. The bathroom is over there. Get dressed, Sonny; then I'll show you the office and how we keep inventory."

# *Chapter Twelve*

The first day at Petty's Auto Parts and Accessories flew by for Jamie. Artie was a kind and patient instructor. He was easy to approach with questions and never tired of going over the instruction Jamie requested as he learned the new job and Artie's expectations.

As the day moved along Jamie began to appreciate his boss's kindness and interests and he realized, for the first time, he had a male role model and father figure in his life. Jamie felt a 'Twanger' in his gut and wondered if his life may have been different if he'd had a father growing up.

Around 1:00pm Jamie was in the stockroom when Artie called out, "Sonny, You've got a call on line one." Jamie froze for a few seconds, *Who would be calling me here? No one knows I'm here.* He moved cautiously to the pole near him and reached for the phone and pushed the flashing button marked no. 1.

"Hello, this is Jamie Davis, may I help you?"

A familiar voice came through the receiver, "Oh, hi, Jamie. How's your first day at your new job? Dad says he really likes you and you fit in just fine.

That's great news, Jamie," Maggie Rose said and giggled.

"Thanks," he said watching the door to the front of the store where Artie was working behind the counter.

"I just called to thank you for dinner last night and see how you're doing," her voice softened and began to sound like a dove cooing.

"I hope we can do it again soon," her voice tapered off sharply and she whispered, "Crabapple is coming this way, I got to run. Talk to you soon, and say hi to dad for me." She hung up the phone just as her boss walked by her cubical and peered in as he moved down the hallway – his hands clasped behind his back like a drill sergeant.

Maggie Rose stared at her computer screen and held her breath until the old creepy guy moved down the row of cubicles. Fear and paranoia consumed her. Finally, when she could no longer hear his footsteps, she began to breathe again and thought, *I've got to get out of here. The toxic environment is killing me.,* She thought about Jamie's escape from Crabtree, Weiner and Pyle and whispered, "Good for you Jamie."

# *Chapter Thirteen*

The days passed, then weeks and before Jamie knew it he'd been at the parts store for three months. With each day he had learned the job and he easily mastered the paperwork and inventory tasks to Artie's delight.

Jamie routinely felt 'Twangers' of confidence and felt his self-assurance and pride began to take the forefront replacing fear and self-pity. The later gradually moved out of the spotlight for longer and longer periods as confidence overshadowed them.

Artie had seen the transformation and had shared his observations with Marie, his only daughter and since his wife had succumbed to breast cancer, his only family.

*** 

Jamie was sitting around the dinner table at Artie's home. Maggie Rose, Artie and Jamie were just finishing their meal. Jamie thought it was exceptionally good and he smiled at Marie, knowing she had put a lot of effort into the meal.

Artie was happy to see his daughter becoming close friends with a good man who respected her and was always a gentleman.

While Maggie Rose and Jamie cleared the table and washed the dishes, Artie moved to the den and carefully opened the liquor cabinet where he kept his alcohol. He reached for his most prized bottle – a 30 year old scotch. He gathered three glasses and set them on the coffee table next to the bottle.

Marie and Jamie came into the den and sat down around the coffee table, "I thought we'd have an after-dinner drink," Artie said and reached for the bottle and poured three neat glasses, handed one to his daughter, then one to Jamie and finally reached for the last glass standing alone. He raised his glass and said, "To my beautiful daughter – thank you for a wonderful dinner and to you, Jamie Davis – I'm glad to know you." Artie looked at both younger people and tipped his glass and sipped the amber liquid.

He leaned in and said, "Jamie, what do you like to do for fun, Sonny?"

Jamie looked at Maggie Rose then her father and said, "Sir, I've never really had any hobbies or interests outside of work."

Artie's face filled with a look of amazement. "Have you ever gone fishing, or hunting or camping in the mountains?"

"No, sir." Jamie replied.

"Well I think we should do that – you and I. We could go to one of my favorite spots high in the Sierra Mountains near Lake Tahoe. It's about a four day hike from Loon Lake, over the summit and through Desolation Wilderness to Emerald Bay. It's a beautiful trip and we may only see two or three people the entire time. I used to do that trek with Marie's mother before we had Marie." He smiled at his daughter.

He returned his focus to Jamie and said, "It's an exciting adventure and trust me, when you're finished you'll feel like a new man."

He finished the scotch in his glass then continued, "I know I always returned home feeling stronger and more confident knowing I'd accomplished something very special and, as a result, I became more certain I could accomplish anything after those trips."

Artie was getting excited at the idea of making another trek through the forest – he hadn't done it in the last twenty five years and deep inside knew he needed a younger man to accompany him. He was getting older and the trip could be dangerous.

Maggie Rose said, "That's a wonderful idea, Dad. Jamie has never done anything like that and it'll give you guys' time to do 'guy stuff' together."

Jamie smiled and liked the idea, "Sir, I've never done any of that so I'd need you to teach me everything from pitching a tent to what to wear and what to pack. I'll need to purchase the gear you recommend – I don't even have a sleeping bag." He sheepishly looked at the other two.

Artie jumped to his feet and beamed with excitement and in a booming voice announced, "Well then, we'll leave in the spring after the snow melts."

# *Chapter Fourteen*

Two weeks after they'd agreed to the 'boys trip' to the High Sierras, Maggie Rose called Jamie on a Saturday evening. He answered, "Hello."

In a wavering voice she said, "Jamie," then she began to cry. "Dad had a heart attack and he is in the hospital. It is a miracle he's still alive." She began to ball uncontrollably.

"Where are you? I'll be there as soon as I can," he said. A 'Twanger' emerged and intertwined with his concern for Artie and Maggie Rose.

Between sobs she said, "I'm in the emergency room at the General Hospital." Her breathing was heavy and labored.

"I'm on my way," he said then he blurted out, "Maggie Rose, dear, he'll be okay. I'm on my way and will stay with you until we get through it."

*** 

Artie suffered a severe heat attach that would result in a triple bypass and four weeks in the hospital.

The doctors would be satisfied with the outcome but Artie would never fully recover and on-no-uncertain-terms, the doctors told him that he would never be able to camp or hike in the high country again.

Artie was devastated. He was healthy one minute and after the heart attack his life profoundly changed with severe limits to his activity and life style.

During his convalescence at home Maggie Rose and Jamie came by to visit him. Maggie prepared a meal for him and Jamie kept him company and they talked about the business and made small talk that carried them through dinner.

After the meal, Artie became serious and said, "Sonny, I was really looking forward to our camping adventure. I had dusted off my equipment and the maps for the trip but this damned heart has kicked my ass." He looked deeply into Jamie's eyes and said, "Now Sonny, I want you to do the trip for the both of us."

Jamie's eyes showed his concern and even a hint of fear, "But Artie, I have never done anything remotely close to hiking and camping – let alone in the wilderness where there are very few people. I can't even read a map let alone make a fire or pitch a tent."

Artie smiled, "Don't worry I'll teach you everything you need to know before I'd let you go up there and get yourself killed!"

He laughed until his chest began to hurt where weeks before the surgeons had split open his sternum.

Jamie began to relax and laughed with his friend. Maggie Rose entered the room with a tray of coffee and gelato.

"What are you guys laughing about?" she questioned with a curious smirk that Jamie thought looked cute.

"Awe nothing, Jamie, here, is going to make the Desolation Wilderness trek for both of us. Now that the damn heart thing has relegated me to being the coach and not a player… damn it," Artie grumbled under his breath.

"Oh that's fine, you two can tell me all about it over coffee and dessert," She giggled. Then she reached for the coffee mugs and said, "Dad, decaf for you like the doctor ordered."

"Damn," he mumbled.

"And for Jamie, your coffee with cream and sugar." She cooed like a dove and smiled for Jamie. She continued, "And now for dessert." She reached for a small bowl – "Daddy, sugar free Jello," he looked at the green soft cubes wiggle as she placed it in front of him.

"Damn, how's a man supposed to survive Marie? You're taking all the fun and flavor out of being alive." He pretended to protest then winked and said, "Seriously, thank you sweetheart."

She leaned over and kissed his bald head then reached for the remaining two bowls. "Jamie, we have mocha gelato." Her father grumbled in a good natured way.

After several minutes of silence, Artie said, "Sonny, we'll start tomorrow after breakfast."

***

Three weeks later, Artie and Maggie Rose drove Jamie and his carefully prepared backpack and gear up highway 50 to the Icehouse Grade, then climbed the winding 30 mile road to Loon Lake. The forest was tall and lush – the air was warm and dry and nature abounded all around them.

Artie turned off the main road onto an unimproved gravel road toward the Van Vleck Bunkhouse, one of Artie's favorite places in the high country.

They continued until they reached a heavy chain hung across the road between two steel poles. They stopped and Artie smiled, "Well Sonny, this is where your adventure begins."

They climbed out of the truck and Artie laid-out Jamie's gear and backpack on the tailgate. He reached for the topographical map and then looked around him. "Sonny," he pointed to the map, "here we are."

He pointed to the tall mountain in the distance, "That's Tell's Peak. Desolation Wilderness is on the other side. Always hike east and you'll end up at Emerald Bay, Lake Tahoe."

Artie looked at Jamie and said, "Follow the road beyond the chain for two miles until you see a clearing on your right – it was a landing strip years ago." He pointed to it on the map.

"From there you are at the base of Tell's Peak. Make your way up to the summit here," He pointed to the location on the map. "Just remember, walk slow, step carefully and keep your eyes and ears open. We'll be waiting for you in four days near Emerald Bay."

He faced the younger man and put his hands on the younger's shoulders, "Call Marie's cellphone when you come out on the other side and we'll pick you up and I'll buy you a big juicy steak."

Artie's eyes welled up with tears, "Damn, I wish I was going with you," and he hugged Jamie.

Maggie Rose's face had tears running down her cheeks. She hugged him and kissed his cheek. She wiped her face with the back of her hand and in a serious tone said, "Jamie, you be careful and remember everything Daddy taught you about the wilderness. I'll be waiting for you on the other side."

# *Chapter Fifteen*

Jamie donned his pack and hung his canteen on his belt, grabbed the well-used hiking stick Artie had given him. He felt a 'Twanger' in his gut and he waved goodbye to his friends and began the climb up the trail.

He looked back over his shoulder from time to time until Maggie Rose and Artie where hidden by the forest surrounding him.

The first several miles was an old timber road – the graded surface made walking easy and he moved quickly in long strong strides.

As Artie had said, the air strip became visible when he came to the crest of the road. Jamie found a fallen tree in the shade and sat for a few minutes sipped, for the first time, from his canteen and looked over his map. He marked the map with his location and the date and time – just like Artie had taught him.

After a brief rest he moved across the open field Artie warned was a marsh so he walked around the outer edge on higher ground. It took longer but he kept his shoes, socks and feet dry. "Keep your shoes and socks dry or you'll get large painful blisters, Sonny," Jamie could hear Artie's warning.

## WALKING THROUGH HELL

He made it to the base of Tell's Peak by noon. Looking up, it was a steep climb. The map told him it was 1002 foot climb to the summit from his position.

He started up moving much like a mountain goat moving in a number of zig zags where he could get solid footing. He remembered Artie's guidance, "Walk slow, step carefully and keep your eyes and ears open."

Progress was slow and the weight of his pack became heavier with each step. He realized he was having some trouble breathing but Artie had warned him, "You'll be above the tree line as you make your way to the summit and the air gets pretty thin. You'll be alright it may just take a few hours for your body to adjust. Just move slowly and step surely."

Jamie found a rock about halfway up to the summit, dropped his pack and enjoyed the view from his private vantage point. He looked off in the distance and saw Loon Lake. He found it on his map. Behind it was Hell's Hole and Devil's Slide. He found them on his map with his index finger.

So far his adventure was going smoothly. It was at that moment of joy and exhilaration, fear and anxiety broke down the locked door in his mind and his 'Twanger' was run over by thoughts he'd lived with for so long.

He was in the middle of nowhere in the middle of a full blown panic attack when he heard a voice, "Hello there."

Jamie jumped to his feet and saw a rugged, handsome man and an attractive woman by his side with a black Labrador sitting at their feet. His pink tongue moved in and out of his mouth as he panted.

Jamie was caught off-guard and looked at the three of them. "Where are you headed?" the man asked in a confident voice as he studied Jamie.

"Sir, the summit then down into Desolation Wilderness. I plan to make my way to Emerald Bay." Jamie said with reemerging confidence.

The man took several steps forward, his partner and dog followed. Jamie watched them closely but he felt they were good and he was not in any danger. The stranger extended is hand and said, "The name is Max Loften, here is my wife Wendi and that 'Meathead' is Jake."

Jamie grabbed his hand and they shook, "Sir, my name is Jamie Davis."

"Well Jamie that's an ambitious adventure you're on. We live nearby and know these mountains pretty well." He sized the younger man up for a second time wondering if he was up to it or not. He thought, *Jamie, you don't look like you have done anything close to this before. Are you up to it or are we going to be pulling you out of trouble in the next few days? You seem like a good man with good intentions, we'll keep an eye on you albeit discreetly.*

Max said, "Good Luck."

"Thank you, it was a pleasure to meet you Max, Wendi and Jake," Jamie said.

The trio moved easterly along the granite rock and thinning forest as Jamie watched them until they disappeared from site.

His chance meeting with them had dashed his fear and anxiety and he felt the sensation of confidence and courage push the weaker sensations back within his mind where he wanted them to remain forever.

He tossed his pack on his back and with a deep breath he began to move up towards the summit and the ridge saddle Artie had instructed him to head for.

The grade became even more difficult and the soft dirt replaced by granite pellets and sand made footing more challenging. All the time the sun beat down and the dry air became increasingly warmer – his body responded to the physical exertion and the sun by perspiring. It felt good.

He kept Artie's advice ringing in his ears, "Walk slowly, step carefully and keep your eyes and ears open." He continued upward two or three steps at a time then stopped and looked for the next three steps as he navigated the steep face. His unwavering objective was the summit. He kept thinking about what Artie had told him, "The view from there is remarkable. You may never see anything else so spectacular."

# *Chapter Sixteen*

Jamie neared the summit saddle ahead. He looked up and thought, *only fifty more feet or so.* At that instant his foot slipped off a loose rock, he lost his balance and began to slide down the near vertical face covered in loose pebbles and sand.

He tried frantically to stop his rapid decent by grabbing at brush, limbs and rocks as he slid by. He frantically dug his fingers into the sand in hope of keeping from continuing his uncontrolled decent.

It was no use, he fell 50 feet or more until he was stopped by a sapling he snagged and hung on to with all his strength.

Minutes later he rose to his feet – dejected and afraid, he looked up at the summit and said, "Damn you."

This time without the sense of courage he'd had moments before he assented the face of the summit once again. "Walk slowly, step carefully and keep your eyes and ears open," he kept repeating to himself.

Jamie adjusted his pack on his shoulders and resumed his climb to the top. He moved upward one step after another until he crawled to the top and froze. What should have been a moment of triumphant was electrified with loneliness and fear.

He fell to the ground, dropped his pack and forced himself to work through the anxiety he felt. He spoke to himself, "You can't cave now you're in the middle of nowhere alone. This entire trip is all about building and reinforcing your confidence and courage. Work through your fear, Jamie."

He sat there for a long time, looking at the incredible view, looking at his map and struggling to rekindle the courage he'd needed to walk down the other side of the mountain and his decent to Desolation Wilderness.

He saw Forni Lake below and heard Artie's voice, "Once at the summit move down as quickly as you can. It gets dark fast in the basin and get to Forni Lake before dark. That'll be your first camp. Watch for loose rock and cracks in the rock that may twist or break your ankles."

On the way down the steep granite boulder face, he slipped twice, falling on his butt and the sharp rock dug into his soft flesh. He grimaced in pain then climbed to his feet and dusted himself off and continued.

Twice he fell face first and scrapped his palms and the tip of his nose. Once he mildly twisted his ankle and as he placed his hand on a granite rock at eye level, he heard a frightening sound, he froze and his heart nearly exploded out of his heaving chest. The sound he focused on was the threatening warning only a rattlesnake makes. He looked at a snake coiled, its head moving from side to side, a long tongue darted in and out of his mouth – it was prepared to strike and undoubtedly lunge at Jamie's face or neck – both fatal and the serpent was on a rock at eye level and only three feet away.

Jamie remained perfectly still except for his lunging chest, perspiration pouring down his face and torso for what seemed like hours but after the snake decided he posed no threat, the serpent carefully moved between the rocks and disappeared. At the instant the reptile was out of sight and its rattle stopped Jamie moved slowly until it was clear then moved quickly keeping a sharp eye on the rocks and the ground around him looking for other snakes.

Later, as his heart beat slowed to normal and he reflected on his encounter he thought, *yes, I was scared but then I was in control and faced the danger with courage and resolve and stayed focused.* He smiled and felt his chest swell with pride and self-confidence and yelled out in the great wide open – "That's a 'Twanger' and I like this new feeling: hell yea!"

He felt growing confidence in his stride as he reached the bottom of the rock face and moved along a barely visible trail towards Forni Lake; a broad smile filled his handsome face. He stood at the edge of the lake around 4:00pm, he dropped his pack and felt the relief in his back and shoulders – the whole time he looked at the lake and to the west where he'd come from and the steep rocky decent, he'd traveled. He was completely alone – not another human was visible as far as he could see. "Chances are rather good you won't see another person for most of your adventure in the back country. It's unnerving at first but you'll get used to it and after a while I'm sure you'll enjoy the time by yourself to reflect and grow," Jamie could hear his mentor and friend Artie's voice in his ear.

He sucked clean air into his lungs and allowed his mind to absorb the sights and the feeling of being alone. It felt good and empowering and he felt a tingle of excitement run down his spine. He smiled and thought, *it's a Twanger.* He twisted his waist several times to stretch his sore muscles and looked at the sun quickly falling behind the granite face he'd just descended. He rolled his shoulders and focused on the task at hand and in several minutes assembled his tent and rolled out his sleeping bag just as Artie and Maggie Rose had taught him.

A short look around the small lake in the dimming light confirmed; HE WAS ALL ALONE.

Exhausted, Jamie ate a little and drank water and crawled into his bed roll. By then the basin was dark and the nocturnal animals were beginning to move around. He was too tied to care and was asleep before his head hit the pile of clothes he used for a pillow. He was too exhausted to worry about being in the wild with creatures in a place resembling the surface of the moon.

## *Chapter Seventeen*

Early the next morning, with his eyes still tightly closed, Jamie arched his back as he stretched. Initially, it felt good then his lower back began to protest from the previous day's trek. The heavy pack he'd carried over the difficult trail had strained muscles he wasn't sure he'd ever felt before. He grunted and continued to stretch inside his sleeping bag until the discomfort subsided.

As his senses began to awaken he became aware of the cold crisp air surrounding him. The tip of his nose and cheeks, the only parts of him exposed to the elements, tingled on this chilly morning. His wool cap snuggly pulled down over his ears and neck, kept the rest of his head warm but then it happened… it started as a little itch then his entire scalp itched in urgency to be released from hours tightly covered with the hat. His hand moved out of his sleeping bag and in a quick thrust grabbed the hat and tossed it on the ground beside him his fingers dug into his scalp until the itchiness was gone. *Ahh, that feels good. Now I'm awake,* he thought, and he looked around, still warm inside his bed.

A glance at his wristwatch confirmed it was early, only 5:30am. The morning sky was bright and clear. The trees and bushes around his camp where an endless combination of greens and browns. He focused on the lake for several minutes. Almost in a trance, his eyes absorbed the stunning images of dark blue water, granite boulders randomly erupting through the water's surface. The water was still and as he looked around the parameter of Forni Lake, he was reminded, he was all alone.

Jamie climbed out of his bag and was instantly reminded of the chill in the air. He reached for his coat then quickly laced up his boots and thought, *I could sure use a cup of coffee now. I'll get the butane stove out of the pack and brew a nice pot of Joe.* He looked over at the tree where he'd leaned his pack the night before and froze. His eyes filled with fear and his jaw dropped – his pack was gone.

Momentarily forgetting everything else around him he ran to the tree where he'd left his pack the night before. His mind raced, everything I need to survive this trip was in that pack. My clothes, my stove and my food. He felt a panic attack coming as he approached the tree and he gradually felt the stress in his neck and the knot in his gut subside when he looked beyond the tree and saw it lying on a grassy knoll 10 feet away.

## WALKING THROUGH HELL

He rushed to his pack and began to laugh when he saw a young raccoon's face pop out from inside. The little critter gave Jamie a mischievous stare, realizing the 'jig was up', he quickly found an escape route and high tailed it to the nearest bush and disappeared. Jamie reclaimed his pack and brought it back to his camp before inventorying its contents.

A feeling which was becoming more common began to come over him again. It was his 'Twanger'. He smiled and thought, *this trip is working. I can feel my self-confidence growing with each moment.* He smiled and no longer felt the morning chill. His senses focused on the beauty surrounding him, the smell of the forest and he thought about Artie and of course his friend, Maggie Rose.

He dumped the pack contents onto the dusty ground and sorted through the pile  placing food to one side, clothes to another and the remaining contents in a third. Jamie said to himself, "Now you little four legged thief, let's see what you've stolen or destroyed." As he said it he realized, he wasn't angry or even bothered, he was amused at the raccoon's valiant effort to steal something larger and heavier than himself.

It became clear at once the focus of the attempted theft was his food. Several Ziploc bags with nuts and dried fruit were opened and partially consumed, but to Jamie's surprise, most of his food was untouched.

Jamie smiled and looked the direction of the thief's hasty retreat and said, "I guess it's lucky for me I caught you before you got into the good stuff," and he chuckled to himself.

The clothes and other items were unmolested and in moments Jamie had refilled his pack, lit the butane stove and began to boil water for coffee and breakfast. The water struggled to boil in the high altitude, Jamie sat on a nearby rock and looked back at Tells Peak and the sheer face of the massive granite rock he'd come down. It was an ominous site, much of the vertical surface was still in partial shadows – still hidden from the rising sun to the east. He felt as if he were in a cathedral and realized how small and how temporary his life would be as he admired the mountain which had survived since the earth was created. In awe and reverence, he quietly spoke to the image in front of him, almost as in a prayer. "You are powerful, gracious and beautiful and stand confidently against the elements for all time. You are immortal."

He heard the water beginning to boil, his attention shifted to the stove as he made coffee.

With an aluminum cup of coffee in his hand he returned to his seat and looked back at the mountain and quietly watched the morning sunlight slowly push the shadows up the face as the sun climbed. With each moment, Jamie could feel the temperature rise and soon it would be warm if not hot and he would wish for the cool of morning.

He'd think about that later, at that moment, he sat quietly, gazing at the mountain and thought about Maggie Rose. The thought of her warmed his heart and alone in the forest he was beginning to realize he was developing feelings, strong feelings, for her; feelings he'd never felt for anyone before. Jamie allowed himself to relax as he thought about his friends and how they'd helped him on his journey of discovery and growth.

## *Chapter Eighteen*

Jamie broke camp and studied his topographical map for several minutes and looked at the compass Artie had given him. Carefully setting down the compass to line up with the highest point on Middle Mountain. "Zero nine five," he said when he read the compass card and wrote it on a piece of paper which he placed in his pocket.

He and Artie had discussed the route he should follow a number of times. Artie had recommended taking the second day slow through Rockbound Valley and make camp by mid-day near Camper Flats. Jamie realized, to this point, all these places were nothing but names – he'd never seen them before but he trusted Artie and carefully folded his map then put his compass in his shirt pocket.

Jamie took his canteen and filled it in the pristine lake and pulled his pack up onto his shoulders. As the pack settled into place, his shoulders ached and the small of his back protested. "Suck it up, Jamie," he said to himself – sounding more like a drill sergeant than himself. "No pain, no gain," He said and began to walk towards the peak five miles ahead.

# WALKING THROUGH HELL

He observed the terrain was markedly different, than the day before. Shortly after he left the lake he found a foot trail moving east and decided to follow it. The crude but welcome trail made the walk easy and soon Jamie had forgotten about the soreness in his shoulders and back. With Middle Mountain visible and directly in his path he began to relax as he admired the scenery. He began to reflect on his life, his choices, so far, and where and what he wanted to be and become in the future.

He found thinking about the future was empowering. Without realizing it, his stride grew stronger and more confident. Jamie smiled, all the future plans he was milling around in his head had one common thread, "Maggie Rose and Artie are part of them," he said and stopped under a scraggly pine tree to catch his breath. He dropped his pack, reached for his canteen and fell to his knees, rolling over and leaning against the tree's trunk. He drank from his canteen then surveyed the minor scrapes and bruises and sore muscles.

He was tired and sore, but the sense of adventure and self-confidence reminded him of why he was glad he'd set out on this trek. Jamie pushed his back into the trunk and lifted his face until he felt the warm sun. He closed his eyes and drifted off into a gentle sleep. The dreams, he wouldn't remember were no longer of fear and danger but adventure and courage.

***

Jamie felt warm breath and a moist tongue on his face, and he jumped to his feet. His heart raced but he wasn't afraid – instead he stood tall and defiant then smiled and began to relax when he recognized the man, woman and a black labrador in front of him.

"Hello Jamie," the man said. His wife smiled and Jake, the dog barked playfully and came to Jamie, stood on his back legs and kissed the young man again.

Max laughed and said, "Jamie seems you really made an impression on 'Old Jake'." Max stepped forward and extended his hand, Jamie took it and they exchanged greetings. Wendi, followed her husband and greeted the lone traveler.

"We came across your camp at Forni Lake and thought we'd check in on you," Max said. His wife's hand found his and their fingers entwined. By then Jake was moving around the area with his nose near the ground looking for a Chipmunk or Ground Squirrel to play with – his tail moving in a gentle rhythm back and forth.

"How's your adventure so far?" Max asked. Jamie motioned to the shade under the tree and sat down, "How much time do you have?" he asked.

The couple sat across from him and were both skilled at reading 'tells' and non-verbal communications. They sat quietly and listened and observed his body language. Jamie, saw what they were doing and tried to ignore it as he said, "Seriously, I'm having a wonderful time and except for a raccoon who tried to rip me off this morning everything is going exactly to plan."

Wendi, a Park Ranger and familiar with the Desolation Wilderness asked, "Jamie, where are you planning to make camp tonight."

"Camper Flats," he blurted out almost too quickly.

"Good that's only a few more miles to the east. This trail will get you there and be careful crossing the creek, this time of year the rocks have algae on them and are slippery," she said and smiled.

Max looked at his wife and thought, *Honey, you really are good at your job.*

Jake came over and sat next to Jamie and began to lick his face playfully.

Max stood up, Wendi followed his lead. Max called Jake over to them and then he looked at his young friend and said. "Jamie, we just wanted to check on you and make sure you're okay. It's nice to see you again." They shook hands and the couple and their dog moved north.

Jamie stood there silently as he watched his wilderness friends move gracefully, in near silence, into the distance. The strong agile man moved with the motion of a large cat, his wife moving confidently alongside him and the happy-go-lucky dog, having the time of his life, moved in random directions ahead of the couple only looking back from time to time to see if they were following him.

Jamie waited until they were out of sight, he hoped they'd meet again. *There's something about them. I'd like to get to know them better someday,* he thought.

He reached for his pack pulled it over his shoulders and continued along the trail until he reached the creek and even with Wendi's warning slipped on a rock and fell into the water – slightly twisting his ankle in the process. "Damn," he said under his breath, got up and soldiered on.

An hour later he limped slightly into Camper Flats and made his camp for the night.

# *Chapter Nineteen*

The campsite was nothing like the word had implied to Jamie. In his mind he'd expected an area the Rangers had graded and made pathways, fire pits and toilets with fresh water to wash with. When he turned the final corner on the rugged and unimproved trail he'd followed all day and saw a wooden sign leaning to one side near a dying pine tree that read in faded color 'Camper's Flat', his heart momentarily dropped in disappointment.

He leaned on the dying tree with one arm and shifted the weight of his pack on his shoulders resulting in some relief, although it was short lived. Looking forward, Camper's Flat was an unshaded area he guessed was about fifty yards square. The ground was littered with granite boulders erupting from the ground making the area uneven leaving little ground suitable for pitching a tent. And worse, it offered no protection from the blazing afternoon sun.

Jamie felt a pit in his stomach and began to wonder why he'd come on this trip. His breath became shallow and he began to feel anxious and frighteningly alone. Another quick look around the rocky knoll and he saw and heard nothing. There were no other campers for miles – he was alone.

The lone hiker moved around the single dying tree until he found a modest patch of shade from the sun and he dropped his pack and sat down with his aching back against the rough decaying bark. His hand reached for his canteen and he drank the tepid water. It tasted good but the warmness of the water offered neither refreshment nor relief.

He let his mind push through the anxiety attack he was experiencing and concentrated on the throbbing pain in his left ankle from his fall. He arched his shoulders and stretched his back against the tree in a vain effort to ease his discomfort from carrying the pack all day.

As he stretched, he realized he was actually enjoying the adventure and a smile came over his sunburned and dusty face. "Hell yes, this is a great time," he whispered to himself and his anxiety and fear faded away and confidence and courage filled the void. He smiled again feeling much better and began to move his shoulders and ankle, they didn't seem to protest any longer.

Jamie climbed to his feet pulled his pack back over his shoulders and moved towards the knoll looking for a suitable site for the night. After several minutes looking around he decided to move north off the trail, "Why not," he told himself and headed toward Middle Mountain where he hoped to find water and some trees for shelter.

It was nearly dark when Jamie found a campsite and he hurried to set up his bedding, ate and prepare himself for another night in the high country before the last of the light left the evening sky.

He realized he was miles from another person. This time he hung his pack in a tree with his food supply tucked away inside. It hung nearly twelve feet in the air from a nearby tree.

Satisfied, Jamie climbed into his sleeping bag, pulled his wool cap down over his ears and forehead and waited for the bag to warm up. He relaxed and listened to the forest and watched the stars and planets in the perfectly clear night sky. *There are millions of lights in the sky,* he thought as he watched them in amazement and awe.

His body was tired yet his mind was alert and agile. Closing his eyes for several moments he concentrated on the sounds surrounding him and the orchestra amused him. He heard the buzzing of nates and flying insects moving in straight lines around him while others seemed to be moving in erratic circles.

In the distance Jamie could hear the faint muffled sounds of padded feet moving slowly. In the soft dirt he'd noticed a number of holes dug near a fallen tree. In the dark the inhabitance were busy moving around feeding and improving their homes. Jamie, smiled as he listened to the chattering and social activity where the ground squirrel community erupted with movement. "Note to self," Jamie whispered to himself – and the ground squirrels froze in silence at the sound of his voice. "In the future don't camp near a ground squirrel colony if you want to sleep," he finished his sentence and after several more seconds the squirrels resumed their evening activities.

Jamie rolled over on his side and just before he fell asleep he felt for the folding knife in his pocket. *Good,* he thought and fell asleep.

\*\*\*

As the lone camper slept soundly on the ground the eyes of the forest watched him with caution, some with curiosity and others with cunning. The muffled sound of padded feet in the distance had slowly circled around the camp coming closer each rotation. The faint aroma of food had found the animal's large flaring nostrils and his stomach drove his brain to locate the food.

The large male brown bear was fully grown and stood nearly eight feet tall. His teeth and claws were fully developed and he was a strong healthy example of his species. From the shadows near the sleeping hiker the bear examined the camp site. He'd visited many of them in the past and this one was laid-out in similar fashion to most of the others. He smelled Jamie before he saw him bundled up in his sleeping bag. His steady breathing told the intruder he was fast asleep. His nose continued to pull the unusual senses from the air – the focus was the smell of food. The bear sat down quietly and scratched his belly with his large paw and ebony colored claws while he pin pointed the location of the food. It was then, he saw the pack hanging from the tree directly over his head.

With a grunt of satisfaction he stood up on his hind legs and leaned against the tree and easily reached up with his paws and clutched the pack and with a tug pulled it down to the ground. It was heavier than he'd anticipated and it dropped to the ground with a loud thump. So much for stealth. Jamie bolted upright in his bed and looked at the bear pulling and tearing at the canvas bag. The bear was focused on the contents of the pack and hardly gave notice to the man as he climbed out of his sleeping bag and began to move towards the bear reaching into his pocket.

Jamie knew better than to approach the bear. The contest was over before he was awaken. The nine-hundred pound bear, his claws and teeth tore apart his pack as he rooted out the food contained inside and Jamie, armed only with a folding knife, was helpless to stop the thief. To threaten the bear would most certainly result in the bear mauling him.

All that was the thoughts of a rational man but Jamie was not thinking rationally at the moment. He was two days from Emerald Bay and food, he was

alone in the forest and miles away from help and he
was angry. Jamie moved closer to the bear and began
to yell, "Get out of there you thief," he growled at the
bear and began to move aggressively at the bear – his
knife open and tightly gripped in his right hand.

The brown bear sensed the man approaching
and looked up from the torn and tattered backpack
and growled, his eyes glowed red. Jamie continued to
approach. The bear refused to back down. The bear
tossed the pack aside and turned towards Jamie
showing his teeth and twisting his neck. In a final
effort to scare off the approaching human, the bear
reared up on his hind legs and stood two feet above
the man. Even that didn't seem to deter the
challenger. The bear, no stranger to conflict, prepared
for what promised to be a short and one sided fight
when out of the shadows the bear saw two bright
flashes of light then two more, then two more. The
deafening sound of gunshots rang out in the forest
and the massive bear felt his body ravaged by the
bullets penetrating deep inside his neck and lungs.

No longer did the bear want to fight, his body
was becoming weaker by the second and all he
wanted to do was move away and rest.

Jamie froze when he heard the gunfire and
watched silently as the bear recoiled from the bullets
striking him. Jamie, as if in a slow motion movie,
watched the fierce bear, ready to shred him into

pieces instantly become docile and move away into the forest leaving a trail of blood behind him.

Jamie heard a dog bark and turned to see Jake come running into his camp. The dog ran up to Jamie, jumped up and licked the shaking man then looked into the direction of the bear's retreat and barked as if to say, "Stay away from my friend."

A few seconds later, Max and Wendi came into the camp each holding hunting rifles. All this was overwhelming for Jamie and he fell to his knees his body shaking as the adrenaline ran through his veins. Jake ran up to him kissing his face and then sat beside his friend. Max and Wendi sat in front of him and set their rifles down and silently watched Jamie until he began to recover.

Max had seen the effects of combat and he was no stranger to the physical and emotional impacts that confronting death for the first time had on a man. He patiently waited for Jamie to recover. When he judged Jamie was ready he smiled and said, "Damn Jamie, I don't know whether that was stupid crazy or brave as hell. What was in that pack, your mother's cookies or something?" He laughed and Jake barked playfully. Wendi's eyes searched Jamie's for answers.

Jamie looked at his wilderness friends and finally said, "Yea, I guess that was pretty stupid." Then he reached for the dog and gave him a hug and said, "Thanks for coming along when you did. If you hadn't I would have probably been mincemeat."

Looking at Max he said, "How is it you happened to be here and carrying rifles?"

Max smiled and after looking at his wife for a moment said, "We have been hunting that bear for nearly a week. He has been making a habit of terrorizing campers and has mauled two dogs and one man. He's been moved three times deeper into the wilderness and he continues to endanger people so we're here to end his reign of terror."

He took a breath and finished, "After we're sure you're okay we'll finish off the bear."

Wendi said, "That bear mangled up your pack pretty well. Let's see what you have left. We have extra food and equipment if you need it." She rose to her feet and retrieved his pack and carefully removed the remaining contents, tossing away the food the bear had already damaged or partially eaten.

Several minutes later she asked, "How many more days are you planning on camping in the high country?"

Jamie, by then feeling much better said, "Two more nights then I will meet my friends at Eagle Falls."

Wendi looked at the contents again and said, "I think you should be okay," and she reached into her day pack and pulled out two candy bars and set them down with his gear. "And these will help you with the munchies; our brave friend." She smiled.

Max tossed the contents into Jamie's, damaged but functional pack and pulled it high up in the tree. "There you go, now Jamie go back to sleep and we'll go finish off the wounded bear."

Max grabbed his rifle and with a final look at the lone camper said, "Jamie that was a very brave thing you did tonight but take it from me, it's a fool's errand to come to a gun fight with a butter knife," He smile and grabbed Jamie's shoulder with his large hand. "Take care my friend."

"Thanks, I hope to see you all again." Jamie said as he watched Jake lead the way. The hunters moved into the shadows and disappeared into the darkness.

# *Chapter Twenty*

Jamie couldn't sleep after all the excitement and lay in his bag quietly thinking about the events hours before. He kept thinking about what the man who he'd grow to respect very much had said, "That was a very brave thing you did…", and he felt a 'Twanger' and his shoulders arched backward, his chest leaned forward and he felt the sense of confidence. He smiled and thought, *This empowering feeling is becoming more familiar. I like it.* Then his thoughts moved to his friends, *thank you Artie, Maggie Rose and you my mysterious friends Max and Wendi – its knowing you and all the things you've done for me has helped me understand and grow as a man; My life is changing for the better.*

Though his eyes were tired and irritated from the lack of sleep his body was relaxed yet alert. He felt his nose protest from the cold air surrounding him. The bite of cold coupled with the constant running of the fluids from his sinuses was a constant reminder -- he was at nearly eight thousand feet above sea level and his body was still becoming adjusted to the severe change from sea level.

\*\*\*

# WALKING THROUGH HELL

The morning sun began to brighten the sky and as it did the darkness surrounding Jamie gradually changed from a black curtain to faint shadows which quickly exploded into clear shapes. The colors around him changed from blacks, greys and whites to a rainbow of bright vibrant colors. Jamie sighed and without protest climbed out of his sleeping bag and began to make himself a coffee and a modest breakfast.

He reached for the coffee boiling in a cup over his butane stove when in the distance he heard a rifle shot and then another followed by a third shot. He knew Max and Wendi had located the rogue bear and with the kindness and mercy any animal deserves had killed it. He felt sad for the bear but knew it was the only solution and he had come dangerously close to becoming the next victim of a bear attack.

All of a sudden he had a strong urge to call Maggie Rose and tell her about the night before and his new wilderness friends. For a long moment he sipped his coffee and thought about how nice it would be to hear her voice and share his adventure with her. Slowly his euphoria subsided and he whispered to himself, "I guess that will have to wait for a couple more days when I see you in Tahoe."

He gathered up his gear, retrieved his pack from high up in the tree, where Max had placed it, and prepared for the third day hiking in the Desolation Wilderness. Jamie studied his map and noticed it was slightly damaged from the bear assault the night before and unfortunately part of the map he needed to navigate to his next campsite was missing, "Damn," he whispered under his breath. "Damn bear." It didn't faze him and he took note of his confidence. He knew before this trip a little set back like that would have crushed him and he would have cascaded into a panic attack.

He smiled and said, "Guess I'll be humming a few bars and faking it – I got this." He reached down for his pack and tossed it over his shoulders and moved eastward toward Velma Lake. His pack felt lighter this morning and his back and shoulders didn't protest as they'd done the morning before. He felt strong and confident and moved with increasing self-assuredness. He moved with one step in front of the other whispering words he'd never had the courage to acknowledge before… "In two days I'll end this journey for my Maggie Rose to see. I walked across the Desolation Wilderness for my true love to be with me." He blushed and looked around to make sure he was alone – he was. He repeated his song over and over and each time he said it more loudly and confidently.

By early afternoon he climbed over a rocky berm and looked down on Velma Lake. It was a beautiful sight and he paused for several moments to soak in the view. The lake was crystal clear and shades of blue from dark sapphire to nearly white as the submerged boulders reached for the surface. The trees around the lake were vibrant green and their trunks many shades of browns and tans. The bushes were a cornucopia of colors from blue greys to greens and bright colored flowers and berries.

He listened and looked around for several minutes to catch the sounds or sights of other people nearby. The air was full of sounds but he decided none were human. He moved down the berm towards the lake and chanted his song until he found a suitable location to camp for the night.

The sun was still high in the sky and Jamie had his camp set up with experienced ease. He listened again for the sound of other campers and heard nothing so he looked one more time longingly at the lake stripped off his dirty clothes and walked naked into the water.

It seemed like a good idea to him until he stepped into the water and realized it was freezing cold. By then he was up to his knees and decided. "A real mountain man wouldn't be afraid of the cold." Jamie took a deep breath and dove in.

His heart pounded and the air evaporated in his lungs. He fought for breath as he stood on the bottom. His body was colder than he could remember. He struggle to breathe until the shock began to subside and except for the discomfort in his groan, it began to feel fine. He felt the bar of soap in his hand and began to bath and once again he realized he was on an adventure miles from another human being and he was okay – in fact he said to his surroundings, "I'm doing more than okay, I'm doing great."

Just then he heard two women laughing as they watched him in the lake without a stitch of clothing.

One yelled out, "Hello handsome, take your time, we'll wait until you finish."

He blushed but the 'Twanger" he felt couldn't be stolen by a couple of curious women camping on the other side of the lake.

Jamie finished bathing and looked at his camp twenty feet away realized, *No woman except my mother has ever seen me naked before.* He felt confident and without modesty walked out of the lake to his camp and dried himself off with a shredded towel and dressed in plain view of the women across the lake.

# *Chapter Twenty-One*

Jamie relaxed in his simple camp-site and enjoyed the surroundings. The animals, birds and even the insects fascinated him. For an hour he watched and listened and thought about how lucky he was to have friends like Artie, Max and Wendi and of course Maggie Rose – who, by now, he'd accepted he was falling in love with.

He prepared dinner over his butane stove and was finished before the sunset behind the mountains to the west. He looked around as the darkness surrounded him and noticed a dull yellow glow outlining the mountains in the direction he would be heading in the morning.

*It must be light from the communities on the California side of the lake.* He rationalized, "I am only 5 or 6 miles away from Eagle Lake." His eyes were heavy and he fell asleep with the thoughts of Maggie Rose keeping him warm.

***

What Jamie and the other campers, around Velma Lake and the area west of Eagle Lake, didn't realize was they were in serious danger. The glow barely outlining the mountains was in fact a fire accidently started by a careless camper. The fire was growing quickly and in a few hours would be out of control and moving west directly towards Velma Lake.

***

Jamie was sound asleep in his tent when the two campers from the other side of the lake ran into his camp and pulled open his tent, "Get up, get up there is a large fire and it's coming our way," they cried from the fabric entrance they had hurriedly pulled back.

Jamie looked up at the two women and instantly saw the fear in their eyes and worry etched their faces. His senses became alert – his lungs were filling with smoke and his eyes burned. He jumped out of his sleeping bag and stood before the two woman naked then rushed to put on his clothes and grab his pack.

"What are we going to do?" One of the women said. Jamie looked at the two of them, they were frightened – he would have to be their leader. He felt a 'Twanger' and he resolved he would find a way to protect these women and get them to safety.

He was calm and in control they could sense it. It gave them the courage to follow him. "My name is Jamie," he said.

The tall blonde woman said, "Hi, I'm Sally and my friend," a shorter brunette, "is Donna. We're from Placerville. It's about fifty miles from here."

Jamie, smiled as he threw on his pack and said, "I'm from Lodi, near Sacramento." He looked into their faces and ask, "Where do you think the fire is coming from?" They both pointed towards Eagle Lake.

Jamie reached into his pack for his cell phone and check to see if he had service. The light blue screen flashed a warning *NO SERVICE.* He turned off his phone and put it in his pocket and reached for his map. After orienting himself he lined up the map and the glow from the fire in the distance and said, "Ladies can you both walk quickly and do you have food and water for one day?" They looked at each other, glad they had a leader and nodded, "Yes. What's your plan, Jamie?"

He set his map on a nearby rock and held it in-place with his left hand and began to move his free hand over the map as he spoke. "Here is where we are," he pointed to Velma Lake. "And here is where the fire is." He pointed to the area north and east of their position. He saw Eagle Lake in the area of the fire and hoped Artie and Maggie Rose were safe.

He continued, "The winds are blowing to the north and west so we must assume the fire will come our direction and hopefully stay slightly to the north." He waited for a moment.

"I propose we move south to separate ourselves from the fire then move east," and he pointed at Fallen Leaf Lake.

97

Jamie took a breath and continued, "Most of the trail will be level or down so we can make good time and we'll be moving towards population centers where we can find help." He leaned back and watched the women consider the idea. They looked at each other, then, in unison responded, "Yes we agree with your plan. Lead the way."

"Okay, we'll take trails so we're near the lakes during our evacuation just in case we get overrun by the fire. If necessary, we'll take refuge in the water." The women's eye showed their lack of enthusiasm for the idea of getting into a lake to avoid being burned to death.

Jamie saw their concern and smiled and calmly said, "If we walk fast and with a little luck we should be fine. Let's go."

## *Chapter Twenty-Two*

The smoke was heavy and Jamie's lungs revolted as the acrid air filled them. His eyes burned but he stayed focused on his task. *Get these ladies to safety,* he kept telling himself.

Motivated by a growing forest fire behind them and the minimal packs on their backs, the three of them moved quickly. Jamie used his compass to blaze a trail to Fallen Leaf Lake. He moved as fast as Marie and Donna could because he knew they were close to the fire on this leg of their escape.

They neared the lake as the sun began to rise and they could see that Desolation Wilderness Basin was beginning to fill with smoke and the fire was now clearly visible to the north. There was little time to enjoy the scenery – they were in a race to save themselves. They continued until Fallen Leak Lake came into view. "Let's stop here for a few and fill our canteens and eat something," Jamie said then reached for his phone. He powered it up and the screen warned *NO SERVICE.* He forced himself to remain calm and put his phone back in his pocket. Then he thought about the candy bars Wendi had given him several days before. He pulled them from his pack and handed one to Donna and the other to Sally. "Eat these – I don't like chocolate," he said with a smile that showed he remained confident and calm.

Sally took the candy and smiled. Soot and dust smudged her face – it did little to hide the worry etched across her forehead and cheeks. She coughed and in a hoarse voice said "Thank you," Jamie felt a 'Twanger' that reinforced his calm and clear thinking. She could feel his strength and it gave her the courage to continue.

Jamie dropped to the ground and pulled his pack around in front of him. He reached for his map and compass to orient himself and site a course to the next point, Azure Lake and then down a steep incline to Tallac, where there were improved roads that would lead them to the Ranger Station at Baldwin Beach and Lake Tahoe where there would be help.

He motioned for Sally and Donna to come near him and look at the map. They did and he explained where they were and the next leg to Azure Lake, then Tallac and then security at Baldwin Beach.

They listened silently and nodded. "Good, let's rest for another fifteen minutes then move on. If all goes well we may be out of danger by later this evening," he hoped he was right.

The remainder of the rest break the three of them sat next to one another with their back against a fallen log and watched the fire in the distance. The bright yellow and orange flames grew higher and higher and lashed upward violently into the sky with defiance. Smoke bellowed from behind the leading edge of the fire rising up and moving over the flames – directed by the winds.

Jamie watched it closely and discreetly bit his lip when he saw the winds beginning to shift from northwest to west; almost directly the direction they were heading. *Oh no, this could be bad*, he thought and came to his feet. "Let's get moving, we have a ways to go ladies," he said and didn't mention the wind shift. *Why make them any more anxious than they already are?* He thought.

The short hike to Azure Lake was through a wooded area and Jamie had to rely on his compass to keep moving in the right direction. With some luck, and his growing expertise with his compass, put them on target. He smiled when they cleared the ridge and saw the lake below confirming his relief they hadn't lost time and energy by getting disoriented.

Jamie looked behind them and it was clear the fire was gaining on them. He felt the wind fanning the fire against his face. Jamie reached for his phone and powered it up, *work you damn thing*, he thought to himself. The phone came to life and he couldn't contain himself, "Hell yah," he exclaimed and his smile told Donna and Sally something good was happening.

Jamie sat down on a rock overlooking the lake and dialed the phone. The first person he called was

Maggie Rose. *Ring Ring,* Maggie Rose answered the phone, "Hello?"

Jamie got right to the point, "Maggie Rose are you and your father okay? There is a major fire that started near Eagle Lake and we are moving southeast to get away from the fire."

He took a breath and said, "I can't talk much, I need to save my battery. There are three of us and we are at Azure Lake. The fire is over taking us and we need help. Can you call the ranger station and ask them if they can get us out of here. I'm afraid we may not be able to out run or out maneuver the fire. Winds are driving it down over us."

"Maggie Rose again, there are three of us and we are on the north side of Azure Lake. We can't out run the fire so we'll wait here and if not rescued, move out into the center of the lake, there is a small island, and take cover in the water and wait for the fire to run over us. Please call the Ranger Station and tell them all this."

"I love you Maggie Rose and can't wait to see you after this," Jamie said and hung up the phone. He looked at the women there with him and their stares said it all – *we are about to get overrun by a forest fire and you call your girlfriend?*

Artie looked over at his daughter, Maggie Rose, what was that. She looked at him from the passenger seat of his old Ford Pickup and she began to cry and she violently fired a barrage of words at him, "Jamie is in trouble he is running away from a forest fire at a place called Azure Lake. He asked me to call the ranger station and asked for help. Jamie said the fire is over taking them and they are going to swim out to the island in the middle of the lake and let the fire run over them if they can't be rescued."

"Damn, we need to get on the phone with the rangers now," He exclaimed.

"Dad, he told me he loves me too." She began to cry again but quickly dried her eyes and began to dial 911 and asked for the local ranger station.

Artie and Maggie Rose had left early that morning from Lodi to ensure they were waiting for Jamie when he called from Eagle Lake. When Jamie had called they were on highway 50 about an hour away from their original destination.

"911, what is the nature of your emergency," a calm professional voice answered Maggie Rose's call.

"I need to be connected to the nearest ranger station. There is a forest fire near Eagle Lake and my boyfriend" Arties eyebrow lifted and he gave his daughter a look then a smile, "and two other campers are running away from the fire. They are at Azure Lake and the fire is overtaking them. They need to be rescued," Maggie Rose gasped for breathe like she'd completed a marathon.

"Okay, I will patch you through to the local ranger station and stay on the line until I know you are connected to the right person," the professional dispatcher said and several seconds later the phone was ringing.

"Ranger Wendi Loften may I help you?" A voice answered.

"This is the 911 operator. I have and emergency call on the line. There are three campers in danger by the Eagle Lake fire. Miss, Ranger Loften will get you the help you need. I am signing off," the operator said and she hung up the phone.

Ranger Loften said, "Hello, how can I help you?"

"My name is Maggie Rose Petty. My boyfriend is camping in the desolation Wilderness Basin and he called me several minutes ago. He and two other people are in serious danger. They are at Azure Lake and a big fire is overtaking them. He told me to call the ranger station for help. They can't out run the fire so they're planning to swim out to the island in the middle of the lake and make shelter or get in the water and let the fire burn over/around them. If they can't be rescued before. Can you help them please?" She pleaded.

Ranger Loften was already two steps ahead. "You said he just called you and he is at Azure Lake. Yes?"

"Yes on the north side," Maggie Rose said.

"Your boyfriend and two other campers, correct?" Loften asked.

"Yes."

"What is your boyfriend's name?" The ranger asked.

"Jamie."

"Jamie. Was he making his way from the Van Vleck ranch at Tells Peak to Eagle Lake," Wendi asked.

Maggie pulled the phone away from her ear and stared at it for a moment then carefully put it back against her ear and asked, "How did you know?"

"Maggie Rose, my husband and I ran into Jamie several times over the last three days. He's a fine young man and very brave." Wendi said as she studied the map on the wall – pinpointing the location of her friend. Jamie.

"Maggie I need you to give me your number and Jamie's number so we can contact him," Wendi's voice had the blend of calm, friendliness and authority. Maggie did as she was told.

After Wendi confirmed the numbers she said good bye and that she would stay in touch and hung up the phone.

Maggie Rose – exhausted and emotionally spent leaned against the truck door and nodded off. Artie kept the Ford heading east up highway 50 and quietly worked on a plan to help his friend Jamie.

# Chapter Twenty-Three

Wendi hung up the phone and thought about the information she'd received moments ago. She reached into her pocket and retrieved her cell phone. She called Max.

Max picked up on the second ring. "Hello dear, working late at the office, I see," he said in a light hearted voice. He was in the barn tanning the bear hide the two of them had retrieved after killing the rogue bear several nights ago. "I just finished…" and Jake barked in the background… "Okay, Jake, 'we' just finished tanning and stretching the bear's hide. It will make a nice rug by the fire place," he said.

She had no time for such games and her voice told him the same. "Max, Jamie is in serious trouble," she said. His face became serious and instantly he was all business.

"How do you know? Where is he? Is he alright?" He peppered her with questions.

Wendi would have normally gone on the defensive but she let his intensity go unchallenged. She said, "A freak call from his girlfriend, the north side of Azure Lake and yes he is okay for now." Wendi caught her breath and continued. "His girlfriend Maggie Rose; a funny name if you asked me, said he is in the company of two other hikers who are running away from the Eagle Lake fire. According to her the fire is moving in their direction and they are preparing to swim to the island in the center of the lake and prepare for the fire to run over them, if they can't be rescued before the fire overruns them."

Max grunted, confirming he understood and thought for a moment, *Jamie that's a pretty good plan for a tenderfoot.* Max smiled and said, "Wendi, can you get a helicopter to his position in the next hour and a half?"

"I'll try but most of the national forest assets are dedicated to fighting the fire near Eagle Lake," she said.

"Okay Wendi, try and make the call. I'll make a few calls myself and see if I can call in a favor or two," he said and before he hung up he softened his voice and said, "Wendi I love you and we'll get Jamie out okay – I promise."

Wendi returned to her office and began dialing the phone. Each call she received the same response – "No way they're all committed, sorry, we can't help you" and so on.

Max walked quickly to the log cabin and into the bedroom and faced the door to his walk-in safe. He rolled the tumbler right, left and right again then put his right thumb against a thumbprint reader. A mechanical click told him the door was unlocked. He pulled the door open and Jake rushed into the room like it was a game – his tail moving with delight.

"No not now Jake," Max said and he reached for the encrypted cell phone and pulled it from it charger. He dialed a number and waited for the other party to pick up.

"Max, you old sack of guts. How is retirement and how is Wendi? Did you call to tell me you're ready to come back inside?" His old agency friend Wilber Johnson said. "Hey, Max I still haven't gotten over you shooting me and throwing a desk on my legs. I still have a limp you bastard," the big man on the other end of the line began to laugh in a booming voice that let Max know all was forgiven and that was a strange and bazaar op they worked together years before.

Max got right to the point, "'Boa'", Wilber Johnson's call sign, "I need a favor immediately. There are three hikers in the Lake Tahoe area who are being overrun by a forest fire. There are no forest service or local government helicopters available. I need one of your black birds and a pilot to fly me in and if possible retrieve three additional passengers. I need the bird to pick me up at the Van Vleck landing field as soon as possible. We only have an hour and a half to get to them – understand?"

"Wow, that's a tough order Max. I just happen to have a bird near you. Keep this number the pilot will call you in a few minutes. Do you need any gear, 'Viper'?" 'Boa' asked.

"No I have what I need," Max said and laughed, "No one has called me Viper in a long time. Thanks and when this is over, let's catch up. I appreciate you coming through for me. This is important to Wendi and me." He knew better than to say too much, but after all 'Boa' was one of his closest friends left in the agency. "One of these hikers is a close friend of ours."

"Enough said. Be careful and keep that phone handy," 'Boa' said and hung up the phone. Before Max had removed his phone from his ear 'Boa' was listening to the phone ring,

"Hello," a calm and professional voice answered.

"This is 'Boa' authentication number 578209456. This is an immediate classified deployment. Wheels up in five minutes first stop west of Lake Tahoe twelve miles one passenger waiting at the Van Vleck landing strip – he's one of us, call sign 'Viper'."

"Shit, the 'Viper'?"

"Yes you will take him where he wants and depending on the situation when you arrive at the objective you may need to extract three additional passengers."

The pilot replied, "Copy, I have a little bird and cannot carry four pax at this altitude. Sorry, it's not possible; but I can make two trips, sir."

Wilber Johnson was getting tired of being in the middle and said, "Work it out with 'Viper'. He is monitoring agency comms: alpha-papa-sierra. His number is 234-234-2343. Call him once you're in the air."

"Yes, sir." The pilot turned several switches on his dashboard and the helicopter came to life.

'Boa' yelled into the phone as the helicopter roared in the background. "This is a classified op and it never happened – understand?"

"Yes sir, I'll be airborne in two minutes, headed to the Van Vleck Ranch landing strip."

***

Max gathered up the gear he'd need from the vault and instinctively reached for his Glock model 19 and four magazines and stuck them in his pack.

He looked down at his buddy Jake and said, "Sorry Boy, this one is not for you." The dog looked sad and wined and moaned.

Max thought about it for a moment and changed his mind. "You're right, Jake. You need to be there, my old friend. But you need to know that it'll be scary, the water cold and the fire hot. Are you still interested?" The dog knew he'd won the argument and he barked and wagged his tail.

"Okay let's get going we need to get to the landing strip for our ride," Max said as he closed the vault and carried his pack to his Jeep.

On the way to the landing strip Max called Wendi. She picked up the phone and he could instantly tell she was frustrated and disappointed.

"Honey what is it?" He asked.

"I've tried every angle I could to get a helicopter and I have run out of options," She said and her voice told of her despair. "Poor Jamie," She said and began to choke up.

"Wendi sweetheart, don't worry. I called in a favor from a friend of mine and Jake and I will be leaving in a few minutes to get them out," Max said. He could have gloated but he didn't and listened.

"What? You and Jake?" She said and nearly broke down in tears.

"I can't give you the details over the phone but I want you to know that our dog is very brave. I wanted to leave him home and he would have nothing to do with it. He insisted he'd come and save Jamie," Max chuckled. "Wendi, we love you and I must go my ride is on the other line. Jake and I will be safe. See you in a day or two, Bye"

Max hung up the phone and rubbed the dogs head sitting beside him in the Jeep. "I never liked long goodbyes," he said. The dog bark in agreement.

\*\*\*

111

The young pilot wearing dark aviator sunglasses made famous by the military pilots from the Second World War put his buckskin gloved hands on the controls and in his capable hands the engine began to accelerate, the blades began to lift the bird and soon it was hovering above the airfield in the far corner of the aviation complex. Without communications with the tower the small, agile black bird leapt into the air rotated until it was pointing west, then leaned, slightly forward and began to accelerate.

"Damn secret squirrel agency jockey. Why don't they have to call in before they takeoff," one of the middle aged men in the tower, overlooking the air field, said. No one was listening.

The pilot flew low over Lake Tahoe and gathered speed. His aircraft was fully fueled and perfectly maintained. The young man was still new to agency work and this would be one of his first assignments without another pilot. He felt the adrenaline rush and the hair on the back of his neck bristled with excitement.

As the helicopter closed in on the western bank of the lake he pulled back on the stick and the bird soared up like an eagle clearing the tall pines by less than 50 feet. *Now that's flying*, he thought to himself. He was an experienced pilot, a daredevil at that and he was in command on one of the most agile and maneuverable birds ever built.

The pilot leveled the aircraft off above the trees and immediately saw a large fire to his right and dark dense smoke moved from left to right in front of him. He pulled up and flew above it until it was behind him and he dove down where he was happiest skimming the tree tops.

The pilot reached for his phone and called the number 'Boa' had given him. It rang once and a cold hard voice answered. "Yes."

"This is 'Black Bird 12 Alpha'. I am inbound to your destination and will be overhead in two minutes. Status?"

"This is 'Viper' I am on the north end of the LZ. Do you need smoke?"

"Negative, 'Viper' I know where you are. See you in 60 seconds," the pilot said and then thought, *Wholly shit, 'Viper' the most famous operator in the company and I get to take him to work.*

Max hung up the phone, Jake sat beside him looking up to the east. Max was used to waiting on a helicopter to pluck him out of the jungles around the world but this was different. His home was only three miles away. Jake began to get antsy and whine then he began to bark and get agitated.

Max looked up above the trees and there was the Black Bird and right on time.  Max kneeled, pulled his pack up under him and pulled Jake in tight and held him close covering his eyes while the pilot landed next to them.

The bird settled and powered down, Max, holding the dog approached the aircraft and put Jake in the back seat, looked at the pilot and said, "Hold my dog while I get my pack."

"Yes Sir," the pilot responded then immediately thought to himself. "What the hell, I'm not your doggie daycare, 'Viper'."

Max returned with his pack and tossed it into the back with the dog then climbed into the front seat next to the pilot.

"Thanks for the lift young man. My name is Max."

"Yes sir, 'Viper', It's a pleasure to meet you. My name is Bettencourt, John Bettencourt, sir. Where can I take you? I'm afraid my tasking from 'Boa' was incomplete and he told me you would fill me in." The young man said as he reached for the controls and powered up the bird and with the slight movement of his wrists it jumped into the air like a bird of prey.

"Are you familiar with Desolation Wilderness?" Max asked.

"Yes sir, I grew up in Truckee."

"Great, Get us to Azure Lake, ASAP and I'll fill you in with the details on the way," Max said in a calm but urgent tone.

Bettencourt was all business and he pointed the bird to the saddle in Tells Peak and pushed the throttle all the way forward. Max looked at the young pilot and thought, *I like you kid. You've got what it takes to make it in this corporation.* Max leaned back for a moment and enjoyed the rare opportunity to see his home from the air close and personal.

Max looked to the right as the helicopter rose and could see barely hidden by the trees his log cabin – his private oasis and where he, Wendi and Jake lived off the grid. Max looked over his shoulder and saw Jake sitting in the seat, panting and looking back and forth between the sites below and Max. "Jake you're doing fine. So I see you like to fly too. You're just an amazing dog." The dog barked – he knew what Max had said.

The pilot flew over Tell's Peak almost too closely for Max's liking but in a man's game, the one who flinches looses.

Max briefed Bettencourt on the task at hand. It was agreed Max and Jake would stay behind with Jamie and Bettencourt would take the two hikers to safety and deliver them to the station at Tahoe for debriefing before being released.

Max, Jake and Jamie would stay in touch via the agency encrypted phone and wait for a later evacuation.

# *Chapter Twenty-Four*

The Black Bird approached Azure Lake from the West. The pilot flew the bird fast and low over the granite boulders and the weathered and rugged trees in the Wilderness Area. The growing fire and the massive smoke cloud it produced was dark and covered all that it passed over.

"Shit, this is going to be close, Bettencourt." Max said into the intercom. "Come in from the north and look for our hikers if we see them put me down as close as you can and I'll bring your pax back."

"Yes sir." Bettencourt heard his voice calm, strong and in control. He smiled, *maybe I'm really cut out to be one of these guys after all*, he thought.

Jake saw Max looking out of the window and he looked down too trying to pierce the smoky barrier between them and the ground. He was the first to see Jamie and Jake began to bark.

"What do you see," Max asked his dog and looked at him clawing at the window and looking down.

"Damn, Bettencourt. Jake found them over there to the right."

116

"Got them, I'll land on that boulder over there," and he brought the helicopter around and lined himself up on an approach landing. As the bird approached the ground the rotors cleared the smoke and Bettencourt landed smoothly atop a massive grey rock dome. Max and Jake leap from the helicopter and ran in the direction of the stranded hikers. Jake rushed ahead barking as he ran head on into the smokiness. Both his vision and sense of smell became hampered.

"Jamie, Jamie." Max called out while Jake barked and barked as they closed on the position they'd seen the hikers moments before.

"Over here," a voice called and Jake came rushing out of the smoky fog. The dog momentarily stopped when he approached a strange woman then he saw Jamie behind her and rushed in.

"Jake is that you," Jamie asked but he knew the answer as Jake lunged at him and tackled him then covered him with affection. Seconds later, Max came out of the acrid smoke and said, "I hate to break up this reunion but…" he looked at the ladies and said, "You ladies have a flight to catch. All of you, please follow me." He turned but not before he smiled at Jamie and said, "Nice to see you again young man."

Max moved quickly but carefully ensuring the hikers were following behind. As they approach the boulder they could hear the sound of the idling helicopter. The closer they came the clearer the black aircraft came into view. It was unlike any they'd seen before. It was small and aggressive looking. They noticed it had no numbers or identification on the sides either. *It doesn't matter it's our escape from this hell,* they thought. Max escorted them to the bird and opened the door and yelled over the idling engine. "Ladies, one in the front and one in the back. The pilot's name is Captain Bettencourt and he will take you to safety. There they will make arrangements for you to return to your families and friends." He smiled at them and they hugged him then Jamie and climbed. Donna reached down and kissed Jake on the forehead. Her eyes were tearing from the smoke and emotion as she closed the door and the pilot powered up. Max pulled Jamie back clear of the rotors and waited for the bird to leap into the air and move away.

When the noise of the Black Bird subsided, Max looked at Jamie and put his massive hands on his shoulders and asked, "What's your plan, son?"

# *Chapter Twenty-Five*

Max stood there over the young man – a massive and intimidating figure. The forest was intertwined with heavy smoke and the orange and yellow glow of fire as it changed shape and color through the acrid fog; inching closer with each second.

It was another moment in his life where in his old life the old Jamie would have caved and given up – a coward. But now he felt another 'Twanger' of confidence and assurance and he rose to his feet and looked Max in the face and said, "Sir, before you arrived we built a raft to move to the island in the middle of the lake and there we can seek shelter and safety from the fire until we can be rescued."

Max looked at him and waited a moment for his reply then said, "Jamie, that sounds like a good plan. Good enough for Old Jake and I to bet our lives on. Lead the way."

Jamie stood there for a moment and looked at Max – Jake was sitting by Jamie's side with his head on the young man's thigh. Jamie had known from the first time they met that there was something special and powerful about his friend Max but he couldn't put his finger on it. *Now this man comes out of*

119

*nowhere and lets me decide how we are going to survive this fire. Hell, I don't even know what I'm doing and he could have easily stayed home – but he came to save the ladies and endure this danger with me. And for what reason or purpose?* Jamie asked himself.

He had no answer so he said, "Max we should get going if we are going to get out of here before the fire arrives." Jamie turned and began to walk back to the edge of the lake. Jake was walking beside him; he understood the young man needed reassurance. Max walked behind him adjusting the weight of his pack on his shoulders – occasionally wiping his eye to relieve them and stifling a cough from the heavy smoke surrounding them.

Jamie found his way back to the site where the raft was waiting. He turned to face Max and said, "Here is the raft sir, I think it will get us to the island and then we can figure out where to hide out until the fire passes by. I was thinking we should find a protected place on the downwind side and if it gets too hot slip into the water."

All of a sudden Jamie face filled with humility and he said, "But I've never had any experience at this and it's only my first time in the forest alone, sir."

Max looked at him and like a bird looking down from above could see so much more than Jamie could have imagined. He focused on the younger's eyes and said, "Jamie, your plan is sound. You take the lead."

Jamie and Jake rummaged around the available woods for something that would work as paddles to propel the vessel across the water. Max took the opportunity to assess how close the fire was and the speed it was approaching. He figured they had no more than 30 minutes to get into open water or risk being burned alive. He looked at the fire. It stood 60 feet high and the orange and yellow flames rose like angry dragons in defiance. The smoke was getting heavy and denser as its source grew closer. Max felt himself getting anxious. He'd never worried about death but the thought of burning haunted him. *Anything but fire is fine – just no fire*, he thought and noticed Jamie had two large pieces of bark and Jake carried a stick in his mouth; happy to help.

"These should work and from the looks of that fire over there I think we should start to paddle over to the island any minute," Jamie said. Jake barked in agreement.

"Think your right. Let's go," Max replied and reached for the raft made of two logs about ten feet long. The logs were tied together with rope and Max was satisfied with its construction. It was heavier than the two of them had thought. They dug in their heels and heaved until it began to float and became easier to pull into deeper water.

Jake was the first aboard. He made a show of trying to jump up but fell back into the water several times until Max lifted the animal and placed him on board and he sat balanced in the center of the log. Max sat behind Jake and Jamie climbed forward. The two men began to paddle with the pieces of bark and soon the raft began to clumsily move in a drunken sailor's course in the direction of the island approximately 75 yards distant.

By the time the raft was halfway across, the brush and saplings near the water's edge were beginning to smolder and soon were burning. "Looks like we got out of Dodge just in time, Jamie," Max said and chuckled under his breath as he thought, *Damn that was close.* Max could feel the heat on his back. It was just hot enough for him to notice and send a shiver down his spine. He pulled harder on the paddle to distance himself from the heat source and didn't look over his shoulder until he felt the temperature subside.

The hastily made raft neared the island and Jake couldn't contain himself any longer. He lunged head first into the frigid water and swam the remaining twenty feet, walked up onto the course granite sand and shook himself several times then barked and turned in circles as he encouraged the men to follow. Soon after the three were standing on the beach looking across the water at the fire consuming the area they'd occupied only 20 minutes before. The flame was now beginning to move around the lake on both sides and soon Max and Jamie would be surrounded but hopefully safe with the lake there to protect them.

Jamie grabbed his pack and said, "Max we should move around the island and find a suitable place where we are protected. He reached for his cell phone and hoped to talk with Maggie Rose but he had no reception. "Damn," he muttered.

"Here let me try mine phone," Max said and he pulled out his agency encrypted phone and it linked right up.

"How come yours works and mine doesn't?" Jamie asked.

"It a satellite phone, here but make it fast. We need to find a hide site soon." Max grunted. He needed to let Wendi know where they were too.

"Hello Maggie Rose? It's me, Jamie," he said.

"Are you okay," she blurted out and Artie gave her a look over the rim of his glasses then looked back to the road ahead.

"Where are you," she insisted.

"I'm fine, I'm with my friend Max and his dog Jake and we are safe on the island in the middle of Azure Lake. The fire is surrounding us but we are safe... the lake will protect us from fire and there is nothing on this island that can burn anyway. It's all granite, rocks and sand.

"What about the women you were traveling with, are they okay?"

"We put them on a helicopter two hours ago and they are safe," He said and felt proud he'd helped save them from danger. "I got to go, I'll call again when the fire is past us. I Love You, Maggie Rose."

"I love you too, Jamie," she said and the phone was dead. She looked over at her father and told him the news. He listened silently.

Jamie handed the phone to Max, "Thanks that is really a special phone."

"Yea kid, it's really something alright," Max said and dialed Wendi.

"Hey Wendi, Jamie, Jake and I are on the island in the center of Azure Lake. We're safe and hunkered down. There are two women we put on the black bird and they should be at the airfield – you know the one. I got to run. Luv ya," and he hung up the phone.

On the other end of the severed conversation, Wendi looked at the dead phone and simply said, "Goodbye to you too." Then she thought, *damn, I love that guy. He's always in the thick of it and never gets harried. Be safe Max and bring Jamie home safe.*

She closed her phone and scolded herself, of course he'll be safe and he'll bring Jamie back safe and sound. She smiled and looked at the map which covered her office wall to locate Azure Lake and the red grease pencil drawn on the piece of Plexiglas that covered the map she used to approximate the area of the Eagle Lake Fire. She had updated the map just minutes before. Her heart climbed into her throat. The red line she'd drawn crossed over the lake.

"Oh shit," she muttered and thought about Max, Jake and Jamie and the danger they were facing at that very moment. *It was so much easier when you were an agency guy and you'd go away – I wouldn't know where or what you were doing until you were safely home again. That was hard, not knowing but this is much worse,* she thought and wiped a tear from her cheek.

In walked the Station Chief, Ranger Wilson, "Wendi, what's the status of the Eagle Lake fire and the rescue efforts in the basin?" he asked. His face showed he'd seen her wipe the tear from her face and he knew about Max's private initiative to go back into the fire to help.

Wilson was vexed by Max. Wendi's husband appeared to be a humble mountain man; quiet and reserved but there was much more to him buried deep inside. He was much more than he appeared and every person who met him felt the strength and power he carefully controlled.

Max seemed to have an endless number of friends with assets he could leverage when needed. Like the helicopter he'd flown into Azure Lake, in front of the forest fire when the National Forest

Service with its federal, state and local power had come-up empty.

Wilson tried not to let the mystery surrounding Wendi's husband distract him, he reminded himself, *Wendi is an excellent ranger and a person I can depend on. The story behind her husband is really of no concern.*

His face softened, "Was that Max on the phone? Is he okay? Where is he?" He fell into a chair across from her and waited. Wendi sat on the edge of her desk. Her pistol and holster dug uncomfortably into her hip. She was used to the weight and awkwardness of carrying a weapon.

"Yes, Max has a satellite phone."

Wilson couldn't help but envy Max, "Damn cell coverage is just about nil in the entire high country and Max has satcom. Your husband has all the toys." Wilson smiled.

"If you only knew," she said and quickly continued to update her boss. Not before Wilson's eye brow raised for a brief second.

"Max evacuated two female campers from his LZ just north of Azure Lake. He, Jake, our Labrador, and a third camper, a young man named, Jamie are being overrun by the fire. They have constructed a raft and were shoving off just ahead of the fire line to make their way to the island in the middle of the lake." She pointed to the location on the map behind her.

"The island in nearly free of vegetation and is mainly granite boulders and course sand. It's no closer than one hundred yards from the fuel source. They intend to find a place on the leeward side of the island to protect themselves from the heat and smoke." She took a breath and for the first time in twenty years wished she had a cigarette.

Wilson looked at the map then at Wendi. "Can you call him on his satcom device?"

Her eyes dropped to the floor, "No. He can only call out." Feeling like she needed to defend Max she said, "And he is pretty busy right now. He'll call us when he can or has something to report." She arched her back and stood defiant.

"Okay, relax, I didn't mean anything, I just wanted to know if we could reach out to them." Wilson scanned her face to see if she'd cool down – and she did.

He climbed out of his chair and said, "Keep me posted and let me know when he calls again." He looked at his best ranger and smiled, "Keep doing a great job. I know that between you and Max everything will be okay, eventually." He turned and left the office – he needed to get into the fresh air for a few minutes and clear his head.

As he moved towards the front door he shook his head and thought, *who in god's name has a satellite phone.* His mind began to wonder for a moment.

# *Chapter Twenty-Six*

Jamie walked ahead looking for a cave or enclosed place where the three of them could protect themselves from the heat and smoke. There were a number of acceptable places but he continued to look until near the water on the other side of the island there was an opening at the water's edge.

He looked over his shoulder and said, "This looks promising. I'll take a look." He dropped his pack and walked into the water up to his waist then entered the opening.

Jake rushed to the water. He sat barking loudly; visibly agitated. Max waited patiently, his senses told him time was running out. The air was full of smoke and the air temperature was continuing to rise.

Inside the cave Jamie looked around with his flashlight. The cave was dry and large enough for the three of them to stay. There was a small opening near the rear of the cave in the ceiling for ventilation and additional light.

Jamie looked back at the opening into the water. The opening was small enough that they could cover it with the blanket he had in his pack to keep the smoke from finding them inside. He smiled and said, "I think this is a winner."

He turned off his flashlight and came back out into the lake. Jake jumped to his feet and barked with excitement and moved in quick jerky motions of glee.

Jamie approached the dog and gave him a hug and said, "Hey boy, I think we found a new home." He looked up at Max and said, "Sir, I think this will meet our needs. It's large enough for the three of us, its dry, there is a small vent in the back of the cave and the entrance is small enough I think we can cover it with a blanket to keep the smoke out. Please come take a look and let me know if you agree."

Max, knowing they didn't have much time to hunker down before the effects of the fire were over them, dropped his pack and climbed into the water and entered the cave. A quick look around confirmed the young man's assessment. This time Jake was in the water next to Max looking in the cave with the unbounded excitement of a Labrador Retriever.

Max called out from the cave, "This will work nicely Jamie. Let's get our gear inside and set up and do any final preps before we are forced underground." Max came out of the cave with Jake right behind him and made his way back up onto the shoreline then to his pack.

He reached into his simple canvas pack and retrieved the sat phone and called Wendi. She grabbed her phone and urgently said, "Max?"

Max laughed at her intensity, "Honey, it's okay and we're just fine. We are on the island and have found a safe place on the southeast side at the water's edge. I will leave three rocks stacked on one another over the cave. The entrance is at the water's edge. We are going to ground in a few minutes, the smoke and heat is beginning to get intense. Don't worry, we're fine. I love you. Goodbye." Click and Wendi was holding her phone against her ear willing him to still be there, "Damn you, Max," she said and began to cry in her hands.

Max looked at Jamie and tossed the phone to him, "Here make it fast we need to save the batteries and get into our hide site." He winked and asked, "When are you going to introduce Wendi and me to your lady friend?" Max grabbed his pack and laughed as he and Jake returned to the water and after a few strides through the icy water were back inside the cave.

Max called out, "Jamie when your done gather some firewood so we can dry out our clothes." He didn't wait for a response. He thought, *if this young love struck kid remembers the firewood great, if he doesn't because his mind is focused on his girlfriend; fine too.*

Max sat on the sandy cave floor and relaxed. Jake sat beside him quietly – happy to be on an adventure. Max looked around the cave and there weren't any major preparations needed so he took the opportunity to go through a mental checklist to ensure they would be as safe as possible. After several more moments he was satisfied they would be fine.

Jake's ears perked up  several seconds before Max heard Jamie sloshing through the water and when his face peered into the cave Jake barked a friendly greeting.

Jamie's arms were full of wood most of it drift wood that had washed ashore. He smiled and said, "This should allow us to dry our clothes and take the chill out of the air." He entered the cave and dropped the wood in the rear under the vent then handed the satellite phone back to Max, "Thanks, Maggie Rose says hi."

Max rose to his feet, "Maggie Rose, that's a pretty name." He looked at Jake and said, "You stay here with Jamie, I'll be back in a few minutes."

The dog growled in disagreement but with a whimper gave in and walked over to Jamie and sat beside him.

Max looked at the two of them and said, "Jamie, start a small fire while I go out and take a look around. I'll be observing from the top of the island and should be back in thirty minutes." He turned and moved out of the cave.

\*\*\*

Max climbed to the top of a jagged boulder – the highest point on their island. Without thinking, he moved slowly and quietly to the edge on his belly and peered over. He brought his phone and his binoculars.

Reaching for the binoculars he looked at the distant edge of the lake the fire was raging and had engulfed the northern quarter of the shoreline. The smoke was slightly deflected to the east of their position so for the time being smoke wouldn't be a threat – that could and would change as the day progressed and the winds shifted to the north.

He reached for his phone and called Wendi. "Wendi, we are safe. The fire has reached the shoreline over the northern quarter of the lake. For now the winds are keeping the smoke to the west of us but we are prepared for that to change. I love you. This will probably be my last report until the fire is past us."

He hung up and took a moment to think about the woman he was talking too and how much he loved her.

He returned to the cave, Jamie and Jake had a nice fire burning which vented nicely through the ceiling. Max took off his boots, socks and pants and placed them near the fire and sat near the flame and told Jamie about what he'd seen.

They were as ready as they could be. Each of them drifted off into private memories of the women in their lives – through the memories they gathered strength and determination to overcome whatever would come over the next twenty-four hours.

## *Chapter Twenty-Seven*

The small fire gradually died but not before the clothes hung nearby were dry and the cave was comfortably warm. It had been several hours since Max had returned from his climb to the top of the boulder to check on the fire.

Max had dozed off to take advantage of the time they had – he'd learned years ago how to sleep almost on demand to stay alert and strong when he'd need it. The absence of crackling and the gradual temperature decline brought him out of a light sleep.

He looked over at Jamie and he was sound asleep. Lying next to him was Jake curled up in a ball against Jamie's torso. "Trader," Max said and rose to his feet. He smelled the air and could sense the heavy odor of burning wood – *the fire was approaching,* he thought.

Max looked through the cave entrance and could see the forest to the south directly across the lake was still intact. *For how much longer,* he wondered.

He returned to the camp area and knelt near Jamie and put his hand on the young man's shoulder, "Jamie, I'm going out to see what's going on. I should be back in less than thirty minutes." He pulled out the sat phone and handed it to Jamie, "Here you hold onto this – just in case."

"Just in-case what?" Jamie asked.

"Ahh, nothing kid," Max put his pants on and laced up his boots then slipped out the entrance. Jamie remained silent – Jake, rolled up in a ball and fell asleep again.

From the entrance Max looked across the lake and could see the fire had flanked their location and was closing any exit quickly to the south. *Shit, we're surrounded,* he thought. He looked up at the sky, it was dark and the wind generated by the fire was gusting, *there's no way a helo can get here now and pull us out. We'll have to ride this one out and hope for the best*, his eyes squinted and he pulled a bandana up over his mouth and nose. He wished he had brought goggles to protect his eyes. *Hell a guy can't think of everything now can he?* He stepped into the cold water and quickly moved to the left.

Max sloshed to the beach and moved with military precision and focus until he reached the boulder which offered the best vantage point on the island.

Soon after he moved away from the water the heavy smoke found its way through the bandana and filled his lungs and irritated his nose and eyes. The ground level visibility had become increasingly impaired by the grey layer which hung over the ground like a heavy blanket. The sun above was partially obscured and a halo was visible around the orb.

He reached the summit and his heart sunk. The water between the burning shoreline and the island he looked on from was churning with the frantic movement of animals swimming away from the fire and certain death.

The thought, *it's surreal to watch big cats, bears, deer, and small rodents set aside their instinct to hunt or hide and run from predators for a common urgent need to survive the fire and death.*

Deer swam beside large predators – neither cared about anything except getting to the island. Most of the smaller animals drowned in a valiant effort to make it to the distant shore. He saw a growing number of animals who had already arrived on the island trying to find shelter as the air continued to respond to the effects of the raging fire.

Max realized the temperature had risen and he suddenly was warm – no very hot. He'd seen enough and returned to the cave. He passed several animals bedded down finding whatever refuge they could from the fire. Max calmly spoke to them and said, "You'll be okay. Keep your heads down and stay calm little guys."

He reached the water's edge and as he put his foot into the cold water he looked over his shoulder and froze. There was a small fawn looking around a bush at him. The baby deer stood only several feet tall. It looked at Max with large moist eyes that telegraphed fear. It was clearly alone separated from its mother, scared and confused. Max knelt and put his hand out. The baby deer slowly moved on wobbly legs into the opening and towards Max. "Come here boy," Max said and waited. Several seconds later the fawn was standing near him. Max reached around the little guy, lifted him into his arms and walked into the water and through the cave entrance. "Look who is joining us for dinner," he said with a hint of cheer in his voice.

Jamie looked up, his jaw dropped and he gasped, "Holy cow, where did you find that little guy?"

"Right outside the entrance. I figure he lost his mother." Max, still holding the fawn in his arm reached into his pack and pulled out a length of line and made a leash and tied the little guy to a rock where he'd be safe and near the fire and a comfortable place to make his bed.

Jake waited patiently for permission to approach the deer and make his acquaintance. Max saw and was pleased at his dog's self-control. Okay Jake, you can introduce yourself to our new friend. Jake stood up and slowly approached the fawn and soon the fawn began to relax and they laid down near each other.

Max looked at Jamie, "We are nearly surrounded by the fire and the smoke is too dense and the winds to gusty for a helicopter." He smiled and continued, "Guess we are going to be here for a while. I hope you brought a good book," and he chuckled.

"Jamie, it is quite a site, the water is full of animals of all descriptions and sizes swimming towards us." He winked, "Looks like they all had the same plan as you, my mountain man friend. It's something to see them swim side by side – but," and he stopped for a moment while Jamie's eye's focused on his mentor. "There are already all types of animals here and many more on their way. All will be looking for shelter. This includes bears and large cats so we need to be prepared to defend our cave if challenged."

Max smiled and laughed, Jake and his new friend looked up at Max then dropped their heads and rested. "You my friend you have already fought a bear in hand to hand combat," Max smiled a big toothy grin. Jamie wondered, *how can you be so relaxed when we're surrounded by a forest fire and we may have a bear or cougar fight us for our shelter?*

Max reached once again into his pack and pulled out his pistol and set it down. "This may come in handy if we have an intruder but it will make one hell of a bang in this cave – trust me."

"Jamie, have you ever fired a pistol before?" Max calmly said.

"Once at a range in Lodi."

"Good, here is the safety and there is a round in the chamber." Max reached into his pack again and retrieved two more loaded magazines. "Just in case he's a big bear." He laughed again, set the additional magazines next to the pistol. "I'm hungry, let's see what we have in the pantry," again he reached into his magic pack and removed an assortment of packaged food and candy. He spread them out on the ground between them and said, "Help yourself."

Max pulled out some dog food and made two dishes and a bowl of water for Jake and 'Little Guy', the unofficial name given to the newest addition to their team.

Jamie grabbed a package of food and leaned back against a rock. Max did the same after he threw more fuel on the campfire. They silently ate and stared at the small flames – it was a waiting game now. There was nothing else for them to do except wait out the forest fire – and listen for intruders.

# *Chapter Twenty-Eight*

Outside the cave the lucky animals, who'd survived the swim, peacefully gathered, too exhausted to worry about the close proximity of predators and prey, they hunkered down in whatever shelter they could find.

The air temperature continued to rise and soon was nearing the summer temperatures found in the great deserts of Southwest Asia. The wind blew with growing intensity and mounting gusts came at them through the violently burning trees with a demon-like howling sound.

The smoke, now so dense it obscured the sun from the sky and the animals, still alive, struggled to breathe – instinctively, they took rapid shallow breaths between frequent coughing spells. Fear filled their eyes as they crouched low to the ground – many digging shallow holes in the soft red dirt to lay in.

***

Back at the National Forest Service regional office, Wendi was the first to notice the weather map and the unusual and quickly changing weather pattern developing and moving rapidly from the Pacific Ocean to the Sierra Mountains – headed directly towards Lake Tahoe and the raging fire everyone in the area was focused on.

Wendi recognized a fast moving cold front carrying moisture laden air up from sea level shoved by the rugged terrain to clear nearly eight thousand feet at the mountain summit near the lake. She exclaimed with excitement, "It's a rainmaker and its coming fast."

Senior Ranger Wilson looked up from the screen of the fire progression and the junior rangers beside him looked her way.

"What did you say Wendi," her boss asked.

"Look at the real-time weather Doppler map, and she moved the screen on her desk to face them. They moved over to her desk for a better view.

Wendi nearly cried with excitement, "There's a cold front coming from the Pacific and it's moving like a freight train." She took a deep breath and said, "It should be here in a few hours and it's expected to be a major rain event. The forecast calls for it to rain all over us – and of course the fire." She could hardly contain her enthusiasm, "The forecasters are calling for nearly four inches in a three hour timeframe." She leaned way back in her chair, she was exhausted from both the excitement and her concern for Max, Jamie and, *that dumb dog, Jake,* she thought.

Senior Ranger Wilson looked at the map and rubbed his chin for a few seconds then looked down at Wendi, "I hope you're right. This will give us the upper hand to contain and extinguish this fire." He looked down at her and his eyes softened and he said in a whisper, "Nice work, you're the only one who didn't get hypnotized by the fire and kept your eyes open." He smiled and said, "Any word from Max?"

"No," Wendi wiped tears from her eyes.

"Try calling him on his 'super spy phone and let him know god has sent in cavalry – and hold on we'll get them out as soon as we can if I have to fly the helo myself." He stood tall and arched his back.

Wendi thought, *you look ridiculous, Wilson,* and she smiled. "Okay, I'll try," she said and reached for her phone but she knew the effort was futile. *Max will turn on his phone when he had something to say and you'll have to be patient – old dogs don't learn new tricks*, she thought and dialed her cell phone anyway. *Maybe they do?* She thought until it rolled into voice mail and she hung up, set down the phone and whispered to herself, "What were you thinking silly girl."

***

Back in the cave, Max had finished sharpening his spear and set it by his bed. Jamie watched quietly. Jake and 'New Guy' curled up together and were fast asleep.

Max looked at the entrance – the air outside the cave was grey, dark and laden with particles of burned forest. He noticed the smoke was moving away from the entrance but a small eddy caused by

141

the air moving by and curling back was beginning to enter the cave. *This could be a serious problem,* Max thought and looked over at Jamie. "Jamie, it's time to wet your blanket and cover the entrance to keep the smoke from making its way inside."

He looked at the young man and thought, *If Wendi and I had a son, I would have hoped he'd have been just like you, Jamie.* He smiled and silently watched the young man jump to his feet and install the moistened blanket as a curtain like they'd discussed during their preparations.

Jake looked up with sleepy eyes for several seconds then put his head back down. 'New Guy' took the opportunity to snuggle up closer to his new friend and continued to sleep.

The men watched the blanket for several minutes until they were content it was working to filter the air and keep the smoke out. Max was the first to lay down, dig a shallow hole for his hip then roll on his side and close his eyes. "Jamie you keep a watch for an hour then I'll relieve you."

"Okay Max," Jamie said and he felt a 'Twanger' as he thought, *he trusts me enough to sleep and leave me with the responsibility for our safety.* He felt strong, confident and he liked the feeling he was beginning to have with regularity.

Jamie remained alert as his friends slept. It was an hour to the minute, Max's eyes opened and he was awake. He sat up without stretching or yawning.

His eyes were clear and focused and his body moved fluidly. "Hey kid, anything happen the last hour or so?" Max asked and he pulled his knees up and leaned forward on them.

Jamie was amazed at how fast Max had transitioned from sound asleep to wide awake – he'd never seen it before. *It used to take mom hours to wake up in the morning. And even then it took a pot of coffee and four or five cigarettes before I could have a conversation with her,* he thought.

Jamie smiled and said, "Max someday I would like you to teach me how to do that."

Max looked confused for a second, "What are you taking about?"

"How you can be sound asleep in one second and the next be wide awake. Everyone I know it takes hours or at least 20 minutes before they can function in the morning," Jamie said.

"Kid, its mind over matter. I sleep because I need to recharge my physical and mental batteries. I'm not one of those people that loves to sleep or lounge around in their fuzzy slippers." He smiled and put the conversation back on point, "Anything happen while I was recharging my batteries?" he smiled just a bit.

"No, it was quiet. The blanket seems to be working and I just put a little fuel on the fire. And those guys," he pointed his thumb at Jake and 'Little Guy', "They haven't moved a bit – talking about the

143

fuzzy slipper club; they must be life-time members," he smiled and felt another 'Twanger' of confidence.

"Kid, grab some sleep, I'll take over," Max said and stood up and stretched his back and twisted his torso and for the first time since he'd awaken looked critically around the cave to familiarize himself with it and their defensive position should it become necessary.

By the time he sat by the fire he heard the gentle and rhythmic sound of Jamie sleeping. "You must have been tired, my friend," Max quietly said and faced the entrance, his spear by his side and his pistol beside that. He sat and listened. All he heard was the quiet sounds of his companions.

## *Chapter Twenty-Nine*

Outside of the cave entrance, Max heard the water splashing and labored grunting. He reached for his spear and nudged Jamie, "Kid, get up, we may have a visitor at the door," Jamie sat up and rubbed his eyes.

Max tossed the pistol to Jamie, "remember how I taught you to shoot it if we need to. I'll use the spear first – you only shoot him if I tell you or I'm over run." Max's eyes were serious and his jaw set. He held the spear in his right hand and walked towards the blanket covering the entrance.

Jamie clinched the pistol and watched in fear and excitement. He kept his finger clear of the trigger. He could hear his instructor at the Lodi range tell him, *never put your finger on the trigger until you're ready to shoot.*

Max listened, the splashing outside grew closer, then abruptly stopped on the other side of the blanket. Max could hear the labored breathing of the beast on the other side of the camping blanket – hurriedly hung to keep out the smoke.

Max raised the spear and pointed it at the center of the blanket and listened and waited. His body was as tight as a piano string.

145

On the other side of the blanket, up to its belly in the frigid water was a large male black bear. He was hungry, cold, miserable and being forced from his home had made him angry. His keen sense of smell had brought him to the entrance. He instinctively knew inside there was food, shelter and protection from the fire. He knew there would be risk and he considered for a moment whether the reward would be worth the fight. A shiver of cold ran through his body and his belly growled – it was worth it.

The bear growled and with a powerful violent swipe of his paw tore the blanket away and he charged into the opening. Jake jumped beside Max and stood ready to fight alongside his boss.

Max waited until the bear was crossing the threshold and could only move forward or backward and he thrust his spear under the bears chin along the massive neck and into the rib cage – the target was the animal's heart. Max leaned into the spear and drove it deeper and deeper into the massive animal.

The bear drove against the spear then clawed at his opponent with his huge clawed paws and sharp teeth covered in foaming saliva.

The bear knew he had few options – stuck in the entrance he had to go directly into the spear or retreat and regroup. He was to tired and angry to retreat and he thrust forward in spite of the pain of the spear driving deeper into his body. He became crazed with battle and the bear drove onward intent to claw and mangle the opponent who calmly stood there driving his weapon deeper and deeper into the bear's torso hoping his aim would pierce the heart and kill the 800 pound beast.

With each thrust the spear drove deeper and Max came closer to the thrashing claws of the wounded predator.

Jake barked and moved around the bear careful to stay out of the range of the sharp claws and teeth.

The bear, whether he was able to rationalize it or not, in the adrenaline driven moment of combat, drove himself with all of his might against the spear in an act that would certainly kill him but it would close the distance to his opponent and allow him to attack and injure or kill the human and the pesky dog.

Max was caught off guard by the bear's fatal decision as it charged – the spear drove deeper into its chest until the tip penetrated the heart. The bear would be dead in seconds but not before Max was within striking distance.

The dying bear struck Max with his paw. The sharp claws tore open his arm and left long deep cuts from his left shoulder across his chest and abdomen. The bear was dead but as his body relaxed in death its left paw inflicted a similar wound from Max's right shoulder down across his chest.

The bear was dead – its limp body lay face down with his forward feet before its head. The claws were still dripping with blood and pieces of flesh.

Max collapsed on the ground several feet ahead of the animal on his back. His chest was torn and bleeding. Jake sensing his opportunity jumped on the bears back and bite the bear then ran to Max – he knew his owner was in serious trouble.

Max, struggling to remain awake said, "Jamie in my pack is a first aid kit. Put the gauge bandages over these wounds the best you can then wrap my torso with the rolls of gaze as tight as you can to hold the bandages in place." He tried to get comfortable, but it was futile. "Jamie, get the phone out of the pack and call Wendi tell her what happened. The pass code is 895623." His breath was jagged and he was losing consciousness, "You're going to have to keep me alive until the fire is over and help can come – do you understand?"

Jamie nodded and reached for the pack and pulled out the first aid kit and did as he was told. The wounds were deep and blood flowed with abundance. He did as he was told and was relieved to see the blood loss slowed down and eventually stopped.

By then Max was sleeping. Jamie pulled out the phone and punched in the access code then pushed the redial button and listened to the phone link up and soon it was ringing. Wendi answered on the second ring, "Max are you alright?"

Jamie cleared his throat and said, "Wendi, this is Jamie. Max is in real trouble. He was mauled by a black bear and has massive wounds across his chest." He stopped and listened to Wendi's jagged breath on the other end of the line.

"Max instructed me to dress his wounds with the first aid stuff we have and I have done the best I can. I think most of the bleeding has stopped or at least slowed way down. He is asleep now and I don't know what else I can do for him." This time he was listening to Max's jagged breathing for a moment.

"Wendi, we are still on the island on Azure Lake in the cave. The forest fire is around us and the smoke is still pretty bad. We have a blanket to cover the entrance to keep most of the smoke out. We have little food, plenty of water and only the medical supplies Max carried in his pack."

He listened to himself and was proud of his calmness as he passed along the information. "Wendi, I need to hang up and save the phone batteries. I will call you again when he wakes up or if he gets any worse." Jamie decided to adlib and ended with, "Wendi, Max wanted me to tell you that he loves you and Jake is okay. Please, if you can contact Maggie Rose, tell her I'm okay and I love her. Bye for now," and he hung up the phone.

Jamie carefully set the phone down next to the loaded pistol and looked at Max and Jake lying beside him. By then 'Little Guy' had timidly moved from where he'd hidden from the bear and lay next to the dog with his little head resting on Jake's back – his doe eyes were moist, large brown pools of emotion and fear. Jamie looked at him and his face softened and his voice was soft and soothing as he whispered, "Hey, 'Little Guy' don't worry, we're all going to be alright. Jake, your new buddy is right there with you and you're safe – I promise."

Jamie choked back his tears and thought, *all the calming words in the world and false confidence didn't change the fact we're in real trouble and the one man who could have saved us is lying there unconscious and badly injured by that angry bear.* Jamie's eyes roamed over to the large dead animal blocking the entrance with his massive body. "What am I going to do with you?" He asked the corpse. Jamie felt fear muddle his thoughts and undermine his confidence.

Jamie stood up, shook his head and focused his mind and forced himself to remain calm by repeating in a whisper, "What would Max do, what would Max do, what would Max do?"

# *Chapter Thirty*

Jamie took several deep breathes then sat next to the fire. He looked around him with calm that caused a surge of confidence – a 'Twanger' as he'd started to call the empowering feeling. Looking around the cave it was no longer a tomb but a safe place that provided security from the raging forest fire and predators.

The fire was no longer a chore to keep fueled but it provided light, warmth and hope. Jamie allowed himself a moment to draw spiritual strength from the flames and the glow of light that promised they would survive.

Jake and 'Little Guy', still lying near Max, were watching Jamie. He looked at them, they'd become close friends and both relied on him for their protection and safety – he knew he couldn't let them down. Jamie looked down at Max wrapped in bloody bandages. He was sleeping on his back near the fire. The expression on his face was calm and relaxed. Jamie thought, *Max you're amazing. You're brave, strong, confident and resourceful. I will protect you and get you to the hospital – I promise my friend.*

Jamie looked at the bear and where it had been an unsurmountable problem blocking their eventual exit from the cave, now Jamie saw it as a challenge he could overcome. He studied the bear and where it had died. Jamie moved around the bear looking closely then began to smile and he felt a senses of excitement and the hair on the back of his neck tingle.

He looked around the back of the carcass – the bear had nearly broached the entrance. His head and body were inside the cave and his rear legs were extended fully behind in the narrow entrance. Jamie thought as he looked at the bear, *remove your legs and maybe the hip joints and there'll be enough room for my friends and I to leave the cave when the time is right.* When the thought concluded a calm deadened his excitement, he realized what he needed to do – butcher an animal. It was something he'd never done or ever thought he would do – not the old Jamie, but today, and for some time, there was a new Jamie evolving and now he could, no he must do it if they were going to escape.

Jamie reached into his pocket and retrieved the pocket knife Arty had given him and looked quizzically at it for several seconds as he considered the small blade and the large animal he needed to butcher. "Talk about coming to a gunfight with a butter knife," he mumbled. He looked over at Max's pack and wondered aloud, "I wonder what you have in your pack – maybe you brought a hunting knife." He crawled over on his hands and knees and began to carefully open the pack and there it was. He pulled a large sheathed hunting knife. He carefully removed the blade and gently ran his finger over the blade. "Figures," he said. "This knife is really sharp – thanks Max," he whispered.

Jamie put some more fuel on the campfire and checked on his patient. It looked like the bleeding had stopped and Max was breathing evenly. Jamie gently pulled the blanket over the bandages and under the sleeping man's chin.

Jake, sensing there was something going on sat up and arched his back. The fawn, uninterested rolled into a ball and continued to sleep.

Jamie reached for the knife and crawled toward the bear – Jake was right beside him. With the knife in hand, Jamie examined the massive leg and imagined what it would be like to cut into flesh and bone. *Where should I cut to deconstruct the leg into pieces I can move?* He reached for Jake, sitting behind him and said, "Here goes nothing, Jake." The dog's tail began to move steadily back and forth.

Looking at the bear, Jamie said, "Sorry bear but you did this to yourself when you attacked my friend." Jamie, placed the knife near where he imagined the ankle joint and drew the knife over the fur. It cut easily and the joint was exposed. The foot came off and Jamie tossed it through the small opening into the lake. He continued to remove the leg piece by piece throwing them into the lake. Each time he looked out of the entrance at the distant shore and momentarily watched the brilliant flames consume the forest.

By the time Jamie had removed the legs, there was enough room to exit the cave. Exhausted but content, Jamie crawled out and sat in the entrance with his feet in the cool water and washed the blood from his hands. Jamie watched the fire burn on the shore across the lake. The smell of smoke surrounded him – regardless the air was better than the stale air in the cave.

Jake came over and sat next to Jamie looking out over the water and Jamie put his arm around the dog. At that moment Jamie felt something on his face and he froze then looked into the skies above. He felt the sensation again and could hardly contain himself – it was raining. He threw his head back and let the rain strike his face.

The dog looked at him with curiosity then returned to the dry warm cave and laid down next to Max.

After several moments, Jamie was soaking wet. Thunder began to rumble in the distance and slowly the crackling sound of the forest being consumed by fire lessened; gradually being replaced by the hissing sound of fire fighting for its life as it drowned in the heavy downpour.

Jamie jumped to his feet and ran into the cave, dropping to his knees beside Max and said in and excited voice, "Max, Max it is raining, a heavy rain and it seems to be putting out the fire around us."

He reached for the sat phone, "Max I'll call Wendi and let her know."

Max opened his eyes and looked at Jamie. "That's good news. Help me sit up and please bring me some water."

Jake began to bark and turn in tight circles when he saw Max move. He moved right next to his owner and without knowing better climbed on Max's chest until Max pushed him off and groaned in pain. "Sorry Jake you wouldn't understand but my chest and shoulders are off limits for a while, buddy." Max reached out with his hand and rubbed the happy dogs head as he waited for Jamie to help him sit up and deliver water – Max was as thirsty as he'd ever been and he knew why. He'd lost a lot of blood.

Max was no longer groggy and his senses began to function – thanks to the jolt of pain complements of his dog's enthusiastic greeting. His eyes registered his surroundings and his nose told him there was still a hint of smoke in the air. His ears reported the rhythm of rain striking the water now visible through the entrance beside a partially butchered bear. The blanket no longer hung over the entrance and water cascaded creating miniature water falls as the island shed the rain.

Jamie carefully lifted Max's head and shoved his pack under it then eased him down until he was propped up several inches. He crawled quickly to the water's edge, retrieved water in a cup and returned to his patient. "Here's some water; fresh as the mountain snow." He said and smiled to see Max awake.

Max drank three cups of water and may have had more but he knew better that overdo it.

"Jamie, Looks like you've been busy while I've been taking a nap."

He forced a smile and realized even that muscle movement in his face hurt and he grimaced a little. "Young man, tell me what you and the..." he looked at Jake and 'Little Guy' "kids have been up too?"

Jake moved from sitting next to Max and sat next to Jamie as if to show that he had helped too. Jamie rubbed the dog's ears and told Max about the last 8 hours. Max smiled again and instantly regretted it and grimaced. "Damn, even my face hurts. That bear really kicked my ass." He looked at the partially dismembered bear and asked, "Where did you learn to do that?"

Jamie pulled the dog under his arm and said, "Jake and I borrowed your hunting knife and we figured it out as we went along."

Jamie smiled, "we're sure glad to see you are okay. You've been asleep for nearly eight hours and... well... it's good to see you're okay."

"Thanks kiddo, but I don't think I'm okay just yet. Do you have a plan for us to get out of here?"

Jamie was instantly embarrassed that he hadn't thought beyond the confines of the cave. "No, sir."

Max looked deeply into his friend's eyes and said, "Jamie that's okay, I need you to keep doing what you're doing and keep us safe. Call Wendi and see if we can get a bird out of here soon or if we need to get ashore and make our way to an exfil location."

"Max what is an exfil location," Jamie sheepishly asked

"Sorry partner, it's a military term for a location where help can meet us."

"Okay," Jamie felt his confidence returning. "I'll work with Wendi to get us out of here."

Max's eye closed and he mumbled, "I'll go back to sleep for a while. Good luck."

## Chapter Thirty-One

"Wendi? This is Jamie. Max briefly woke up and I gave him some water, we talked for a few minutes then he fell asleep again. I'm afraid he's really bad. The bleeding has stopped – I think." Jamie was out of breathe and his voice reflected his concern.

Wendi kept her voice calm and even, "How are you holding up, Jamie?"

"Okay, it's raining really hard up here and I believe it's knocking down the fire. Max asked me to call you and see if we can come up with a plan to get off this island."

Jamie heard himself and thought, *slow down and stay calm. You have to keep your cool and protect Max and the animals.*

He continued forcing himself to stay confident and calm, "the smoke is lessening but the rain and low clouds have reduced visibility."

Wendi listen and said, "I've been looking for a helicopter and EMTs to come. No one is crazy or good enough to land on the island so far and the weather forecast calls for heavy rain for another day then dense fog that will keep the helicopters on the ground. Do you think you could move Max by raft to the south side of the lake? We could get to you and

158

help move him to a point where an ambulance could met us."

Jamie thought, *Exfil Location.* He thought for several seconds and said, "We can do that. If our raft is still intact on the other side of the island or if I need to cobble one together afresh, Wendi it will be done… but."

"But what, Jamie?" I don't have a map any longer and don't know the area. How will I find the Exfil location?" He felt a 'Twanger' when he heard himself use the term.

"Get to the other side with Max and Jake and I'll work out the details. Call me when you're ready to move and again when safely on the other side." Her voice was calm but authoritative. He knew she was in control and he could trust her.

"Jamie, before we sign off there is someone here that wants to talk with you," Wendi said and a hint of excitement filled her voice.

"Jamie, oh Jamie my dear are you okay?" Maggie Rose's voice hit him like a freight train.

"Maggie is that you?"

"Of course dear, Dad and I have been in constant communication with Ranger Wendi and all three of us are at the ranger station watching gigantic TV screens with the weather on one the fire on another and where the firefighters and others are in the danger area. Your location is circled in red."

"Maggie Rose I want to talk with you forever but I need to save my batteries for now. Know that I love you and I will bring my friend Max and Jake and 'Little Guy' out safely and then I'll tell you all about it. My best regards to your father and remember – I love you Miss Maggie Rose. Goodbye and talk with you again soon."

He clicked off the phone and looked at the battery life – it was at 20 percent. "Shit," he said and carefully placed the phone in a safe place next to the pistol.

He was still feeling excited and emotions ran wild in his mind from his conversation with Maggie Rose. He found it hard to sit still and began to walk in circles around the cave. His mind was running in hyper drive and his heart pumped quickly – pounding violently against his sternum.

Several minutes later he forced himself to sit and relax as he kept silently chanting, *what are you going to do next, what are you going to do next?*

It came to him, he needed to see if the raft was still on the island and bring it around to the cave. With the thought came a 'Twanger' which told him it was the right decision. He looked at Max who was sound asleep and he decided to leave the cave and check on the raft. Without a word to Max and a whisper to Jake, "Stay with Max, I'll be right back."

# WALKING THROUGH HELL

Jamie shimmied by what remained of the massive black bear and slipped into the water and splashed his way up on the sandy beach nearby.

The rain was driving downward in heavy dense drops that pleated his face and clothing. It made it difficult for him to see but he was glad for the weather. It had subsided the smoke and he could sense the fire was dying – the bright yellows of flame being replaced with steam and light grey smoke.

He retraced the path he and Max had taken. This time the island was covered in ash and overrun with animals who had swam across the lake to avoid the fire. They looked scared and exhausted. Most had hastily made beds while some moved aimlessly over the rocky terrain.

In powerful strides he climbed over the summit and descended to where they'd abandon the raft. He was relieved when he saw the raft where they'd left it. After a brief moment of excitement, he thought, *what did you think? It's not like anyone was going to steal it.* He chuckled and closed in on the makeshift craft. "All I need is a paddle," he said out loud. Several of the animals milling around looked up at him and returned to their new and traumatic reality.

Aware of his surroundings and potential danger from another angry lion or bear, he walked along the shoreline looking for a suitable paddle. He found what he was looking for and returned to the raft.

The rain continued to fall from the sky. He pushed the raft off the beach, climbed aboard and began to paddle – slowly the raft responded and moved along the shoreline in the direction Jamie intended. The rain had long ago drenched his clothes and his eyes stung from the water running into them. He was uncomfortable but kept focused on the task. He willed the fatigue in his shoulders away and ignored the soreness in his back and stroked steadily fighting the water and wind until he wrestled control, and in the end, he saw the cave entrance and the beach alongside. He beached the craft, pulled it up and secured it to a tree.

He allowed a few seconds of quiet satisfaction and relief then returned to the cave. The fire was nearly extinguished, Jake was sleeping in the same place Jamie had left him an hour ago. He looked up, barked then stretched and approached him.

Jamie used his remaining strength to greet his friend and fuel the fire. He checked on Max – he was still sound asleep, his breathing remained even and steady. Jamie checked his wounds and the bleeding externally had stopped. He sighed with relief.

Jamie removed his wet clothing and hung them by the fire. He crawled under his blanket and fell asleep as Jake laid beside him.

***

Two hours later, Jamie bolted upright from his sleep. A haunting vision had flashed through his mind

– he was being watched. He looked around the cave all was the same. He looked over at Max and saw his dark blue eyes watching him. Max had managed to lift himself and his face was turned toward Jamie. "What's going on? Why did you jump up? A nightmare?"

Jamie shook his head, "Na, I felt like someone was watching me and I guess I was right." He tried to smile as he ran his dirty hands through his matted hair. He sat up and raised his knees. His young chest and arms were exposed – he didn't notice.

Max grinned and said, "Sleeping in the buff, you're becoming one of us mountain men." He shifted a little and asked, "How long have I been out?"

"Four hours."

"Have you talked with Wendi?"

"Yes, and we have a plan."

"Okay, I'm all ears." Max struggled to find a comfortable positon; but it was futile.

Jamie told him about the phone call, the plan they'd agreed too and the raft sitting outside the cave when the time was right.

"Good," Max said and continued, "Jamie when can we go? I need to get to a hospital soon."

"I figure, as soon as the rain stops, we'll paddle to the south shore and move towards an exfil location." Max cocked an eyebrow then gently lowered his head on his pillow.

"Jamie, wake me when its time. You're doing a fine job, son." Max closed his eyes and was soon sound asleep.

Jamie held Jake near him and looked out at the lake and the distant skies wondering when the rain would stop.

## *Chapter Thirty-Two*

Jamie began to doze off as he sat beside Jake. The dog had given in hours ago and was curled up and quietly snoring. It was still raining outside the cave entrance. He could hear the hissing of the forest as the rain gradually overwhelmed the massive fire. Jamie struggled to stay awake, but his body was exhausted and began to shut down when his eyes began to close. His mind began to register thoughts he was just too tired to consider.

Just as he fell asleep, Jake jumped to his feet and began to growl and bark aggressively. Jamie's eyes opened and he was instantly awake. Standing in the entrance was a mountain lion. Bearing his teeth and clawing menacingly with its right paw – claws extended.

The large cat was moving cautiously into the cave. Jamie jumped to his feet then slowly moved towards the pistol sitting on a rock near the fire pit. Jake continued to bark and growl at the intruder. Jake knew he was in a fight he couldn't win.

Jamie moved slowly the entire time keeping eye contact with the cat. The cat continued to enter the cave moving around the bear carcass still obstructing the entrance. Under the tan coat the skin was ripped by muscle and tendon – a magnificent killing machine.

Jamie reached down for the pistol and hoped he remembered how to use it. He checked that it was loaded by slowly pulling the receiver back – it showed a round in the chamber. Slowly he closed the receiver and pointed the gun at the lion. Jamie's calm movements only angered the cat who began to fold back his ears and all his teeth and claws were exposed.

Jamie knew what he had to do. He aimed at the center of the cat's chest and squeezed the trigger. The pistol made an incredible sound inside the cave. He missed the animal but the sound caused the cat to retreat in such a hurry by the time Max opened his eyes and said, "What the hell is going on," the mountain lion had sprinted back through the entrance literally ran over the water and disappeared beyond the bank. Jake followed him to the entrance and made a show of barking loudly as if to say, *Take that you lousy lion. Come back and I'll take care of you myself.*

Jamie turned his attention to Max and dropped to his knees by his friend, "Max, I'm sorry but a mountain lion came into the cave and … and… I shot him."

Max looked around the cave and said, "Where is he if you shot him?"

Jamie dropped his eyes embarrassed, "I guess I missed."

"Well, good job protecting us from the lion. Remind me to teach you how to shoot when we get out of here."

"Okay, I'd like that."

Max tried to sit up but gave up after several attempts, "It sounds like it's still raining pretty hard. Do you have enough fuel to keep the fire going?"

"Yes," Jamie replied. He was proud he'd done that on his own.

"Jamie, what is the remaining battery life on the satcom?"

"Twenty percent."

"Good, will you dial Wendi and give me the phone, please."

"Yes, sir" Jamie said and reached for the phone and called the number he'd memorized. When it began to ring he handed it to Max.

Wendi grabbed the phone and said, "Jamie is Max okay."

Max listened to his wife's voice and her tone told him she loved and cared for him. "Wendi it's me," he said in an unstable and hollow voice.

Wendi began to ask a seemingly endless number of questions in a barrage of disjointed sentences.

Max cut in and said, "Honey, I only wanted to hear your voice. I'm in bad shape and we need to get out of here. I need medical attention soon. Can you send a para EMT or military corpsman to fast rope onto the island?"

Wendi began to cry as she said, "Honey, we have looked at that and many other options and we can't do any better than have you and Jamie get to the south side of the lake and move down to Baker's Creek. We can meet you there with an ambulance. I promise I'll be there waiting."

"Okay, we'll see you at Baker's Creek. We will cross the lake within the hour and check in with you when we're 'feet dry'. I love you and by the way … this kid is really doing a great job. I can't thank him enough for everything he's done. Bye for now."

He was fading fast and forgetting where he was or who he was with, "Viper, over and out."

Jamie listened and wondered what that meant but Max was asleep with the phone still clutched in his hand. Jamie retrieved the phone and turned it off.

He began to fill the pack with their belongings and began to load the raft. Max had said they would be underway within the hour and Jamie was damn sure it would happen or at least nothing within his control would cause a delay. *Max, hang in there my friend, I'll get you out of here and to a hospital – I promise.*

Jamie kept telling himself that over and over again until he was certain he could do it. He felt a

'Twanger' giving him the strength to get through the next phase of this adventure.

## *Chapter Thirty-Three*

Hastily, and with amateur results, Jamie partially skinned the bear to make two blankets he then put them under and over Max as he lay on the raft. Jamie hoped the skins would keep him dry and provide some warmth during the transit across the lake.

He pulled the raft around to the entrance and lifted one end putting it on the rocks so he could slide Max on a blanket to the raft and pull him aboard. Max tried to help as best he could but his strength was limited and Jamie had to do most of the work.

It took them time but Max finally lay on a bear skin blanket and was covered with a wool blanket and a bear skin over it. Jamie's plan had worked the rain didn't penetrate the skin and Max was comfortable and dry. Jamie brought 'Little Guy' out of the cave with some encouragement and put him on the raft and Jake jumped aboard without being called.

Jamie placed his makeshift paddle aboard and pushed the raft off the beach and let it settle in the water before he knelt near the stern and began to paddle. With a compass around his neck, he kept the raft pointed south. 'Little Guy' and Jake laid down, their eyes wide open – too excited to sleep, they looked forward.

Jamie paddled and periodically checked his compass to keep on course. The rain and fog made seeing the other side of the lake difficult, so he couldn't use a landmark to steer by. The rain remained heavy and everyone was soaked except Max who laid under the blanket quietly as he watched Jamie pull on his paddle.

He pulled stroke after agonizing stroke until he could make out the shoreline ahead and fixed his course on a large granite boulder partially extending into the water to greet them. He looked over his shoulder to see if he could still see the island but it had been obliterated in fog and rain. He stopped paddling and fixed his eyes on something in the water behind them.

At first, he wasn't sure what it was then he focused hard and willed his eyes to see what was trailing them. "What is it?" Max asked.

Jamie, squinted and looked again, then he smiled and said, "Well, I'll be," and looked at Max. "There's a doe swimming behind us. I bet its 'Little Guy's' mother."

"Could be. Let's get to shore and find out," Max said and closed his eyes.

Jamie looked forward, found his landmark and resumed paddling to the beach. Occasionally he looked over his shoulder – the doe was still there swimming along careful to stay a safe distance from the boat.

It took another hour for Jamie to propel the raft to shore – one stroke of the paddle at a time. He was exhausted and his arms, shoulders and back ached and his mind was beginning to drift into thoughts far away. He continued to pull the paddle almost without thinking any longer when the vessel bumped the shore and jarred him out of the dream.

The fawn and dog jumped ashore and splashed their way to the beach. They were glad to be off the water. Jamie stood up, stretched his back briefly then quickly secured the boat to the beach. Jamie knelt near his friend and asked, "Are you ready to get off the boat?" Max nodded. Together they worked to get the injured man ashore and beneath the landmark where there was a dry spot.

Jamie made Max as comfortable as he could. He began to look around after Max was resting. The immediate area on the beach was somewhat intact but ten feet inland, the forest was a charred blackened mess. The ground was covered in grey ash. The trees were torched, their limbs gone, trunks burned, blackened, but they stood straight upward in defiance of death. The brush, which once covered the ground, was incinerated with only the sturdiest bones still surviving the inferno. The air was scented with the heavy odor of burned forest and flesh. The forest was littered with glowing ambers and smoldering logs.

## WALKING THROUGH HELL

Jamie thought they had found themselves in hell. "I guess we're Walking through Hell," he said to himself.

After several moments he turned and began to look for young trees and saplings to make a stretcher – a stretcher like the ones he'd seen at the Native American Museum in Sacramento during a high school field trip.

The ones he'd seen were pulled by a horse – "Oh well, I'll get to be the horse too," he chuckled and canvased the area for suitable lumber. He put his hand on Max's knife – the knife he'd borrowed and strapped to his side since he'd begun using it nearly two days prior.

Searching along the shoreline he found the tree limbs and saplings he needed, he gathered them and brought them back to the hastily made base camp where Max, Jake and 'Little Guy' waited. The doe carefully off in the distance watched her fawn closely.

Jamie began to build the stretcher and reused the line he'd used to hold the raft together. The small black braided line, Max had referred to as 'parachute cord' had worked well to keep the raft together and Jamie hoped it would prove up to the task of holding his stretcher together too.

He worked steadily until nearly dark and when his hands could no longer work and his back and shoulders were cramped in protest of hours of kneeling and crouching.

Jamie looked over frequently at Max who slept and occasionally woke up long enough to look over at the young man and say, "How's it going, son?" then he'd close his eyes and drift off again into a sound sleep. Jake came over periodically to offer support and encouragement with a nudge of his shoulder and a few strategic licks across Jamie's face then he'd return to the makeshift bed he and 'Little Guy' shared near Max.

Jamie didn't mind, in fact he had begun to feel comfortable with the responsibility he'd assumed to protect and care for his injured friend and the two four-legged companions who had become part of his family. He looked over at the doe in the distance and called gently to her, "Are you 'Little Guy's' mother. I bet you are. Why don't you come over here and see him and rest. You're safe. Jake and I will protect and take care of you."

The doe looked at him and cocked her head to one side and slowly dropped down to the ground but kept an eye on Jamie and the others the entire time. Jamie smiled and said, "If you don't mind, we'll call you, 'Mother'."

Jamie examined the finished stretcher and smiled. He stretched his shoulders and back to work out the cramps and aches of the day. He walked around the camp and gathered more firewood and was glad to have Jake right alongside him the entre time. "Jake, you're the best friend a guy could have," Jamie said and the dog bristled with excitement as he pranced next to Jamie.

When they returned to the camp Max was awake and sitting up slightly on his side facing the waning flame of the fire. "Where have you two been? I was beginning to get cold and hungry," Max said and he tried to smile but it soon turned into a grimace. He slipped on his back and looked into the darkness above them.

Still holding the firewood, Jamie said, "Max how are you feeling?"

"To be honest I feel like shit," Max grunted. "Have you talked to Wendi lately?"

"No, I was going to feed the fire and feed you then thought we'd call her together, Max." Max smiled.

Max said, "I'd like that, I miss her," and his face twisted in pain.

"Max are you alright?" Jamie asked again – Max grunted then slowly relaxed.

"Jamie, you're a good man. You've come a long way from the guy I met a week ago. You were alone and afraid and trying to overcome your fears and insecurities. Look at you now – you're confident and brave and have taken charge of the situation. I'm sorry I've become a burden. Save yourself and Jake and the fawn. If you must, leave me to save yourselves."

Max gasped and closed his eyes. He forced his body to relax and willed the pain he felt to move out of his mind. Jamie watched the discipline and emotional strength his friend displayed. Tears came to Jamie's eyes, "Max that's good of you to say but we will all get out of this together or we will die together. No man is left behind. And that is the end of that story." Jamie said with confidence, strength and resolve in his voice. He punctuated his word by dropping several logs on the fire and laid the remainder of the wood nearby. He stood up and said with all the enthusiasm he could muster, "Now it's time to see what we have for dinner."

Jake heard the word, 'dinner' and he jumped to his feet and ran over to Max – nudged him with his nose then ran over to Jamie who by then was rummaging through the backpacks for food. He found a Ziploc bag of dog food – Jake recognized it and his tail began to fan back-and-forth. Jamie dug deeper and found a can of peaches and beef jerky. He held them up and with glee proclaimed, tonight we'll dine on California Peaches and Beef Jerky from…" he stopped and read the back of the container and continued, "from Redding, California. Who would have thought?" He said then looked at his four-legged friends and said, "But the children eat first." He opened the Ziploc and poured its contents into two piles, one near Jake and the other near 'Little Guy'. Jamie looked into the shadows and could see the doe lying there and he took some of the remaining food and slowly moved towards her. She sat up then came to her feet prepared to flee but stood her ground as if she felt that Jamie wasn't a threat. Jamie moved slowly talking calmly as he approached the mother. He set the food down several feet away then slowly moved back away. By the time he was back in the camp he looked over his shoulder and the doe was eating.

He smiled and said, "Okay, Mister Max, its peaches and jerky for us guys. Wendi and Marie Rose would cringe if they saw us tonight."

"So they would, my young friend," Max whispered.

The men ate slowly and when they finished Max said, "Thanks for the gourmet meal. Before I pass out again let's call Wendi."

"Okay," Jamie said and jumped to his feet and moved to the back packs. His hand dove into Max's pack and retrieved the satcom. He turned it on and pushed the redial button. Seconds later the phone rang and on second ring Wendi answered "Max?"

Jamie answered, "Wendi it's me, Jamie, hold on I know a guy who wants to hear your voice," He handed the phone to Max and helped place it next to his ear.

Max struggled but managed to say in a raspy voice, "Hello darling, Have I told you I love you lately?"

"Max, my darling I love you too. How are you? Know we are doing everything we can to get to you."

"I know, Wendi but we need to save the batteries and here is Jamie… he is in command." Max pushed the phone into Jamie's hand. Jamie froze for a second and thought *Jamie is in command. Shit.*

Then without a thought said, "Wendi, Listen Max is really in bad shape, but he is eating and drinking water. He sleeps a lot but wakes up frequently. I am running out of bandages and I have no more antibiotic to fight infection. I have Jake and an abandoned fawn with us. I've made a Native American style stretcher and tomorrow we'll begin to hike out due east towards Lake Tahoe."

He took a breath and continued, "We have little food and the forest we'll be transiting is like walking through hell. There are still small fires and smoke, ambers and ash six inches deep but we'll make it – that I am sure. Can you send a party to meet us? Max needs to get to a hospital very soon."

He bit his tongue and said, "Wendi, he loves you very much and he is a remarkable man but that bear really tore him to pieces and I can only do so much without help."

Wendi had tears running down her cheeks when she said, "I understand, call me in the morning and I hope to have a plan to meet you by then."

"Okay," Jamie said and was ready to sign off.

Wendi said, "Just a moment there is someone here that needs to talk to you. A familiar voice came over the phone, "Jamie, is that you?"

"Maggie Rose… is that you?"

"Yes darling. I know we can't talk long but I love you Jamie and I am thinking about you every moment. Please come home to me. I need you." She burst into tears.

Jamie's heart swelled and froze at the same time. "Maggie Rose, I love you too and I will make it back to you. I promise. I love you but I must sign off now to save our batteries. I love you," and the phone went dead. Jamie turned off the phone and gently placed it into the pack then looked at Max – who was watching. "Kid, it sounds like you've got it bad. I remember when I fell in love with Wendi. It was the best thing that has ever happened to me. Good luck and I heard we'll leave in the morning. Get some sleep – you'll need it."

Jamie laid down; Jake had been watching from across the campsite. He stood and stretched his legs then walked over and laid down next to Jamie. Together they quietly looked at the campfire. Their minds were mesmerized by the bright colors and rhythmic motion of the flames. Their minds wandered to memories of places and people far away. Unspoken, they shared the warmth and calm their memories brought them. In the early hours of the morning, they finally slept – too tired to dream.

# *Chapter Thirty-Four*

The smoke continued to blanket the forest. The density was such that the morning sun was nothing more than a dull orb on the Eastern horizon. The light was dim, but the shapes of the burned and tortured forest became more visible with each moment.

Jamie opened his eyes and his lungs immediately protested the smoke and ash which had settled in his chest during the night. He sat up and coughed. Jake jumped to his feet and looked eye to eye with Jamie, licked his face and began to stretch as animals do.

"Good morning, Jake. How did you sleep my friend?" Jamie climbed to his feet – his body ached from the heavy labor the day before and sleeping on the hard ground hadn't helped. He stood up slowly and stretched repeatedly until his body began to move without pain. He looked at the dog and said, "I can see why you always stretch before you get going. It really works to get the kinks out."

Jake knew Jamie was talking to him and he responded with a stifled bark and excited motion of his tail.

"Let's see how our patient is doing," Jamie said and began to move over to Max. "Good morning Max, how do you feel today?"

Max was still, covered in the bear skin blanket. He was lying on his back and his breathing was steady but shallow. Jamie knelt by him and asked again, "Max, how do you feel? Can you hear me?" He began to fear the worst when Max opened his eyes and said, "Good morning, Sunshine. What's on our agenda today?"

Jamie was relieved, his friend was awake, "Max, I think we need to change your bandages and then we'll eat some food. Then we'll check-in with Wendi and see what she can tell us."

He looked around and said, "Max, we are still in a tight spot. The forest is still smoldering and there are small fires around us. The ground is covered in inches of ash and debris. The smoke still fills the air and makes it hard to breath." He looked at Max with concern, "Jake and 'Little Guy' seem to be okay and the doe, I have begun to call 'Mother' is still with us keeping herself at a safe distance from our camp."

Jamie turned to his side and looked at the stretcher he'd built the day before and said, "and over there is your chariot." He smiled. "I made it. It comes with a forty-mile guarantee. Labor and parts are covered," and he tried to smile at his humor.

"Great, I can't wait to take it for a test drive," Max said, and he tried to smile. "What does it have under the hood?" He asked.

"One young Lodi motor," Jamie replied referring to himself. "Now let's look at those wounds and replace your bandages before the crew become's impatient for breakfast." Jamie grabbed the pack and pulled out the first aid kit, opened the lid and looked at the remaining contents.

Max watched Jamie and said, "Jamie, I'm proud of you. You have really stepped up to the challenge and it suits you to be the alpha. I trust you and the decision you'll make. I just wish I was able to pull my own weight."

Jamie was overwhelmed by a massive 'Twanger' as it rushed through him and nearly lifted him off the ground. To hear words like that from a man who he admired, as a role model of the man he wanted to become, filled him with pride and courage. He thought back for a few seconds, *this transformation into a confident and self-assured man was the original goal of this solo hiking adventure into the wilderness.*

Jamie's eyes teared slightly and he looked down at his friend, "Max that was very kind of you. You can't imagine how much that means to me," he choked his words then said, "If you only knew. I promise I will get you back to Wendi safely."

"I know you will – now cut the emotional crap and let's dress my wounds, eat and get a move on. I have a date." Max kiddingly growled.

They shared a smile and Jamie pulled back the blanket and the loosely fitting shirt over the ravaged chest. He carefully pulled open the shirt exposing blood-soaked bandages that crossed his chest from Max's large muscular shoulders to his tight rippled abdomen.

The bandages were dark red, and in some cases nearly black. Jamie worried there may be an infection beginning. He looked at Max and said, "I need to remove these bandages and it will no doubt hurt. I'm sorry in advance."

Max nodded and braced himself.

Jamie carefully removed the bandages from the left shoulder to the right abdomen. The wound was deep, jagged and raw. He reached for the remaining antibiotic and bandages and sparingly used them to ensure there was enough for the other wound.

When he finished, he carefully completed the same task on the other wound running the length of the right shoulder to the left abdomen.

He looked at Max and said, "Well my friend, that's done. I am no doctor, but we need to get you to the hospital. Your wounds require surgery, lots of stitches and more antibiotics than we have."

He looked into the first aid kit and said, "Max we are out of bandages and antibiotic."

Max nodded.

Jamie redressed Max and shifted him onto the sleigh he'd built. Max was sandwiched between two bear skin blankets and strapped to the sleigh so he wouldn't slip off during the journey.

Jamie leaned the sleigh up on a boulder, so Max was sitting at an incline and he was able to see around him for the first time in several days. "I like this view better than being flat on the ground he said as he swallowed the canned peaches and jerky Jamie fed him.

Jake and 'Little Guy' finished their dog food and were getting anxious to get moving. They moved around the camp in anticipation of the next chapter in the adventure. 'Mother' cautiously ate the food Jamie placed near her and gradually she moved closer to the camp – still at a safe distance from the dog and humans but nearer to her fawn.

Jamie looked around the camp to see that he'd prepared everything for the hike to safety. His compass was hung around his neck. The knife was strapped to his hip and the partial topographic map was in his pocket. Satisfied, he reached into the pack and retrieved the satellite phone looked at Max and said, "Let's see what they've got planned."

Wendi answered immediately, "Jamie, How is Max doing today?"

"He's okay but we need to get him to the hospital. I dressed his wounds this morning as best I could and we are out of bandages and antibiotic. But he sends his love." She giggled like a school girl for a moment.

"Jamie, we have a plan. Do you have a map in front of you?"

"Yes," Jamie replied.

In a matter-of-fact voice Wendi said, "Look to the southeast of your position four point four miles. There is a place called Peterson's Meadow, just north of Snow Lake. The terrain is relatively flat from where you are to the meadow. Can you get there with Max on the sleigh?"

"Just a moment," Jamie said and pulled out the map and found Peterson's Meadow. "Yes, I see it and I think we can get there."

"Good, Max's friends will send a helicopter for you when you arrive. Call me when you're there and I'll call in the helicopter."

"Okay, Wendi. That's great news. We better get started," Jamie said.

"Goodbye and good luck. Tell Max I love him."

"Okay and he knows," Jamie pushed the off button and noticed the battery strength had drifted into the red. *Oh shit,* he thought.

Jamie put the phone back in his pack and strapped it to the sleigh.

He looked around the camp for the final time, focused on Max and in a voice, he forced to sound confident and in control said, "Okay let's get this show on the road. We have places to be."

One last look at the map and he sighted a line with his compass in the direction of the meadow, slipped into the yoke he'd fashioned to support and pull the sleigh around his shoulders and said, "Giddy up." He leaned into the yoke and began to pull the sleigh. Jake rushed to his side then ahead a few yards while 'Little Guy' fell in behind the sleigh. 'Mother' followed her fawn twenty feet behind.

# Chapter Thirty-Five

Within twenty feet from the water everything abruptly changed. Near the water the bushes and trees were somewhat spared from the fire but as the party moved away from the lake the devastation was profoundly worse than Jamie could have imagined.

"How are you doing back there, Max?" he asked.

"Could you try not to hit every bump in the road," Max replied.

"Max, do you think this is what hell looks like?"

"Never gave it much thought."

Jamie looked around him in astonishment. The ground around them was grey – covered in a fluffy coat of ash. Everything around them was unrecognizably burned. The ground cover had disappeared into dust. Only a few charred twigs and limbs remained of a once healthy vibrant forest. The trees were black, charred, and barren poles which stood naked skyward like thousands of giant boney arthritic fingers reaching up in a final, defiant effort to escape death. Many of the wretched, once majestic, trees smoldered or burned. The air was heavy with smoke and the smell of death – death of the forest, the animals and plants which had once flourished there.

There were no visible trails to follow – just a grey, smoldering, pungent surface they trekked over.

In the distance ahead of them Jamie saw an orange glow – the hair on his neck tingled. He knew the fire was still burning ahead of them and they were still far from safe. He moved forward one step ahead of the other. He moved his eyes between the ground to chart a course to minimize the jarring his patient felt when the sleigh hit rocks or fell into holes and Max would groan in pain.

Jamie kept his eye on the direction he was headed to keep from getting lost. He watched Jake and 'Little Guy' who followed several feet behind the sleigh and further back the doe who followed with her head down low to the ground but her eyes always on her fawn.

Jamie balanced the sleigh with his hands firmly clinched to the handles he'd fashioned for that purpose. His shoulders and back ached under the weight of pulling the sleigh behind him – but he didn't mind.

They came over a ridge and looked down at a stand of charred and stained boulders which looked like nature had erected impassable wall across the steep ravine. "Shit," Jamie said and stopped for a moment. Max called out, "Jamie, what's wrong?"

"Looks like we'll have to back track a little and try to find a way around these rocks."

Max said, "Turn this stretcher around so I can see."

"Okay, hold on," Jamie said and lowered the sleigh unhooked himself and then turned it around and raised it so Max could look over his bear skin blanket.

Max grunted then said, "This is Perry's Hideout. See the narrow opening on the left?" Jamie looked then nodded. "That's a cave that opens up to the other side. I'm sure it's big enough for us to get through – even with this damn contraption I'm strapped too."

Max looked over at Jamie and said, "Prop me up against that tree…" he looked over at a charred tree trunk, "and I'll watch you go down there and check it out before we all move further."

"Max, that's a splendid idea," Jamie said as he smiled and thought, *this will give me a few minutes to stretch my back and neck. I wish I had wheels to put on that sleigh – it would have made pulling it a lot easier.*

Jamie leaned the sleigh against the tree, looked at Jake and 'Little Guy' and said, "Stay with Max. I'll be right back."

He turned and began to walk down towards Perry's Hideout when he heard Jake and the fawn running after him. "So much for listening, Guys."

190

Jamie said and laughed and for the first time since they'd started their trek to Peterson's Meadow he had become accustomed to the tortured and burned landscape surrounding them.

He bound down the hill to the entrance Max had identified; the dog and fawn right behind him. He stepped inside the opening and moved carefully when the filtered sunlight was overcome by the darkness of the cave. *I wish I had brought the flashlight,* he thought as he shuffled his feet on the ground to avoid stepping into a hole or off a ledge. He moved slowly; his eye struggled to pierce through the darkness with little success. He felt his heart beat faster and his ears became more alert. He heard the animals behind him crawling on the ground.

Jamie moved slowly until he bumped his head on a rock, stopped rubbed his head for a moment then moved to one side. A light became visible in the distance and he knew he'd made it through.

He moved towards the light and soon he could see the ground and his steps became more confident and his stride lengthened. He came out on the other end with a smile across his face, the dog and fawn right behind him with equally confident expressions across their faces.

For the first time in days, Jamie was glad there had been a fire around them. He quickly found a piece of wood; charred and smoldering which he nurtured into a torch and used it for light to retrace his steps through the cave.

He immerged triumphantly and hustled back up the hill to Max with the good news. "We found the secret passage and there's lots of room for us to get through."

Max looked at him and said, "Good. Peterson's Meadow is still several more miles ahead."

Jamie, reached into the pack and retrieved the canteen and gave Max some water. Max struggled to keep it down but he was able to swallow a few sips. That's a good sign, Jamie thought and smiled. He returned the canteen to the pack and this time retrieved the flashlight. "I should have brought you along the first time," he said to the flashlight and smiled.

"Are you ready Max," Jamie asked.

"Yeap."

Jamie strapped on the sleigh and began to pull it down the hill towards the cave. This time Jake and 'Little Guy' ran ahead and waited at the entrance for the men.

By the time Jamie reached the entrance Jake and his buddy were laying down resting just inside the opening. He reached for the flashlight and turned it on and pointed it into the cave. This time there was an abundance of light and he could see evidence that people had been there years ago. He pulled Max behind him and moved along the foot prints he'd left moments before. This time when he came around the corner where he'd hit his head he stopped in his tracks and froze. "Jake, stay behind me," Jamie calmly said.

"What's going on?" Max gasped.

On the ground between Jamie and the opening was a large rattlesnake. The snake was coiled like a spring. Its head was moving back and forth and left to right – the entire time its eyes and flicking tongue pointed like a weapons guidance system at Jamie. The tail shook it's deadly warning in an almost hypnotic sound.

"Jamie, it sounds like a big rattlesnake. Don't get near it. Carefully lean me against the wall and retrieve the pistol from the pack. Then kill the damn thing."

Jamie did as he was told and moved slowly to not further agitate the snake. He pulled out the pistol. Cocked it and said, "This is going to be loud." He pulled the trigger and the explosion amplified by the enclosed cave made them temporarily deaf.

Jamie hit the coiled reptile. The bullet ripped through it in several places and tore it into three sections that wiggled and twisted in separated spastic motions as it died.

Jamie felt bad he'd killed the snake but he focused on his mission. He needed to get Max to Peterson's Meadow as fast as he could.

He kicked the snake pieces to the edge of the cave careful to stay away from the mouth and the still potent venom in its exposed fangs.

The party emerged from the cave and continued toward their destination.

The glow in the distance gradually became brighter with each step they moved towards Peterson's Meadow. "Max," Jamie said over his shoulder.

"Yeah kid," Max whispered then gasped.

"It looks like the fire is still burning off in the distance … in the direction of the meadow."

Jamie stopped and looked over his shoulder and he felt a rush of fear pass through him like a ghost. "What if the meadow is burning and the helicopter can't come for us?" His hands began to shake.

Max turned his head and looked up into Jamie's eyes and said, "Don't worry, my friends…" and he winked at Jamie and continued, "and that includes you my young Jedi are unmatched in their skills, courage and loyalty. Together we'll find a way out of this mess."

Max grunted and with as much strength as he had left said, "let's move to our objective, recon the LZ and call 'Boa' with an Op Green or Alt LZ request." Max fell silent after his last word and his head fell forward against his sternum.

Jamie immediately released the yoke and pulled the sleigh thru remnants of what was once a massive Douglas Pine and leaned it against the tree. He knew his friend would suffocate if he didn't do something fast to keep his air passage open.

Max's head lay with his chin against his chest and his breathing was shallow and jagged. "Hang in there, Max." Jamie cried out in anxious tones.

He reached for his knife and pulled it out with the same urgency a warrior would as he leaned into a fight. His eyes became focused and dark with concentration as he laid the blade across the bear skin near Max's throat. He leaned in and pulled the fur back exposing his friend's neck. Jamie looked at the neck for a second then carefully slipped his blade between Max's neck and the bear hide and gently cut away at the hide.

When he finished, hanging in his left hand was a two-inch-wide strip of bear skin nearly three feet long. Still unconscious, Max lay still – his eyes remained closed.

Jamie sheathed the knife and rose to his feet. He gently lifted Max's head then with the fur side against max's forehead he tightened the strip around the sleigh to hold Max's head up and allow him to breathe and prevent injury to his neck.

Jamie looked at his unconscious friend and said, "Max my friend you are getting worse by the minute. I promise I'll get you back to Wendi alive. I promise."

Jamie double checked that his friend was securely tied to the sleigh and climbed into the yoke, grabbed the handles and began to move as quickly as he dared towards the fire and the meadow ahead.

"Jake, I need you and 'Little Guy' to keep up. Max is getting worse and we need to get to the LZ, whatever that is." Jamie pulled and pulled the sleigh and continued to talk to Jake.

Jamie thought back to the cryptic thing Max had said when he fell unconscious the last time. *Let's move to our objective, recon the LZ and call 'Boa' with an Op Green or Alt LZ request.* "Jake what did Max mean? What is our objective, what is reconning the LZ mean and who is 'Boa'."

Jake ran beside Jamie looking into his face, barking in support and encouragement. Jamie smiled and didn't think about the pain in his shoulders and back as he moved as quickly through the forest as he dared pulling Max behind him. His mind focused on the last words Max had said. Jamie decided it was a code he needed to break.

He pulled the sleigh and checked his compass as he wondered, *who are you, Max? Why do you seem like there are two of you? The one I know and the one I see when you are nearly unconscious. You are two different people. Both strong and both powerful.*

He pulled and moved ever closer to the raging fire ahead – the entire time Jake and 'Little Guy' were there with him and 'Mother' only several feet behind her fawn. He mulled the coded message around in his head to keep his mind focused.

*What is the LZ?* He thought. We are moving to a location where a helicopter is going to meet us… *Landing Zone*, he thought, and he smiled and a 'Twanger' flashed by. His confidence focused, *Great now who is 'Boa'?* He thought and said to himself, "That one is too hard without more clues."

Jamie continued to *decode* the message. *What is OP Green or Alternate LZ.* He smiled as the puzzle came into focus and he said out loud, "OP Green means we can execute the pickup at Peterson's Meadow and alternate LZ means if it's ablaze or unusable we'll find another place to land the helicopter and get Max to a hospital."

Jamie felt a sense of pride and confidence in solving the riddle and in his joy called over his shoulder, "Max, I broke your coded message except or … who is 'Boa'?"

A weak voice hoarsely whispered, "A friend of mine I'd like you to meet when we get out of here."

## *Chapter Thirty-Six*

Jamie pulled the sleigh and occasionally looked at his traveling companions. He laughed when he saw Jake. The dog's body was covered in a thick coat of grey ash. And his face appeared to have aged – it was completely grey except around his eyes and mouth that were black. "Hey old man," Jamie called to his companion, Jake barked and sneezed. "When did you get so old?"

Jamie could see and feel they were moving nearer to an active fire. He could see flames where there had only been an eerie glow. The temperature climbed and his body became wet with perspiration.

He found a vantage point and stopped. They needed some water, he needed to check on Max and the animals and do some navigation to determine how far they were from Peterson's Meadow and estimate when they'd be there *First things first,* he thought and reached for the canteen. He tended to Max who was awake and carefully sipped water from the plastic canteen. Jamie spoke briefly with his friend the poured water into a collapsible bowl and Jake and 'Little Guy' drank enthusiastically until the bowl was empty. Jamie looked back at the doe and called out softly, "Here 'Mother' come here and have a drink of water." He slowly set the bowl down near her and filled it with water, then slowly retreated. The doe came forward and consumed the water then backed away.

"Good, everyone has had some water and now it's time to figure out where we are and how much longer we'll be on the trail," Jamie spoke as he wet his lips and fought off the urge to consume the remaining water in the canteen. *Save the water for Max and the kids… they need it more than you do*, Jamie told himself and closed the canteen and focused on the map, compass and charred land ahead of them.

Jake moved beside him and nudged the map with his dirty nose and left a wet, grey smudge on the paper. "Ahhh, Jake," Jamie playfully said and ran his fingers through the dog's fur. "Now let me concentrate buddy," Jamie said, and Jake lay down by his side.

Jamie lifted the compass to his eye and looked through the sight to the meadow. He looked down at the compass face and said, "bearing two-two-four magnetic." He laid the compass near the meadow and looked for the ridge he was on and confirmed it was along the compass line two-two-four and it was. "Good this is where we are… approximately." Jake's head popped up and he looked at the navigator.

Jamie laid his finger in a straight line from his assumed location to the center of the meadow over the map – noted the length by his finger then moved the finger to the legend on the map margin. "We have two and two tenths of a mile to go," he said and folded his map, shoved it into the pack and stood looking at the destination – off in the distance.

Jake was becoming exhausted and the acid in the ash he was walking through was beginning to make his paws sensitive. He walked over to Jamie and nudged him with his black gritty nose and looked up at the young man. The dog knew he could trust Jamie and it showed in the tired animal's eyes.

"Come on Jake, we'll make it and get out of here," Jamie said in a tired voice buoyed up by courage. He checked on Max then lifted the sleigh and began to pull it towards the meadow and the raging fire just beyond. I hope we can get there before the fire and I hope the helo can still make it in for Max; he really needs to get to the hospital now, Jamie thought as he doggedly put one foot in front of the other.

Jake, the fawn and his mother walked behind the sleigh – by this time the doe was walking alongside her fawn unafraid of the dog or the humans she traveled with. Together they made it down a gentle ravine, along a stand of torched trees smoldering from the inferno which had consumed them days before.

Jamie led them to a small creek which was choked with ash and burned debris but under the polluted surface the water was clear cool and inviting.

Jamie thought about whether the water was safe to drink then felt the weight of the canteen – it was nearly empty. "We'll take a chance," he said and opened the canteen, cleared the surface of the creek with his hand and lowered the vessel into the water. When it was full he raised it to his lips and tasted it – it was sweet, cold and refreshing.

He reached for the bowl from his pack and filled it with water. Jake, 'Little Guy' and 'Mother' drank and rested beside the water.

"Max," Jamie called out as he looked at his friend strapped tightly to the sleigh. "Here is some cool fresh water for you." Jamie said calmly. Max opened his eyes and Jamie's heart sank.

"Kid, I can't hold on much longer without medical attention. How far are we from the meadow?" Max asked. His eyes were red and his face smudged from the soot, dirt and sweat.

"We're still about two miles from the LZ. Maybe three hours." Jamie tried to remain calm.

"I can't wait that long Jamie," Max said. "Please call Wendi and ask for a 'little bird' and find a small LZ nearby. The pilot will need to make two trips to get us all out."

"Okay," Jamie replied and pulled out the phone and the map.

Wendi was on the phone instantly, "Are you there already," she asked.

"No, we're still about two miles away but Max is getting worse, and he asked me to call. He asked for a 'Little Bird' and a closer LZ." Jamie swallowed hard and tears began to run down his face. "Wendi, we need to get him to the hospital right this minute or we may lose him." He sobbed into the phone.

Wendi was too scared to react and looked at the map and found Trapper's Ridge. "Jamie, where are you? Can you find Trapper's Ridge on the map," she asked? Her voice was anxious.

Jamie ran his finger over the map looking for the location until he found it, "Yes, I see it."

Wendi sighed with relief. "How far away are you?" Her voice became calm, professional and authoritative.

"I believe we're close – maybe a quarter mile to the northwest. I can see it from here and it looks like an easy hike. I can get Max there in 20 minutes," Jamie's voice was calm and in control. Wendi could hear it in the young man's voice and thought back to her husband years ago when he was young and ruggedly handsome and always in control of himself.

"Jamie, I will call Max's friend and send in a small helicopter with a medic onboard. The bird will only be able to carry Max on the first trip and will have to come back for you and Jake on a second trip. Do you understand?"

"Yes, but the fire is still burning nearby and if the winds shift the LZ will be ablaze by then. The fire is already dangerously close and it will be a horse race getting Max out."

He thought about it for several seconds and said, "And I can't get out yet I have a doe and her fawn with us so let's get Max to the hospital and I'll hike with Jake and our new friends and together we'll get out of this mess." A 'Twanger' rushed over him and the hair on his neck bristled, and his confidence swelled.

"Wendi, if it's possible could you send me another battery for the phone and some more food for Jake, the fawn and doe. They seem to like dog food. Maybe some food for me too, please."

"Sure, the bird should be in the air soon and be there in the hour." Her voice softened and she said, "Jamie, you are an exceptional young man. Thank you."

"No problem, that's what friends do." He said and fell to his knees.

"Jamie, when you hear the helicopter, watch him he'll land where he can and you'll have to move to his location."

"Got it. I better get moving, Max has a freedom bird to catch," he said, and a warm feeling came over him, "and please tell Maggie Rose that I love her."

"I will, and, she already knows, Jamie."

Jamie ended the call and looked at Max. "It's all arranged. We'll move to Trapper's Ridge and a Little Bird will meet us. There will be a medic to help you until you get to the hospital."

Max nodded and said, "What about you and Jake?"

Jamie smiled, "Don't you worry about us. I'll take good care of your dog, anyway Jake and I have two others in the expedition who need to be cared for. Remember 'Little Guy' and his mother. Jake and I will get them out of this inferno and safely back into the forest then we'll come see you in the hospital."

"Kid, you remind me of me," Max grunted and said, "I guess we should get moving over to the ridge."

## *Chapter Thirty-Seven*

Wendi called Wilbur Jackson who was near the 'Little Bird' and its pilot, the same young man who'd dropped Max into the forest fire four days before. Wilbur had recruited the pilot and liked his confidence, talent and courage. *He's a good fit for the kind of work we do,* Wilbur thought.

The phone rang and Wilbur (or as the operators in his organization called him 'Boa' for his tremendous strength. He had literally squeezed a man to death) flipped his phone open with a snap of his wrist and said in a deep voice, "Boa," and listened.

Wendi spoke slowly and clearly, "Wilbur, Max is being delivered to Trapper's Ridge and should be there within the hour. He is reported to be in serious condition and will need a medic. Can you provide the man helping him with another battery for the Sat Phone and some food for the young man and his dog? They'll be hiking out on their own once Max is airlifted out."

Wilbur listened and made a mental list of her requests, "Wendi, consider it done. The pilot will be in the air in ten minutes. I have a medic standing by. And the food and a new phone will be on the bird."

He thought about the young man with Max and how brave and confident he was under pressure and said, "When this is over, I'd like to meet that young man. He might be the kind of guy we need in the snake pit."

"Goodbye Wendi. Don't worry we'll get Max out and to the hospital in no time." Wilbur hung up the phone, barked a few orders and the men around him began to react with professional calm and efficiency.

Ten minutes later, the black helicopter was wheeled out of a covered hanger. The pilot and medic were already aboard and before the helicopter came to rest the pilot had the propellers turning. Moments later the bird leapt into the air and sprinted away out over Lake Tahoe – no more than thirty feet off the emerald, blue water. The pilot calmly pushed the bird to its performance limits and tweaked the controls to coax out every bit he could.

Herbie, the medic, busied himself in the area behind the pilot. Herbie was a combat vet with thousands of hours in the medivac and triage business. He loved what he did and his new job working for 'Boa' was the next best thing to being an Air Force Para – and he thought, *the pay is much better*. He smiled then focused on the work at hand.

He prepared the litter and equipment he'd hastily gathered when assigned to extract a seriously wounded man. A man he'd only heard of during his civilian training as 'Viper' the number one operator in the elite Snake Pit. He'd made the cut and was one of the medical team assigned to support the Black Ops. His call sign was 'Cotton Mouth' or as the guys had done – shortened to 'Cotton'.

Herbie thought, *the poor guy really got the shit kicked out of him by a bear. From what I've heard it must have been one hell of a bear to have done that,* briefly looking out the window at the fires still burning in the direction they were headed. *Ah shit,* he thought and took a few deep breaths, clearing his mind and calming himself. He reminded himself, *dumb shit, remember you're the NFG (New Fucking Guy), fresh out of Quantico and on probation. This is your first op and you better not fuck up or it'll be an office job in DC for you.*

The thought of an office job sobered him, and he doubled checked his gear and reread his notes on the type and severity of the patient's trauma. They would be hovering in a few minutes. He was ready, *this is just like Afghanistan*, he thought, *except the view is much nicer.* He smiled and looked up at the pilot. "Hey, Tony, so this guy is the real deal?"

"Yea, we'll be in the shit forever with 'Boa' if we don't get him to the hospital."

He looked over his shoulder at the medic, "Newbie, you'd better do some of that doctor shit when we get 'Viper'. I understand he's in bad shape and we'll only have a few minutes to land and grab his ass so get ready. We'll be there in five minutes."

Tony grinned, he'd been the newbie until Herbie arrived and on one hand liked no longer being the rookie, but he remembered the pressure and stress of being the NFG, so he knew how his crewmember felt.

The pilot looked forward at the landscape. He was driving the helicopter at two hundred miles an hour straight into a raging inferno. Below him the forest had been consumed by the fire and smoldered in its final act – black charred and consumed. Ahead was a very different picture. The forest was engulfed in flames reaching to the sky several hundred feet into the air.

Ahead of him was a wall of orange and yellow flames and bellowing grey with a black hue clawing thousands of feet in the air. His heart pounded against his chest as he looked into what must surely be Hell and wondered where he would land his bird at the edge of the inferno and recover 'Viper'. *Ah shit, this is really the shits,* he thought and looked around for the poor bastards in the makeshift LZ.

"Hey Newbie, help me look for the assholes we're here to find. That fucking fire is danger close. We'll only have minutes on the ground if we expect to get out of here in one piece." His voice carried a tone of fear and concern. Herbie could understand when he looked up from his medical gear into the Hell ahead of them.

"Tony, I saw a lot of shit in the Sand Box but never anything like this – holy shit man," Herbie said as he forced himself to calm down.

The medic looked down at the incinerated forest and ash that blanketed the ground looking for signs that people had been there or clues to where they may be. He looked left and then right – off the right was a line in the ash that looked like a skier's tracks in newly fallen snow.

"Tony look to your right there are tracks that look like skies and wait… there are footprints too."

The pilot pulled back on the yoke and reduced power as the bird came to an abrupt stop in midair then hovered as they followed the tracks. Off in the distance they could see a man pulling a sleigh with a dog and what looked like a fawn with its mother twenty feet behind.

"That must be them," Tony said, and he turned the helicopter and looked for a place he could land. With the other eye he watched the fire raging a quart mile ahead of them, *holy shit those guys really have guts*, he thought and focused on flying his aircraft. He flew low over the party then moved to the closest landing site he could find. He hovered for several minutes to blow much of the ash from the ground below him.

The action made a large cloud of grey dust but cleared the area for the helicopter to land. Jamie moved quickly pulling Max to the LZ. Jake followed trusting Jamie while 'Little Guy' and his mother were not quite so trusting and waited off in the distance.

Tony lowered his helicopter onto the pad he'd cleared with the prop wash and feathered the pitch and reduced the rotation to an idle. Herbie climbed out of the back with an emergency kit over his shoulder running in the direction of Jamie and the sleigh he pulled behind.

Jake ran towards the medic barking in a combination of greeting and guarded reserve until he sensed Jamie was comfortable with the stranger.

"Hi my name is Herbie and I'm a medic here to help 'Viper' and get him to the hospital. Tell me all you can about his injuries, when they happened and what you've been able to do to dress the wounds. Here let me carry the sleigh, we must hurry the fire is near."

He helped Jamie out of the harness and began to pull it towards the idling helicopter as Jamie downloaded the information he had on Max, his injury and what he had done to dress the wounds and his assessment of Max's condition.

Jake stayed by Jamie's side right up to the door of the helicopter. The down wash and noise scared the dog but he stood alongside his friend and looked on to his master, Max, as he was loaded aboard the small bird. He waited to jump aboard but when Jamie stepped away and the bird roared to life and jumped into the air he stayed by Jamie's side. He trusted the young man – he had sensed from the first time they met that he was a lot like his owner, Max.

As the bird rose off the ground, it rotated to the east then sprinted away at tree level with Max safely aboard. Jamie looked at a black package the pilot had tossed to his feet seconds before the bird leap off the ground. He looked at the package then looked at Jake sitting at his feet. "Don't worry Jake, Max will be okay." He said the words and only hoped they would be true. He hadn't even had a chance to say goodbye to his friend as he was sweep up and flown away.

By then the helicopter was miles away and the noise had subsided. Jamie opened the package and found two Ziploc bags of dog food, some beef jerky, a Sat Phone and an envelope with his name on it.

He left the food and phone in the package and tore open the envelope. In a second, he recognized the handwriting – it was Maggie Rose's. It read,

Jamie,

You are very brave, and I am very proud of you and wish you were here with me. Please be careful and come safely back to father and me. We love you very much and can't wait for your safe return.

I love you with all my heart and
pray for your safe return. I love you.
    Love,
    Maggie Rose

As he finished reading the letter, he held it
momentarily against his chest and tears of joy rolled
down his cheek. Jake sat in front of him looking into
his eyes with a curious look on his face as his tail
moved impatiently back and forth.

Jamie wiped the tears from his face and said,
"Jake, my friend, Max is on his way to the hospital,
and he'll be okay. Now it's time for us to get out of
this Hell and get back to the people we love." Jake
barked and began to dance around Jamie's feet.

Jamie grabbed the food and the new phone
from the package and moved them into his pack, He
took one long last look at the sleigh he'd built to
move Max then threw the pack over his shoulder and
led his party away from the fire in the direction they'd
come. He'd lead them that direction until they were a
safe distance then he turned east toward the lake. Jake
moved steadily alongside Jamie while 'Little Guy'
and his mother followed ten feet behind with their
head hung low – their noses grey with ash soot.

They trudged through the tortured and
destroyed forest. They felt the heat from the nearby
fire and their surroundings were littered with charred
trees, some smoldering while others openly burned.
The air choked them with the heavy smell of

incinerated wood and flesh. The skies were grey and dense with the airborne waste the fire had created – the sun, but a dull masked orb high overhead.

The winds began to increase and the fire in the distance began to react as it rejoiced in the added vigor the wind gave it. The flames grew brighter and the heat became noticeably hotter. Jamie looked over his shoulder at the now raging fire and knew there would not be another helicopter coming for them.

"Jake," he said. The dog looked up at him and barked.

"My old friend, I think we're on our own and we need to outrun this fire and get over towards Lake Tahoe where there will be people who can help us."

The dog barked like he understood and agreed.

"Good, we'll hike to the ridge ahead then turn east to the lake."

The dog barked and walked beside Jamie.

The young man thought, *Man, am I lucky to have a friend like you, Jake. I promise to get you safely home to Max and Wendi and you will help me get home to Maggie Rose and my family.*

Jake barked again and the friends moved with renewed strength towards the ridge – the path ahead was smoldering, grey and black and resembled the visions his Sunday school teacher, Mr. Pratt had brought to mind with his vivid descriptions of Hell.

Jamie began to think about his friend, Max and wondered if he'd arrived at the hospital as Jake and the fawn and his mother followed at something between a jog and a fast walk. *Max, I hope you're doing okay and get to the hospital quickly. I look forward to seeing you and Wendi again with Jake when I get out of this hell,* he focused on the ridge – still a hundred yards ahead of them. Jamie looked over his shoulder briefly to check on his friends. They appeared to be fine – tired and hot but still able to keep up with him.

To the right of the point on the ridge he was moving towards, there was a large tree, actually two identical trees coming out of the same trunk. They were black, smoldering with rapidly rising trails of smoke and higher in the symmetrical trees a fire was burning in bright yellows and oranges. He concentrated on the tree and focused on the fires burning high up in the twins when he heard the crackling of the fire and the popping of the sap from the Douglas Fir as it ignited and like miniature fireworks flew out in all directions and burned following their trajectories until they fell to the ground. *No wonder this fire isn't dying. Each tree it ignites sends a cascading fountain of burning sap to start millions more fires nearby.* Then he said in a mumbled voice, "We must move quickly and get down towards Lake Tahoe and safety." He pulled on the straps of his pack and leaned forward and reached deep inside himself for the strength to push onward.

Jamie felt fear and doubt – his old demons. The ones he hadn't felt for a while when he was around his friend Max.

"Go away, I will not allow fear or doubt to control me ever again," Jamie said with a determined look on his face. Jake looked up and barked with encouragement and moved up alongside his friend for moral support. It worked and soon Jamie had locked his old demons away in the recesses of his mind and he felt his confidence and courage returning. The feeling was warm and comforting. Jake watched him and could sense something good had come over Jamie and he barked again, and his tail moved back and forth with his gait.

When they reached the ridge, Jamie looked to the east towards Lake Tahoe and through the smoke he could see the emerald color of the water in the distance. He smiled and knelt beside Jake and began to rub the dog's neck and back, "Jake there's the lake. I can see it. That's the direction we must move now. And look… about two miles or so that direction the forest is still green. If we can get there, 'Little Guy' and his mom will be safe and they can start their lives over again here in the high country."

Jake sat at Jamie's feet looking intently into the young man's eyes and enthusiastically barked in agreement.

Jamie pulled his pack off his shoulders, shoved his hand inside and retrieved the canteen and the collapsible bowl. In a fluid motion he opened the bowl and filled it with water and set it down in front of the dog. Jake looked down at the bowl and inhaled the water is several seconds. Jamie retrieved the bowl, filled it again and walked slowly towards the doe and her fawn and set the bowl down several feet in front of them. The fawn moved forward towards the bowl after he looked for an approving nod from his mother. He too devoured the water then returned to his mother's side. Once again Jamie filled the bowl and set it down near the doe this time and she drank slowly then nudged her fawn to the bowl to finish the remaining water.

The selfless act of the mother brought tears of joy and hope to the young man's eyes and fueled his commitment to ensure he guided this mom and her baby to a safe place where they could start a new life as free animals in the wild. "I won't let you two down," he said then drew a long pull from the canteen for himself, shoved the container back in his pack and said confidently, "Okay, guys, we'll head directly towards the lake and walk out of this hell together."

Jamie tucked his thumbs under the shoulder straps of his pack near his collar bones and gently pulled forward to relieve the pressure. It felt good and he began to move forward in large powerful strides.

## WALKING THROUGH HELL

They marched from ridge to ridge then stopped briefly to reorient themselves then move forward – occasionally looking over their shoulders at the fire burning in the distance. Jamie had lost track of the time since the helicopter had taken Max away. It was then, he thought about his friend and remembered he'd been given a new phone at the LZ. "Let's catch our breath and let's call to check in on Max." He said as he dropped down on his knees and pulled the pack over his head and dropped it in front of him. He pulled out the new phone, looked at it for the first time, and recognized it was identical to the one Max had. Jamie felt a wave of relief knowing he knew how to use it.

He dialed Wendi's number and the phone rang and rang. Just when he was ready to hang-up she answered, "Jamie is that you?"

"Yes, I wanted to check on Max and see how he's doing." He said and sighed deeply.

"He's still in surgery. The doctor said it was lucky you had taken such good care of him and that he got to the hospital when he did. Much longer out there and he may have gone septic and died," her strong voice weakened, and she began to cry. "Thank you for taking care of him, Jamie. We won't know more until the doctors finish stitching him up and address any infections he may have."

"I'm glad we were able to get him to the hospital in time." Jamie said and looked down at Jake then said, "Your papa is in surgery and the doctors are fixing him right up. Nothing to worry about boy."

Jake barked and began to walk in a tight circle.

"Sound like you and Jake are getting along fine. Where are you and do you still have the doe and her fawn in tow?" Wendi asked.

"Yes, we're one big happy family," Jamie said and laughed.

"Where are you?" Wendi asked.

Jamie thought about the question for several seconds then said, "I really don't know. I can see Lake Tahoe off in the distance and we are moving in that direction. I figure there will be people there and we should be leaving the burned part of the forest in a few hours and I hope to get 'Little Guy' and 'Mother' settled and reintroduced to the forest. Then Jake and I will make a beeline to the water and call again when we figure out where we are."

"That sounds really good right now."

Jamie said "I'll hang up now and we'll continue to hike to the lake. I'll call in two hours or so and check in again. Oh and by the way, thanks for the new phone."

"You're welcome and thanks again for taking care of Max. You're a real friend. Talk to you soon," she said, hung up the phone and pressed it against her forehead for several seconds. She thought, *Jamie. You're an amazing young man and you remind me of*

*Max. You're strong, confident and brave. No wonder the two of you get along so well.*

Jamie returned the phone to the interior pocket in his pack where he kept it and retrieved the canteen and filled the bowl for each of his crew then took a swing himself.

He retrieved the Ziploc bag of dog food and used the water bowl to feed his friends. While they ate and rested, he chewed on a piece of jerky and thought, *This really tastes good.* He quietly watched his family and felt content.

## *Chapter Thirty-Eight*

After a short rest, Jamie led his expedition further away from the fire and towards the vast lake in the distance. His legs were growing tired and his mind foggy from fatigue and exhaustion. He forced himself to put one step ahead of the other as the landscape he moved through became uninteresting and without variation in his tired mind.

As he reached a ridge, he stopped to look in the distance to the lake. For an instant his heart skipped a beat until his eyes focused on the emerald blue ahead of them. "Good we're still moving in the right direction," he said as he looked behind him and realized his traveling companions were rung out and could barely stand.

Jake laid panting in the dusty red dirt. His eyes watered and his lips and tongue were caked in red mud. His tail barely moved and he rolled over on his side and grunted – Jamie had never heard that sound coming from the dog before.

'Little Guy' fell to the ground with his legs tucked under him – his face showed the same signs of fatigue and thirst. Even the doe, normally timid and distance staggered up near her fawn and dropped to the ground – her brown eyes pleaded for a rest, water and food for her fawn.

"Okay, I get the message guys," Jamie said and he sat down facing them and pulled off his pack and set it in front of him. "Let's take a break and have a drink or two and feast on a banquet. What do you say?" He smiled at them and they responded. Each lifted their heads and looked enthusiastically in anticipation.

"Good, now that I have your attention, let's drink first," Jamie said. His voice calmed and reassured them, they'd be okay. He reached for the collapsible bowl and filled it. He passed it to 'Little Guy' first. "Here my little friend, you look like you need this the most." He set the bowl under the lying deer's nose and he rapidly consumed the water.

Jamie repeated filling the bowl and gave it to the doe beside her baby. She seemed to inhale the water and in seconds Jamie retrieved the empty bowl then he filled it and gave it to Jake. The dog found the energy to sit up and drank his ration slowly as if savoring it like a fine wine.

Jake finished as Jamie tipped back the canteen and let the cool refreshing water run down his throat. Instantly he began to feel better and his mind began to clear somewhat. He felt the canteen and decided to give his crew a second ration – which they all gladly consumed.

The water made a noticeable improvement in the animals. *I should have done this sooner,* Jamie thought to himself as he watched his traveling companions begin to move more easily and rest more comfortably. He reached into the backpack and pulled out the bag of dog food and fed the deer and his dog until they were content and resting.

Jamie pulled out a piece of jerky and put the end between his teeth, tore off a small piece and he began to chew it as the dry meat gradually mixed with his saliva and became soft enough to chew and swallow.

He leaned against a tree and it felt cool and he looked around in amazement. The trees were green and the vegetation on the forest floor was alive and in vivid colors the dirt wasn't covered in ash. He sniffed the air – yes there was still the strong smell of fire and burning wood but it was much less than he remembered.

He jumped to his feet and spun around looking up at the forest then down at the ground and in an excited voice called out, "Look, we made it out of the fire. We are in an unmolested forest – we're going to make it my friends." By this time, Jake was running around Jamie playfully barking and wagging his tail. The deer were on their feet and nodding their heads up and down.

Jamie looked at his friends and said, "I know we're all tired, but I think we should press on towards the lake, find a new home for 'Mother' and 'Little Guy' and Jake," Bark, Bark the dog sounded off, "You and I will make our way to the water and get to Wendi and Max." The dog began to playfully turn around in circles and bark with delight.

"Before we go, let's check in with Wendi and see how Max is doing," the young man said. He reached into his pack and retrieved the phone and the animals dropped to the ground near him stealing another few moments of rest before their trek continued.

Wendi picked up the phone on the first ring and said, "Jamie is that you?"

"Hello, the kids and I wanted to check in and see how Max is doing?"

"Jamie, he's out of surgery and still very serious, but the doctors are optimistic he'll recover completely – except he'll have a whole lot of scars, but that's nothing." Her voice was exhausted but her relief rang out loud and clear.

She held back a tear and said, "He was briefly awake when I sat beside him in the ICU. The first thing he asked about was how you were doing and if you'd gotten out yet." She took a deep breath and said, "Jamie, he likes you."

"That was nice of you to say, and please tell him Jake, the deer and I are fine. We are out of immediate danger and are resting in a beautiful green forest. I think we're near Eagle Lake and we can see

Tahoe from the ridge. We're exhausted and will rest for a few hours before we resume our trek east. Oh, by the way, I think Jake and I will be going it alone soon. The mother and her fawn are ready to disappear into the forest."

Wendi thought for a moment then said, "Jamie, Maggie Rose and Arthur will be waiting for you. When you know where you are and approximately when and where you'll come out of the forest, call me and I'll forward the info to them to pick you and Jake up. I'll stay here at the hospital with Max."

"Sounds like a plan," Jamie said in an upbeat voice. "I better hang up and save the batteries. I'll call again soon and tell Max I was asking about him and look forward to seeing you both soon."

Wendi heard the phone go silent and she sighed and prayed they'd be okay.

Just then Wilber 'Boa' Jackson walked into the recovery room. He was wearing an expensive tailored suit with a bright silk tie and Italian leather shoes. His head was cleanly shaved and reflected the artificial light in the room. The fact he'd been a professional lineman for the Raiders was no surprise. He stood, momentarily in the door frame – all 320 pounds standing nearly 6 foot 8 inches tall with arms the size of tree trunks and shoulders that were the width of the opening. "Wendi," he said in a quiet emotional voice. "I came as soon as I heard he was coming out of surgery. The docs think the 'old bird' is going to be just fine and how are you holding up?" His perfectly straight white teeth were especially remarkable juxtaposed against his ebony skin.

He approached her and gave her a hug which nearly crushed her rib cage and she thought, *now I know why Max calls you 'Boa' because with those massive arms you could be as lethal as a constrictor.*

He held her at arm's length and looked into her tired eyes. "Wendi is there anything you need? Just ask and I'll make it happen. Don't worry about Max, he's in very good hands. The doctors are ours and they have access to the very best of everything. I am not kidding when I say your Max will be fine but when he's well enough to travel we'll need to take him back to Virginia to our facility to facilitate his recovery. You are more than welcome to come with him…" he took a breath and said, "and I know he'd like that too."

He dropped his arms to his side and smiled, "Think about it, there is no hurry it will be at least a week or two before we move him."

"Have you heard from the guy that dragged Max across Hell's playground? Is he okay? I'd like to meet him."

Wendi's eyes revealed that she'd just spoken to Jamie. "He's fine and out of the fire for now. He still has a fawn and its mother in tow with Jake, Max's dog, their moving towards Emerald Bay."

She smiled, a tired smile and said, "He's quite a remarkable young man."

"Damn, it sure sounds like it," The big man grinned as he rocked back on his heels.

Seconds later, his face changed, and he looked serious, and his eyes twinkled, "Wendi, let me know if you need anything – promise?"

A smirk came over his handsome face and he chuckled, "Tell 'Viper' I came by and ordered him not to wrestle anymore bears for a while." He laughed so loudly his body moved with each belting roar. His bright smile lit up the room, a tears of emotion filled his eyes.

He quickly wiped his cheeks with a silk handkerchief and turned leaving the room without another sound.

## *Chapter Thirty-Nine*

Jamie arched his back and stretched his arms over his head. As he did, he realized his bottom had become numb from sitting on the ground so long. He jumped to his feet and began to massage his rear until the feeling began to return. Jake looked over with a sleepy look then he yawned and stood up and shook off his coat. Instantly awake he trotted over and sat beside Jamie.

'Guy' was still sleeping as his mother sat beside him watching carefully over her baby while he rested peacefully.

Jamie looked at the deer and realized it was time to part ways. They were safe back in the forest, and now would be as good a time as any to say goodbye. He leaned down and whispered into Jake's ears. "It's time to say goodbye to 'Little Guy' and 'Mother'. They'll be fine and it's time for us to get out of here."

Jamie tossed his pack over his shoulders and stood up beside Jake. He looked sadly at 'Mother' and 'Little Guy' and as a tear of regret and happiness rolled down his cheek, he softly said, "Goodbye. Be safe and I hope we'll see each other again someday here in the forest." He turned slowly and began to

227

walk down the ridge. Jake looked equally sad at their traveling friends and barked once and followed Jamie as he moved down the steep drop-off below the ridge.

After several minutes, Jamie stopped and looked over his shoulder to the ridgeline above where he'd left his friends. They were standing there looking down saying their goodbyes and good wishes, as deer do – silently and stoically. Jamie waved for a moment and continued down the mountain towards the lake. Jake barked again then ran out in front of Jamie leading the way.

The green forest and full ground cover kept the dust down and the temperature comfortable. Moving down the gentle grade made moving easier for the travelers. No longer were they required to weave their course around burning trees or dense smoke or deep ash. They moved in nearly a straight line stopping only long enough to determine their next course by compass, drink water and nibble on a bite of food. They were exhausted but driven to get out of the forest and reunite with the ones they loved.

Jake led the way down the incline making his way around the underbrush and the healthy trees which made up the lush green forest.

Jamie followed his four legged friend and gradually slipped into a mind numbing trance – the result of severe fatigue and lack of sleep over the last four days. His body moved forward step by step and somehow he followed the dog managing not to stumble and fall. For lengthening periods of time his mind was asleep, yet he moved in a rigid – robot-like motion.

Jake periodically looked back over his shoulder noticing the strange way his friend was moving. He finally stopped and patiently sat down – waiting for Jamie to catch up.

To the dogs surprise the young man walked past him without acknowledging him. The dog watched the stiff movement and the zombie-like look in Jamie's eyes as he walked by.

Jake whimpered in worry and slowly rose to his feet and followed – somewhat feeling rejected and confused. His tail down and his head hung low, Jake fell in behind his friend and silently watched. Moments later he stopped instantly and watched Jamie trip on a root, normally in plain sight and fall forward. Jamie struck his head on a large tree trunk falling to the ground. He hit the ground without trying to soften the fall and lay still on the forest floor.

Jake sprinted forward barking in alarm. The man lay without movement. Blood began to pool around his forehead.

Jake, now behind Jamie barked loudly and pushed the man with his nose and paw. He began to lick the man's face, barking loudly and slobbering over the man's cheek. *Come on and wake-up. Come on show me you're okay. We're so close, don't give up ...* "Bark, Bark Bark," the dog pleaded.

Jake saw the cut on Jamie's scalp and though the bleeding had begun to stop by itself, the dog hovered around the body in jerky concerned movements, barking, whimpering and licking Jamie's face.

Several minutes later Jamie began to stir. First his body twitched and his eyelids began to flutter. He opened his unfocused eyes and struggled to see.

"Ouch," he said as he sat up and felt his head with his left hand. Feeling the sticky liquid on his fingers he brought his hand into sight and said, "Shit, I cut my head, Jake. How did I do that?"

Jake smiled as subtle and obscure as dogs can and his barking changed tone from that of worry and concern to elation and happiness. He barked in delight and moved around in quick circles several times then fell to the ground beside Jamie and laid right against him – putting his head on Jamie's shoulder and looked at the injured man as if to tell him, *Let's rest for a while here before we continue and don't you dare scare me again like this ... you really had me thinking you were seriously hurt or even dead.*

Jamie knew exactly what his dog was telling him and after checking his wound – which by then the bleeding had stopped and whispered, "Damn, that'll leave a scar." He laid down, gently laid his arm beside the dog and whispered, "Thanks Jake. You're a great friend."

# WALKING THROUGH HELL

Jake barked softly and watched until Jamie was sound asleep before he looked around the forest to make sure they were safe then he fell asleep. The dog periodically awoke to check on Jamie then fell back asleep.

Four hours, or so, later Jake felt Jamie beginning to move – the dog jumped to his feet; prepared for anything including battle to protect his friend. The dog instantly relaxed when he saw Jamie sit up and look at him.

"Jake, hello my friend. How did you sleep? I had a wonderful sleep and man, did I really need it. I've never been so tired." He said as he reached for Jake's neck and began to pet the warm black fur. Jake relaxed and leaned into Jamie's hand to encourage him to scratch his back from head to tail. Jake softly barked and closed his eyes momentarily.

Jamie and Jake sat together for several minutes. Jamie lifted his hand and felt his wound. "Damn that hurts," he mumbled then reached for his backpack and removed the first aid kit. With the mirror included he was able to put a large Band-Aid over the three inch gash on his scalp. He retrieved the aspirin and tossed several briefly into his hand then into his mouth and drank from his canteen. *My head is killing me. I hope it's just the cut and not a concussion*, he thought and took five more pills.

He gathered up the contents of his pack littered around him and replaced them into his worn and torn canvas pack. He stood up and looked at Jake sitting, ready to resume their trek to safety.

Jamie pulled his compass from his pocket and the map from his shirt. He was lost. The area was unfamiliar and didn't know from which direction he'd come from.

"Jake, I must have been sleep walking for some time before I fell and hit my head. Boy, I think I'm lost."

Jake barked and his tail began to move excitedly from side to side. He jumped to his feet, barked again, and turned around and moved several steps forward, looked over his shoulder and barked again as if to say "I know the way Jamie – follow me. I'll get us out of here."

Jamie watched the dog and knew he had nothing to worry about.

"Jake, of course you know the way out of here. You take point and I'll follow," he said with a smile from ear to ear.

Jake barked and turned facing away from Jamie and began to move through the forest. Jamie followed each step moving them further and further from the fire and closer and closer to their loved ones.

\*\*\*

Max stirred in the hospital bed. Though heavily sedated, he was a driven man who possessed superhuman discipline. Though unconscious, his mind was thinking about the man he'd left in the field. Drugged and confused, his brain worked in vivid dreams that fired around his mind. All related to Jamie and the danger surrounding him. Most took on characters and scenarios from the many missions he'd accomplished during his clandestine career.

Ghosts of the past and locations faraway taunted and threatened Jamie in the veteran's tortured thoughts.

Wendi was reading a novel sitting in the ICU beside her husband. When she noticed his body twitching and his bandaged arms began to thrash about in powerful jagged motion. She dropped the book and moved to his side, called his name and reached for his arm. He was perspiring and he moved his head and moaned in deep guttural sounds.

Wendi frantically called the nurse and doctor to help then resumed trying to comfort Max. He continued to thrash about, by then his wounds were beginning to reopen and weep blood. She looked on calling his name and frantically pleading for him to wake from the dark place his mind had taken him.

Several moments later the nurse and doctor arrived together. The doctor reached for a vial and a syringe on the counter and without delay drove the needle into the vial withdrew the clear liquid into the syringe, approached Max as the nurse tried to immobilize the strong man's arm. She struggled and waited for the doctor to inject the sedative into Max's vein.

The effect was immediate and the patient relaxed and stopped moving – his breathing returned to the steady rhythm of a sleeping person. After several minutes the doctor and nurse left and she sat back down in her chair, holding his hand in hers. She whispered, "Max, where are you my dear? Come back to me. I love you …"

Wendi looked at the cell phone she had set beside the bed. She waited for Jamie to call with his location and a status report on his progress towards the extraction point. She assumed it would be at the Eagle Lake trailhead. She waited for his call to pass the rendezvous location and approximate time to Maggie Rose, the Command Center and Max's friend 'Boa'.

She smiled weakly and thought, *I hope I hear from Jamie soon. I know how worried everyone, including Max, is about that young man's safety.*

She looked at Max, sleeping soundly, his wounds had stopped weeping, "Max, my dear, you gave us quiet a fright earlier – I think Jamie and Maggie Rose are in love. Isn't that wonderful?"

His eyes gently opened as he tried to focus on her face then fell back into deep slumber.

# *Chapter Forty*

Jamie followed Jake through the forest. They were on a steady descent and they were miles from the area of forest that had burned in the massive fire. The cool air, the downhill direction and a growing sense the ordeal would be coming to an end soon reassured them as they moved in a quick cadence towards Eagle Lake and the trailhead only two miles beyond the lake.

Jake reached a small ridge and waited for Jamie to catch up. Jamie looked at his friend and could tell something special was visible. He moved quickly and in short order stood beside the dog. "What's up, Jake?" He looked down and there was a hiking trail. Off in the distance was Eagle Lake.

Jamie dropped his pack on the ground beside him and knelt down near Jake and said, "We did it Jake. We are nearly home."

Jake's tail moved frantically and he walked in excited circles around Jamie. His bark was crisp and bright with excitement. Jamie's smile confirmed he was also happy.

Jamie reached into his pack and retrieved the last of their food and water. "Jake, we might as well finish off our food – we'll be home by dinner tonight." He placed the dog food into a bowl and Jake inhaled the food in seconds. Jamie held the three pieces of beef jerky in his hands and then savored the flavor consuming them one by one.

He opened the canteen and poured most of its contents into the dog's bowl and watched Jake lap up the water. Jamie swallowed the remaining water in several gulps and returned the now empty container into his pack. He looked at the dog and said, "Jake just a few more minutes to rest then we'll be on our way. Let's call Wendi and tell her where we are and see how Max is doing?"

Jamie grabbed the satcom and pulled it from the pack, turned it on and dialed the only number he knew on the phone – Wendi's.

***

The phone began to ring in the hospital room. Wendi lifted the phone and said, "Jamie, is that you?"

"Yes, Wendi. Jake and I are checking in to see how Max is doing."

"He's out of surgery but still in tough shape. The doctor has him heavily sedated and he is sleeping now. The doctor seems confident he'll be okay," She said in a tired but excited voice.

She waited a moment then asked, "How are you? Where are you and when can we come get you?" She couldn't help herself and added, "I know Maggie Rose is anxious for you to emerge from the forest. She wants to be there to pick you up."

"Oh that's wonderful, you know Wendi, I love her very much." He stopped and thought, *Wow that was so comfortable to say – I do love her very much.*

He continued, "Jake and I have rejoined the Eagle Lake hiking trail and are about two miles from the lake. From there it's an hour or so to the trailhead."

He looked down at the dog and said, "I figure we'll be there in several hours."

"Wendi, could you bring some food for Jake? We finished our food for lunch and he'll be hungry by the time we come out of the forest."

"Jake, of course. You are a wonderful guy … always thinking about others first. I'll call Maggie Rose and give her and Artie the good news."

"Wendi, I'll call again when we are getting close to the trailhead. My best regards to Max. And tell him Jake is doing fine. Bye."

Jamie hung up the phone and turned it off to save the batteries. He tossed it back into his pack, looked at Jake and said, "Okay, let's get going we have family and friends to meet tonight." The dog barked and started moving towards the trail. When they reached the trail they turned to the right towards Lake Tahoe. "We're nearly home," Jamie said under his breath and smiled. He was thinking about how much he was looking forward to holding Maggie Rose in his arms.

\*\*\*

His daydream was interrupted by a strange sound ahead of them. He listened closely, it was something large moving clumsily through the forest. He began to prepare for a bear or large cat to appear when he heard, "Aw shit." Jamie smiled and realized it was a hiker on the trail. *That's the first person I've seen in the forest in days,* he thought to himself.

# *Chapter Forty-One*

Maggie Rose and Artie were standing by the trailhead when an exhausted and dirty pair of hikers emerged from the forest. Maggie was the first to see them and she began to run towards the pair. Jamie stopped momentarily and watched her running towards him with tears of joy streaming down her cheeks. In that instant he knew, *she was and would always be the one for him.* They embraced and kissed as lovers do – passionately with complete abandonment. Artie caught up and watched with a smile as his suspicions were confirmed – Maggie Rose and Jamie were hopelessly in love with each other.

Jake, growing tired of the public display of affection moved over beside Artie and leaned in for a head scratch. He was richly rewarded for his forwardness.

Artie called Wendi confirming Jamie and Jake were safe and he'd bring them by the hospital later in the day as the four of them walked to the car.

They drove to the hotel where Artie had rented a room to allow them to remain close during the ordeal. Jamie took a long hot shower then they drove to the hospital to see Max and Wendi.

239

Jamie with Maggie Rose's hand in his walked into the room. Wendi looked up from her book and smiled. "I see you found each other," she winked and rose to her feet. "Jamie, I'm so glad you're safe," she said then tears welled up in her eyes and she hugged Jamie and Maggie Rose.

"Jake is in the car with Artie," Jamie said as tears of relief, exhaustion and joy rolled down his face. With a weak and wobbly hand Max reached out to him and their eyes locked in a silent exchange confirming they had completed the task and were still alive.

Wendi fell to her knees beside the bed and put her head against her husband's shoulders and for the first time allowed herself to cry from the depths of her heart – she knew he would be okay. The sight of Jamie and knowing Jake was fine would fuel him through recovery and, as the doctor suggested, "He'd be as good as new: less a few more scars."

Jamie gently sat on the bed next to Wendi and Max. "Thank you, Wendi, for helping us every step of the way and always being there at the end of the satcom when we needed you."

He looked over at Max and said, "She is the reason you and I made it out alive." Max shook his head slowly then fell back into a drug induced slumber.

Maggie Rose stepped beside Jamie and put her hands on his shoulders and gently squeezed them with loving care. She silently watched the bond between the husband and wife and how easily Jamie was in their presence. *Jamie has changed. He is no longer a young man of doubt and insecurity. He has become a man full of confidence, strength and courage.* Then her thoughts changed and her eyes became soft and her cheeks glowed, *and you're not bad to look at either.*

Jamie looked up at Maggie Rose and could read her mind – she leaned comfortably into him as he put his arm around her waist. "Maggie Rose, I love you. Your memories – memories of everything you've said to me and the way you move when you walk, the way you laugh and the way your face lights up when you're happy kept me moving even when I couldn't put one foot in front of the other."

"Jamie, I love you too and prayed for you and Max every day you were in danger. I can't imagine my life without you in it." Then an exaggerated pout came across her face as she said, "Don't you ever do anything like that again – promise?" The pout left her face as quickly as it had appeared and was replaced with a toothy smile.

Just then the natural light coming through the opened door disappeared and the room became noticeably darker. Max, in his semiconscious state felt the change, opened his eyes as the others looked in unison. In the door frame stood a huge man. He nearly filled the entire opening. He was wearing a silk suit, bright colored tie and expensive shoes. His head was shaved and reflected the remaining light in the room.

In his arms was a large bouquet of flowers. He stood there for a moment and the room was silent. When a broad smile erupted on the strangers face, the room lit up and he said in a deep booming voice, "Young man," looking intensely at Jamie. "Don't be too quick to make that promise to your girlfriend. After the way you performed in the field and brought 'Viper' home, I would like to have a conversation with you and offer you the job of a live time."

He looked at Maggie Rose and said, "Before you get upset, look at how well Max and Wendi are as a couple. We can make it work."

Maggie Rose stood up and said, "I'm sorry, I don't know who you are?"

The man quickly looked over his shoulder to ensure no one was behind him listening, he grinned showing off his large perfect smile. Then, as his mouth formed the words, Jamie spoke, "Boa."

### *The End*
\*\*\*

# Death of a Liberian Seaman

## (A Short Story)

# Rex Inverness

## The End Is Near
### Somewhere in the Mid Pacific -- August 1978

THE END IS NEAR ... Ian shoved a life
jacket under the mattress to wedge himself against the
stateroom bulkhead then curled up with a pillow to
keep from being thrown onto the deck. A heavy wool
blanket tightly wrapped around his body, kept him
warm. There he slept as the motion rocked him like a
baby in a cradle. This night his dream was vivid and
alive. He tossed and turned as he dreamt in
magnificent colors and erotic smells. His body ached
for the touch of a lover. His fantasy had his heart
racing as every detail played out in slow motion.
Climbing into his mind, the story unfolded something
like this:

The Brazilian sun rebounded off her long soft
auburn hair, the summer sea breeze gently stirred
through its length. Her eyes made emeralds dull by
comparison, with the bewitching ability to penetrate
the soul at a glance and leave one's innermost secrets
exposed, naked, for all to see. The soft deeply tanned
skin of her face radiated the youth and beauty that
few have known; yet many have sinned for. She
walked towards him; her slender, well-shaped frame

outlined by the Rio de Janeiro seascape, her body played a symphony of sensuality, poise and eroticism with each step.

A minuscule black bikini bottom drove his stare to where her shapely thighs came together. She wore a wrinkled cotton shirt; secured only around her waist. The fact she had been in the water only moments before left little to one's imagination.

Closer and closer she came as he lay on the beach, helpless in the presence of this approaching goddess. As she drew near, he rose to his feet. From behind her ripe red lips, she produced a porcelain smile. Then to his astonishment her eyes remained fixed on him, her sweet lips drew together and launched a seductive and overpowering kiss, leaving him weak and powerless.

Her delicate hand reached out for his and as if hypnotized, he responded. With the joining of their two hands, his body, his being, his life was taken hostage. She slid up against him and he began to react instinctively. The curves of their bodies seemed to fit perfectly as the animal desire to consume one another erupted. His arms held her ever closer and the passion in their kisses exploded. The young man's desire for this woman's body made him crazy with lust. He didn't even know her name ... they were on a public beach in Brazil and ... he couldn't give a damn, HE NEEDED HER!

Still embroiled in the moment, their kisses became more passionate. They lowered themselves onto the blanket where he'd slept just moments before. She would be his in another moment. In a language he didn't understand, she pleaded for him to make love to her. Her bikini slipped off with the ease of cooperation; her top opened, her breast exposed. His kisses moved down her torso towards her rocking thighs. Just then...

"Third" spoke an old, tired male Filipino voice shattering the young man's dream,

"It's twenty-three-thirty, Sir it's time for your watch."

An instant later Ian's retinas screamed in pain as the excruciating brightness of the overhead lights pierced his closed eyelids. His first conscience thought was to kill the bastard for ruining his dream.

"Get the hell out of here," he yelled as the door closed.

The able-bodied seaman's entertainment for the evening was complete.

Losing his woman once again, the angry man wiped the last bit of sleep from his eyes and realized his stateroom was moving violently. The room, his prison, his sanctuary: was small; no more than eight by twelve feet of dark paneling. In the far corner, his treasured eight cases of Holstein Beer carefully secured and intact.

Good.

Near his beer was the settee with a pile of dirty clothes a week or two overdue.

"Another damn job I've got to do," he muttered to himself.

Next to the settee was the head, its toilet and sink forever clogging, a testimonial to the condition of the vessel and the owner's lack of concern for the crew. To the immediate right was the wooden desk, bolted to the floor. For the last two … no … three days Typhoon Diana has faithfully cleared his desk of papers, pencils and his well-thumbed Hustler magazines. As his ears began to function, his attention was drawn to the deck where the trash can rolled back and forth in sympathetic movement with the vessel. Its contents slid across the deck sounding like percussion instruments. The curtains covering the porthole rhythmically brushed the wood trim as the books in the bookcase flopped back and forth in a frenzied dance.

"Damn," he said under his breath as he braced for another watch on this miserable ship. It was twenty-three forty-five and just fifteen minutes left until he'd relieve the bridge watch. Struggling from the bed got harder each day. "God, I wish I were dead." He said as he shook the grogginess from his mind.

As he weaved a drunken path of least resistance towards the head, the moving deck directed his course from left to right to left. Ian's eyes shut in pain as he turned on the overhead light. He grabbed the sink with both hands to balance against the movement underfoot.

"God" he said. He couldn't believe what stared back at him in the mirror; a dirty and unshaven face. He shook his head and talked to his reflection, "you were born into a wealthy family of position and political influence. You grew up in the finest home in Amsterdam and your mother's family even owns a castle in the country. You're the heir to one of the largest shipping companies in the world. What have you become?"

He took a breath and continued; "But then there was the fact ..."

"You watched as your father was murdered in his boardroom. You were only five. Your mother is hauntingly demanding and the coldest and most unforgiving woman on the planet who tolerates nothing but perfection and ruthlessly crushes anything less."

"Yes, I should have had a charmed life of wealth and position. I had plenty of expensive toys and beautiful women to play with. Yes, I was just an irresponsible playboy and family embarrassment. Thank God for the butlers and lawyers that cleaned up my messes. Why did I join this damn ship anyway?" He asks the face in the mirror.

"I don't know but I can't go home just yet."

He looked deeply at the twisted and tormented face in the mirror. Then slowly his face softened and the storm in his eyes cleared. For a moment, he tried to remember what he used to look like. "I can't." he mumbled. "I can't."

He needed to get ready for watch. Ian struggled out of the head when the motion of the vessel abruptly changed from long, deep rolls to a gut-wrenching motion as the vessel plowed into the monstrous Pacific swell. With each swell, the bow dove headlong into the sea and mercilessly slammed. The vessel surged and violently shuddered in protest to the compass course it was held too. It dove again into a wall of water and moaned as tons of seawater covered the forecastle. The ship struggled and groaned while it shed the unwelcome weight.

"My God, the old man must be nuts to have us on this course. The damn ship will break her back." he said to himself.

"I'll change course in a couple of minutes. To hell with this."

Ian wore his dirty, stained and torn khakis, worn boots and he combed his long unkempt hair with his fingers as he wove his way to the pantry for something to eat. He hadn't used a bar of soap, razor or toothbrush in five days, but he was damn hungry. He had his priorities.

He pulled on the refrigerator door and saw an untouched plate of cheese, cold cuts and a quart of fresh milk. With abandonment, he groped for the bread and made a sandwich.

The sandwich in one hand and the quart of milk in the other, he turned the corner and headed for the bridge. Ian walked down a narrow passageway, climbed the stairs as the violent storm raged on. The walk was a challenge and the trail of crumbs, meat and milk were testimonial to that fact.

"Who cares … the damn steward will clean it up."

Up the last flight of stairs to the wheelhouse and there he stood knowing full well that once he crossed the threshold, the vessel and the lives on board were his responsibility. He took a deep breath as the ship pounded and shuddered then reached for the door handle.

### The Beginning of the End
### Tampa, Florida
### Seven Weeks Before

Ian's plane landed at the international airport in Tampa. Bright sunshine poured through the fuselage windows and assaulted his face. Ian raised a well-read magazine to shield his eyes and groaned. After being in Amsterdam for five months, his eyes stung from the light. They had become accustomed to the dark nightclubs, bars, and brothels he frequented. His liver had been punished with copious amounts of jonge jenever, which the local described as young gin, and beer. His heart hammered in his chest, still reeling from the cocaine and other drugs in his system. He couldn't remember the names or faces of the women he'd run through in the constant blur of self-abuse. Ian rubbed his eyes as the plane taxied down the runway. He pulled out his wallet and thumbed through the couple of bills inside. "Shit, that's all I have left?" He sighed, and shoved it back in his pocket. Maybe he could change with Susan's help, but deep inside he knew he wasn't ready to become what his family expected – no, demanded of him.

When the passengers began to exit, he let them rush by and then slowly followed. Mindlessly, Ian gazed off into the distance until the flashing red light and alarm brought him back to reality. The jolt of the conveyor belt was immediately followed by a metallic sound and it began to move. Moments later he saw the sea bag and luggage that contained his sextant, binoculars and other professional accessories each deck officer carried with them. Elbowing his way into the impatient travelers crowded around the moving luggage, he grabbed his bags and walked away from the horde.

With luggage in hand, he made his way outside and spotted the local shipping agent Arturo Sanchez. He'd be hard to miss, with his ever-present toothpick, white suit, and unbuttoned shirt. He smiled when he saw Ian, showing off his crummy teeth with two gold crowns glinting in the sun. Ian stifled a laugh. "Hey man, good to see you. It's been a while." He put his bags down. "Even though you look like a pimp, you're a sight for sore eyes. You know that gold chain is going to drown you someday. You'll go straight to the bottom with it around your neck."

Arturo puffed out his concave chest. "Dude, I am better than a pimp and you know it. Who does everyone come to see when they need transportation, happy pills, or companionship? Me … Arturo!" He pounded his sternum in a poor rendition of an anorexic Tarzan. He slid his over-sized sunglasses down his oily nose and his beady black eyes took Ian's measure. "It looks like you've been overloading on the good things in life yourself, my friend."

"I've had my share," Ian said, "Too long in Amsterdam can kill a man."

Arturo chuckled. "I can see that. Come now, I have a driver waiting." He turned and headed to a sedan on the curb. Ian grabbed his gear and followed.

The driver was a rather plain looking man in a dirty white shirt, cheap sunglasses and horrible teeth, his filthy cowboy hat sat on the back on his head. His nicotine stained fingertips drummed the steering wheel. He put the window down as they approached and he and Arturo exchanged a glance and a nod. Ian rolled his eyes and got in the back, Arturo slid in next to him and barked, "Hooker's Point – the Cement Terminal."

Arturo's helot responded and put the car in gear and quietly merged into traffic. Ian found the small talk shallow and uninteresting. The peddler beside him pitched his goods … "girls? … drugs? …what do you want?" Ian hardly heard him as the noise of the city sympathetically drowned out the other's voice.

Ian stared out the window. He's been in this city a number of times and hardly knew a thing about it. Tampa seems like a town where there may be tolerance for a man like me to start over. That thought rushed over Ian with warmth and urgency and just as quickly it was gone and then there was nothing. He felt hollow and returned to his private place. A place deeply embedded in his thoughts. He was only semi-aware of the people and places that rushed by the window and the dullards that occupy the car with him.

As the car left the city, the sights became familiar. Beautiful buildings and well-manicured homes were gradually replaced with warehouses, rundown homes, cheap bars and pawnshops. The clean and well-maintained cars were replaced with broken wrecks and burned-out hulks that littered the streets. It dawned on Ian that every port around the world was the same. They stunk with the promise of quick money, crime, desperation, exploitation and misery. A look into the eyes of those that existed there and it was all the same. There were the few that had learned to exploit these dens of misery through crime and violence. Most, however, carried their burdens until their lives were spent. Why did he see this so clearly? He feared he had become one of those creatures himself.

Closer and closer to the ship they traveled. Soon in the distance the Amore Islander was visible above the buildings and warehouses that lined the pier. There she was … his home, his prison, his sanctuary and his hell.

The Amore Islander was stunningly beautiful yet wretchedly ugly. She was pure of soul, yet tormented. She embraced you with love and security then cast you to the devil himself. A rational person would call a ship an inanimate object but to her crew she was as alive as any woman who had graced this earth. She was cold and unforgiving, yet warm and passionate. She was an angel and she was a demon, and so was the love-hate relationship that all mariners share for their ships.

The car moved to the gate at the head of the pier. The driver slowed and briefly stopped. They got a disinterested glance from the fat and sleepy guard in his ill-fitting, sweat-stained uniform and with minimal effort his arm provided the go-ahead. Around the corner, the ship came into full view. It was overpowering. All of its eight-hundred and fifty feet dominated the pier and dwarfed everything around. The driver pulled up to the gangway. Arturo looked at Ian and said, "Home-sweet-home, sailor boy." and smiled. Then without a moment wasted he and his driver bounded up the gangway as they hoped to shake-down the captain for whiskey, cigarettes and a free meal or two.

Ian gathered his things and saw two Filipino crewmembers as they scurried down to the gangway to help him aboard. They were covered from head to toe in grimy and ripped hand-me-down clothing. Long sleeve shirts, long pants, gloves, and oversized straw hats kept the sun off their skin. Their bright and cheerful faces beamed as they excitedly greeted him.

"Third ... welcome back, we heard you were coming back! Many good times? Third ... lots of parties? Have fun on vacation?" The curious deckhands asked.

Ian's head cleared, he was alert and felt alive once more. This rusty sea whore was his home and these were his people. The gnawing emptiness that haunted him for months vanished.

He and the two Filipinos carrying his gear walked up the long gangway. It flexed up and down under their feet as they made their way to the top. They reached the deck and boarded the ship. Forty feet above the water, the view opened up and Davis Island, the City of Tampa, and the vast bay were readily visible. It's nice to be home. Ian thought. The smells, sounds, and vibrations that are the soul of the ship were assimilated into Ian's body and he and the ship became one. Once again the mother and her child were together. He was safe in the warmth of her womb.

With a few friendly conversations, Ian walked along the rusty deck to the house and passed through the watertight door. He casually noticed the watertight gaskets were missing and the door and its hinges rusted and neglected. Inside the Amore Islander was clean and well lit. The stewards department had done a good job keeping up with the hotel services. He walked by the officer's watch mess and saw Herbert, the Third Engineer and Neil, the

First Officer. They raised their mugs to him, both with wide grins.

"Welcome back, you old dog." said Neil

"Screw you too," Ian said with a smile. "You two have been around a lot longer than I have and you guys were geezers when I met you." He pounded them both on the back. "But hell, it's still nice to be back aboard."

Ian offered and they agreed to go ashore later to the local club and catch-up. Ian bid them adieu and continued down the passageway to the ladder-well. Up two flights of stairs and he stepped into "Officer Country." This was where the officers and engineers lived.

With experienced ease he turned to his right and walked down the narrow passageway towards the starboard side and right again, heading aft to the second door on the left. He took a deep breath and walked in. This would be his home for the next six months. His bags were waiting for him in the middle of the floor. To his left was a desk, ahead the bed and to his right the head. This room had been the temporary refuge of every third mate. For twenty years this was where men had slept, cried, written home, lost their humanity and some their sanity. All the time they wasted their lives away ... this was Ian's private hell.

Memories of his previous tours rushed over him and then he looked at his bags and grumbled, "To hell with it!"

Unpacking, he changed into the uniform he'd live and work in until this contract was completed. He had four sets of identical clothes; khaki shirts and trousers. One pair was clean and unstained, the others tormented with spilled paint, grease and rust.

He put on the clean set and tied his boots, smiled at himself in the stained mirror then made his way up to the captain's office with his merchant marine license in one hand and his passport and sea service book in the other. All of which he would surrender to the skipper. He reversed his course to the ladder-well and up another flight of stairs to the "Senior Officer Country". This was where the captain and the chief engineer lived. Again emerging from the ladder-well, he turned right and then made an immediate left, and looked into the skipper's office. Ian saw the captain seated at his desk, reading glasses rested on his bulbous and blood shot nose. The older man was balding, overweight, and dressed in dirty and wrinkled clothes. Ian stood there for a moment as the man concentrated on papers in front of him. He shook his head and smirked. What a wretched mess of a man you are, Herr Captain. Ian straightened his back, squared his shoulders, and knocked on the door frame. The captain looked up, leaned back in his chair, removed his glasses, and squinted as he ran his fat fingers over his bald head.

"Ian … good to have you back … I've been expecting you." He waved his meaty hand.

"Come in and sit for a moment".

Ian sat in the wooden chair anchored to the floor. "Thank you, Captain Strauss for letting me return. I do like the ship, her crew and the run."

"You're a reliable officer and a pleasure to have aboard." Ian suppressed a chuckle. He knew the man was blowing smoke.

After a few minutes of small talk, the captain grew noticeably tired of the conversation. "You're assigned the eight to twelve watch starting tomorrow morning." He shuffled around some papers. "Enjoy your time ashore with Neil and Herbert."

His vacant stare would have normally alarmed Ian, but Ian knew this man. He was a drunk, a loner, and miserable human being. A company man; Strauss was submissive and spineless to his employer and the crew had little respect for him as either a man or a leader.

Ian smiled and handed over his paperwork. The captain grabbed the papers, screwed his eyes into focus with much effort and looked to ensure they were current and complete. Satisfied he set them down and pushed the shipping articles under Ian's nose. He signed the contract. Ian was now officially part of the Amore Islander crew. Once again, his prison sentence sealed until properly relieved. The ink was black but he knew this contract was written in blood.

## *The Man in a Black Suit*
## *Alongside, Tampa*

As Ian left the office, the captain watched the young man leave and then returned to his paperwork. Moments later, Strauss' mind wandered to a place far away. He leaned back in his chair, removed his reading glasses, closed his eyes, and drifted into memories of the tortured youth that led him to the miserable life that consumed him like a cancer.

The owner's representative stood on the dirty pier next to the large ship. He looked out of place. The temperature was nearly ninety degrees and there he was in a black suit, starched white shirt, and dark glasses. He looked back at the black limo that had delivered him to the ship and then he straightened his bright red tie and came up the brow. He knew the sooner he finished, the sooner he'd get out this miserable place. As he boarded, the mate on watch met him and with barely a word escorted him to the captain's office.

The captain expected the visitor. Strauss was convinced he would be fired for incompetence. So this is how it will end. The drunkard thought as he heard the stride of a confident man echo through the passageway.

Out on deck, cargo operations were underway and the Aragonite, white sand from the Bahamas, was poured into the discharge hopper at two-thousand tons an hour. In another six hours the ship would be empty. Neil, the chief mate, had finished up his watch and was satisfied with the progress. He smiled and jotted a couple of comments into his pocket sized notebook then leaned against the rail in his stained overalls and closed his eyes for a moment, facing into the hot Tampa sun.

Strauss wiped his sweaty palms on his grungy pant legs. When the visitor appeared in the doorway, Strauss tried not to grimace at the expensive briefcase and Italian shoes that must have cost a fortune. The man's silk tie was just an added insult. Strauss knew if the ship owner had paid for this metro-sexual to fly halfway around the world for a private meeting, he was in deep trouble.

Still wearing his Armani sunglasses, the visitor struck an imposing figure. He was tall, handsome yet rugged, and extremely fit. Strauss blanched and glanced down at his bulging stomach and rubbed stubble on his chin.

The man removed his dark glasses and looked into the captain's averted eyes.

"I'd like a drink." He said with an efficiency that cut like a knife. Strauss scurried around the desk to a cabinet and produced a bottle of Scotch in his shaking hands.

"Will this do?" he asked, wishing it was a better brand and his desk wasn't sticky.

The man nodded. "Two fingers straight up."

Strauss poured two glasses and asked, "Why did you come out here in person?" He still couldn't look into the man's eyes. "You could have fired me over the phone."

The man leaned back in his chair and laughed. Then leaned in close to the captain, stared through his skull and said, "Is that what you think I am here to do? You think I'm here to fire you? If I was going to do that, wouldn't there be another captain here with me?" He chuckled. "Don't worry, old man, sit down and relax. I came to the filthy ship with instructions. That is all."

He held his glass up and scowled. Taking a handkerchief from his lapel, he wiped the rim of the glass. He still didn't look happy when he held the glass up again, but took a drink. "The owner has a proposition for you and no one, and I mean no one, can know of it. If you play your cards right, you will be well compensated and have the ship of your choice in the Y.G. Yang fleet." The tendons in his jaw line tighten. "Do we understand each other?"

Strauss thought for a moment. He knew he wasn't one of the better captains. What he lacked in competence, he tried to make up for with blind loyalty. But he knew from the look of the man that whatever it was … it was illegal, likely immoral and most certainly criminal. He also knew if he declined he'd be unemployed and destitute. With his reputation on the waterfront, there was no future for him except suicide and he wasn't quite ready for that yet.

Strauss looked up, and nodded. "I understand and I am ready to listen. Let me close the office door and freshen up our drinks." Strauss shook himself and tried to muster confidence as he stood up.

After securing the door lock, he refreshed their drinks and this time he poured heavily. The two men moved over to the couch, sipped their drinks and, after what seemed like an eternity; the man began to lay out the plan.

While the two discussed opportunities and the future in hushed and conspiratorial tones, the engineers were doing what they could to maintain the machinery with the few spares parts and limited tools on hand; the mates and deck gang were discharging the ship and doing what they could with limited stores, and the stewards were staring into a boiling cauldron conjuring up spells to make their meager food taste like something edible.

Several hours later the two men came out of the office. The visitor wore his sunglasses as they walked together to the brow. Strauss thanked him for the visit. The visitor turned, shook the old man's hand and told him he'd see him again soon. Strauss watched as this nameless man in an expensive dark suit, sunglasses, and a designer briefcase left his ship, climbed into the limo and seconds later headed to his awaiting plane. Strauss replayed their conversation. He didn't even open his briefcase.

The limo rolled up to a black corporate jet with no identification markings, the pilot threw some switches and the jet roared to life. As the plane climbed into the bright blue sky an encrypted call was made to Hong Kong.

"Yes …"

"He agreed … the plan is a go."

"Good"… and the phone call ended.

"Bring me a martini, straight-up with a twist." said the only passenger on the luxury jet. He removed his sunglasses and watched the flight attendant with unconcealed lust. The pretty Asian woman smiled. A moment later she delivered him the drink. At thirty-thousand feet he winked at the young lady who was there for one reason … to tend to him on the long flight back to the Far East. He smiled, sipped his drink, and loosened his tie. She steeled herself and thought, a few more rich men with nasty fetishes like this one and I'll be able to move my family out of the Kowloon projects into a small home outside of the city. She slid onto the couch next to him and waited for his groping hands and probing tongue to assault her.

### Last Night on the Beach
### Hookers Point
### Charlie's Bar

After Ian left the captain's office, he thought, *something really bad is going to happen to this ship and the men aboard with such an incompetent in command. If you're smart, you'd cut and run now.* He grimaced and knew he had only one option and that was to go back to Holland and be strapped into the yoke his family had built for him. He shook his head and said, "Not quite yet." Then he walked aft through a watertight door out on deck to clear his head. He looked over towards the center of Tampa. Again, he wondered, Could I start over in a place like this? Could I live a better life or is this life my damnation for eternity?"

When Ian was home, he had visited the family priest in Amsterdam as he looked for salvation and a solution to his anguish. The man of cloth offered little hope. Embarrassed and angry, Ian thought, if a Dutchman can't offer redemption … there must be no hope. That disaster had fueled his most excessive binge of self-abuse yet. Memories of his five months ashore in Holland were absent, or at best, distorted.

The sun warmed his handsome face and it felt nice to close his eyes and soak up the sun. It was nearly time for the evening meal and he could smell the unmistakable stench of atomized lard coming from the galley fry-o-lator. It must be fish tonight. Later he would meet up with Neil and Herbert for a night on the town before departure on the morning tide.

Back in his room, Ian pawed through his clothes for something to wear into town. Nothing too fancy, they were only looking for drinks and a good time with the local working girls. He hoped that Susan would be there. She had been his steady for years and the focus of his dreams and hopes for the future. He knew he would be able to fix himself with her love and support. But he couldn't get his head completely around "how" just yet. He grabbed a clean shirt, shorts and sandals. Might as well be comfortable.

The meal was as good as could be expected. The stewards did their best, but they could only do so much with limited food of questionable quality. Ian saw it in the chief steward's eyes as he fed the crew. Ian and the others knew the chief steward was an amazing restaurant manager and chef. For many years, Cookie Chavez owned one of the finest restaurants in Manila. He had named it after his mother Isabella. For some reason, he left it all and joined the merchant marine and over time ended up on the Amore Islander. He'd been the chief steward on the ship for years. Cookie made it no secret to the crew things had gone to hell in the galley since Strauss became the captain. Everyone knew he clung onto the hope the ship would return to being the first class feeder someday soon.

Neil and Herbert were joking while they waited for Ian on deck by the gangway. They saw each other as Ian walked towards them and the banter started.

"Are you going to wear that clown suit ashore?"

"Screw you too, numb nuts."

"I'm just saying ... the girls won't give you the time of day."

"I'll give you something," and the ribbing continued.

Neil chimed in, "Hell boys, let's get drunk." And with that they all smiled checked the sailing board. *Departure, ten in the morning.*

Down the gangway, they laughed and joked like frat boys. They piled into the waiting cab. "Charlie's Bar." said one of them to the sleepy cab driver who sat up and stretched like a cat and rubbed his eyes.

"Are we keeping you up?" Herbert joked and looked at the others as they laughed with him. The driver started his old Chevy, unshaken by soon-to-be-drunken and obnoxious mariners. The faded car was missing three hub caps and the windshield was cracked. The rolling junk squatted as it moved down the road, its shocks creaking and moaning in protest to the three large men in the back seat.

Charlie's was a well know dive a mile or so down the road from the ship. The owner was a colorful old mariner in his own right. He had spent years sailing around the world as a ship's bosun. He had a colorful and probably true reputation as a hard drinking and wild whoring sailor who found the seediest dives in every port. After his second heart attack, the Coast Guard took away his seaman's document. Undaunted, he decided to marry his favorite hooker, swallowed the anchor, and bought his own bar. Charlie's was dark and dusty, just like any dive in any port town. He made no effort to make the place feel warm and friendly. The old bosun knew from experience that mariners and stevedores go there for two things -- drinks and girls and that's what he catered to.

Tonight the girls had on their war paint, short skirts and poured out of their small blouses as they aggressively hawked their goods. The men cycled through. Some paired up with a hooker right away, others waited until the alcohol took effect, and a few passed the time just watching the action. It was a sad day, the Amore Islander was well represented, and the girls knew they needed to make their money from the crew tonight before this ship left in the morning. The

Amore Islander and her crew, to this point, had been a regular fixture here at Hooker's Point and at Charlie's. The ship was in and out of Tampa two to three times a month and had been for years. Tomorrow the ship and her crew would leave and never return. Thinking back Ian could see the night the ship arrived in Tampa, there were more working girls on the ship than crew. During Ian's first contract, he learned to keep his room locked or a visitor would crawled into his bed. If on watch or away from the room, he knew he could expect to be robbed if the door was left unlocked. These ladies were good in bed and stole whenever given the opportunity.

Ian and his friends paid the driver and ran through the bar door. Ian looked around and thought, *This shithole hasn't changed a bit.* Then he saw a familiar face in the distance and smiled.

Susan was sitting at the bar. She was nursing the first of many drinks and looked off in the distance … clearly in a dream far away. She turned and their eyes met. She'd been in this line of work for about ten years and her youthful beauty was quickly waning. Each time Ian saw her she looked more tired and older. She had been his steady for years. Whether a short-time or the occasional overnight marathon, she knew exactly what he needed. Ian had no claim to her nor she to him … they just seemed to end up together. It was comfortable and satisfied them both.

Ian planned to make it more, but needed to control the demons that tormented him first. Susan was the only one that seemed to understand his struggle with destiny and desire and the pressure, guilt, and regret that stood between the two. He wasn't quite ready just yet, but with her help, he would be soon. He'd already written to his mother about Susan and told her he would bring Susan with him when he was ready to come home.

Susan was once a pretty young girl from up north somewhere. Her naturally blonde hair and her blue eyes were striking, but a closer look reveled years of pain and disappointment. Yes, she was pretty, but she had a class about her that reminded Ian of his mother. Class was a rare commodity in her line of work and he loved her from the first time they met. Over the years, Charlie had told him bits and pieces of her story. She followed her boyfriend to Tampa right after high school, got knocked-up, and he ran on her. Pregnant, pretty, desperate and alone, she became easy prey for the pimps in the area. After the initial shock and horrible guilt subsided, she found it was easy work and occasionally even enjoyed spending time with the men passing through town.

Ian thought, *I want to settle-down with her and start over. We're both so much alike, and yet so different. Would it work or not? I wonder if she ever thinks about me and a possible future together, or am I just another one in hundreds of men that rotate through her bed and soil her sheets?* Ian wanted to ask, but couldn't, and she would never offer up more than the money on the table had purchased.

Ian walked up to Susan and kissed her discreetly on the cheek. He pulled up a stool next to her and looked over at Charlie behind the bar. "Charlie, how are you doing my friend? It really sucks that we are leaving Tampa, I really like this town and ..." he looked at Susan and smiled and her eyes grew swimmy. "I really like the company." He winked at her and she blushed, erasing years from her face.

Charlie chuckled. "What you drinking Ian? I assume you are buying Susan a drink too, right?"

"Of course, Susan my dear, what would you like?"

"Bourbon on the rocks"

Ian looked back at the man behind the bar, "Bourbon on the rocks for the lady and a vodka martini – make it Grey Goose for me."
Charlie bristled and barked back, "Grey Goose -- what kind of a place do you think I run here? If you want that highbrow hootch, go into the city. I've got Smirnoff or Absolute. Take it or leave it."

"Okay ... don't get so sore Charlie ... Absolute is fine." Ian turned back to Susan and they chatted a few minutes while waiting for their drinks. They talked about nothing and everything, as love and passion reflected in each other's eyes. Ian asked about her daughter and she politely told him Sarah was fine and doing well. Charlie delivered the drinks and waited for Ian to drop a twenty on the bar. Once the money was in the till, Charlie moved to another patron waiting for a beer.

Over the years, Ian met Susan's daughter several times and loved to watch Susan talk about her, it made him smile. At the same time, Ian watched as she sized him up. Tonight was a money-making night for her and she needed to choose well. They had been in this mating dance many times and Ian knew what she was thinking, *Will he buy me for the night or an hour?*

He brought all of his remaining money and she would be his for the night. Ian reached into his front pocket and pulled out a wad of bills, gave more money than she expected and she smiled. Charlie looked from behind the bar as he stood next to his wife and poured them another round. "On the house you love birds."

After they both had their fill of drinks, Susan brought him back to her apartment. They made a bee-line for the bedroom where they consumed each other as lovers do. Later, spent and content, they slipped into a gentle sleep cradled in each other's arms. *Is this what it's supposed to be like?* Ian wondered as he dreamed.

Hours later Susan woke him, reminding him he needed to get back to the ship. She poured coffee and they sipped together at the kitchen table. Ian wondered, *Is this the way it's supposed to be? A partner to love and one that loves you in return?*

Quietly she drove to the ship. The sleepy guard recognized her and sent her though. She drove Ian to the gangway and turned off the headlights. Susan turned to Ian with both hands still on the steering wheel, a tear rolled down her cheek. She leaned over and kissed him. They talked and kissed each other for ten minutes in the idling car until Ian asked, "Would you ... ever consider..."

She touched his lips and said, "Don't say anything ... I love you and I'll be here when you return." They kissed again, one long, feathery goodbye. As Ian walked away from her car he thought, *this was the first time I've truly loved a woman.*

## Departure
## Tampa Bay

Later that morning, Ian woke and lay in his bed for a moment and thought of Susan. He remembered how she felt, smelled, and responded to his touch. *Who am I kidding? I paid her to respond that way,* he thought and slowly rolled out of the rack and headed to the sink to wash his face. There was a knock on the door … it opened, the light went on, and a little Filipino face peered around the door, "Third … it's seven fifteen. We sail at ten." With that, the tormentor was gone.

Ian showered, shaved, and dressed in his best khakis. He remembered they would have company on the bridge. Dressed and ready to go, Ian walked out the door and headed to the watch mess for a quick cup of coffee and a couple of eggs and toast.

The watch mess stunk of old grease and filthy men. It was small and this morning was crowded with mates and engineers gathered for the morning meal. The room was popular with the men because the meals were served quickly. Engineers especially liked eating there because they could eat in their dirty overalls and greasy boots. Of course the stewards hated the room because it was so difficult to keep clean.

This was the source of one of many tensions between the departments aboard the ship. Mates looked down their noses at the engineers, who had a healthy distrust of mates, and the stewards were everyone's tool. The stewards, in turn, selflessly tended to the interior living spaces, prepared and served four meals a day, and cleaned the officer's rooms. They tried to ignore their second class status, but carried it locked in their hearts. It burned with such passion that, if unleashed, would result in violence – even murder. Who could blame them? Slavery was alive and well aboard ship and shipping articles were as a binding as a bill of sale was for flesh in the South a hundred and fifty years ago.

His belly full, Ian smiled and thanked the steward. He didn't need the stewards sharpening their knives with him in mind. Ian moved through the maze of passageways and stairs as he made his way to the bridge to assume his first watch and prepare the ship for departure.

During the early morning, cargo operations were completed. Discharging the ship was far less difficult, and therefore, the second mate was left in charge to finish while Neil went ashore. Looking into the deck log, Ian saw the last of the cargo was discharged at four thirty-six. Since then, the watch team had secured the hatches and gear on deck for departure. So routine was the preparation, Ian barely noticed when he came aboard earlier.

On the wing of the bridge, the second mate, Dieter, sunned himself. *Yes, another German.* Ian thought, *I'm surrounded by krauts.* Yes, and Ian hated krauts! It might have been that his family had suffered a number of times at the hands of Germany. But mainly it was their arrogance, superiority, and aloofness. It must be in their DNA.

Even now, they continued to invade Holland in their Mercedes Benz, their modern day panzers, and dominated and controlled Holland. He smirked as he remembered 'keying' an expensive red sedan with German plates on his sixteenth birthday while several of his friends drank beer and encouraged the vandalism.

Even the Germans aboard the Amore Islander had that way about them. Neil and Ian talked about it constantly… but they tried and look beyond it as these krauts had become family; their shipboard family… *Okay, but they're still krauts!*

Ian looked over the deck log, nothing unusual caught his eye. He walked out to Dieter and they started the watch turnover.

"Good morning, Dieter."

"Good morning. Cargo operations completed four thirty-six and the deck was secured for sea. I contacted the engineer on watch and they reported all machinery was tested and ready for sea. The number four winch amidships was still broken, so the spring line must be run to a secondary winch to be retrieved. It should be brought aboard first. The starboard anchor windlass was broken too."

He continued and Ian was only half listening, the routine of standing watch had become second nature. Though his first watch of the contract, he was already back-in-the-groove. Dieter droned on and on. Finally he stopped to catch his breath and Ian re-engaged. "Thanks Dieter … anything else?"

"No."

"Then I relieve you," Ian said.

Dieter bid goodbye, clicked his heels, spun around, and headed down to the salon for his morning meal. A proper German, he was always dressed in clean khakis, polished shoes, and had a cleanly shaven face. He dined by himself in the salon with silverware, linen table cloth, and napkins. The only other person who routinely dined there was the captain. Ian remembered when he used to eat in fancy dining spaces too. That's too much trouble.

Alone on the bridge, he prepared the ship for departure. Ian called his engineering counterpart, Herbert, in the engine room and confirmed all was ready for first bell around ten. He confirmed and commented quickly on his experience ashore last night.

"Yeah … I had a good time too," and Ian hung up the phone.

Next, Ian checked the charts and logs. The charts had stains, and Scotch Tape repaired several torn areas. Ian carefully placed them on the chart table with sharpened pencils, dividers, navigation triangles, and parallel rulers. The deck log's entries were in black, red, and green ink. The captain insisted normal entries be made in black, safety events in green, and key and emergency events logged in red ink.

On top of the other charts was the harbor chart they'd use to transit to the bay's entrance beyond the Sunshine Skyway Bridge. Under that were a few coastal charts that had the planned track down to Panama where a trans-pacific cargo of iron ore waited in Peru.

A quick check of the weather confirmed light winds from the south at five to ten knots, and seas outside were two to three feet in height. Off at the far end of the weather map was a low pressure area that no one was concerned about yet. Ian set the map aside and walked to the bridge wing and looked at the sky. *Alto cumulus clouds overhead, maybe there would be showers later this morning,* Ian thought as he continued the preparations for departure.

Ian turned on the VHF radio and called for a radio check. It tested out satisfactory. He contacted the tug company and confirmed they were sending three tugs; the Alice, Suzie Q and Betty. The tugs were all small so they'd need three instead of the two they usually called for.

Continuing down his check list, he contacted the pilots and confirmed a pilot would arrive soon.

"Carlos," Ian called on the walkie-talkie to his Filipino AB on deck.

"Yes, Third"

"Is the gangway ready to bring aboard?"

"Yes, Third …"

"Make your way to the gangway with Juan and standby for the pilot. I'll be down in a few minutes."

Ian continued, next the ship's whistle and general alarm were tested. It announced to the crew and those on the dock, the ship would be underway soon. The ship came alive and Ian heard auxiliary machinery lit off by the engineering watch. Just then, the captain came through the door onto the bridge. He looked remarkably rested and alert for a change.

"Good morning," Strauss said.

"Good morning, sir."

The captain looked over the chart, the weather report and the deck log. He asked about the number four winch, "No, sir." Ian replied

"How about the starboard anchor windlass?"

Again, "No, sir."

"Never mind," Strauss said under his breath.

"The pilot should be here any moment and the ship is ready for sea, Captain."

"Good … have coffee and pastries brought to the bridge."

"Aye, sir." Ian made a call to the galley, "Steward … Bridge … please bring coffee and pastries for the captain and pilot."

Ian threw a series of switches that lit off both radars; the satellite navigation system and the new navigation tool called LORAN, and efficiently tuned them. *They work, too… amazing!* He smiled to himself.

A car came up alongside the ship near the gangway. Ian excused himself and left the captain to his own thoughts and rushed to the brow to greet the pilot. The pilot came up the gangway huffing and puffing when he reached the top. Ian got there just in time to meet him.

"Welcome aboard the Amore Islander".

The pilot brushed by asking; "Is the ship ready for sea?"

Ian respond, "Yes, and Captain Strauss is on the bridge."

"Strauss, you say," the pilot said, stopping short and looked back at Ian.

Ian confirmed with a nod.

"He's still has a job … hummm." The pilot turned and continued to the bridge.

Out of courtesy, Ian escorted him to the wide expanse of the bridge. He knew the pilot had been on this ship many times, and knew his way around as well as any of the crew. Ian made introductions and returned to his preparations for departure. But first, Ian grabbed the hotel "H" signal flag, and ran aloft and hoisted it. Back down on the bridge, as the captain and pilot talked, Ian called Herbert, "Start the generator and bow thruster and standby for engine orders."

Ian could feel the pressure beginning to mount as departure approached. He hung up the phone and rang the engine telegraph from FINISHED WITH ENGINES to STOP. Up the narrow channel came the three tugs. Ian tested the bow thruster... *It worked, amazing!* Another private smile.

Carlos came to the bridge and assumed his position behind the helm. He was still in his dirty deck clothes, long sleeve shirt and pants. He removed his hat and stood behind the helm. Ian was busy documenting the time the crew turned too, the pilot boarded, the telegraph shifted to STOP, and the locations and time the tugs were made fast.

Ian had Carlos cycle the rudder from left to right and back. Steering system checked satisfactory. The captain and pilot were on the offshore bridge wing looking at the approaching tugs. The pilot was communicating with the boats, and the captain with the mates, as they stood by on the bow and stern with a handful of deck hands. The decision was made ... Alice is forward, Suzie Q aft, and Betty is amidships.

Orders were given and the tugs were made up to the ship.

The crew was moving to their maneuvering stations on deck forward and aft. Their job was to retrieve the mooring lines and stow them below deck. As if on cue, line handlers came out of the dock shadows and tossed the lines off the bollards.

Captain Strauss called the mate forward to bring in the spring line forward.

"Aye, Captain."

A similar order is given to the mate aft for the aft spring lines. Order acknowledged. Ian walked out onto the in-shore bridge wing and watched as the lines were brought aboard. Another task Ian would record in the log. The pilot directed the tugs to "push easy" and they complied. The ship was pinned to the pier as the final lines were brought aboard. The ship settled against the dock, the captain called to his mate aft to bring in all lines. A moment later the same order was given to the mate forward.

The captain called to Ian, "Last Line."

Ian scribbled the time in the log book. The voyage had begun.

The captain and pilot moved back and forth from one bridge wing to the other. The whole time the pilot gave orders to the tugs by walkie-talkie. He yelled rudder and engine commands to Ian in the wheelhouse. The captain was present and engaged but silent.

"Left Full Rudder" the pilot directed. Ian repeated the order; Carlos repeated the order and complied.

"The Rudder is Left Full" Carlos responded after the rudder indicator needle was buried to the left of the gauge.

Ian repeated, "Rudder is Left Full."

And the pilot called for, "DEAD SLOW ASTERN." Ian repeated and moved the engine telegraph to DEAD SLOW ASTERN. Another time for the log … First Bell …

Down in the engine room the Chief Engineer acknowledged the telegraph order and opened a valve that connected the two story slow speed diesel engine with high pressure air contained in a series of large bottles. The air turned over the engine until the diesel fuel began to fire the cylinders.

The ship bucked as the engine coughed to life and the twenty-four foot propeller began to thrash the water, the ship vibrated and began to move. Slowly it backed to the left, away from the dock. All three tugs reversed their thrust and pulled the ship from the pier. The ship was moving. It took nearly fifteen minutes for the pilot to twist the ship in the narrow channel, slowly turning the Amore Islander end for end, the tugs pushed and pulled the ship and the rudder and engine was used to help twist the ship. The channel was only eleven-hundred feet wide in the turning basin and the Amore Islander eight-hundred and fifty feet in length overall. The maneuver was slow and carefully conducted to avoid collision with the other freighters that lined the piers.

By ten-fourteen, the Amore Islander was pointed outbound and the tugs sat idle alongside, still made fast.

"Rudder Midships; DEAD SLOW AHEAD," called the pilot as he and the captain moved into the wheelhouse from the port wing.

Orders repeated; the helm placed amidships and the engine telegraph rung-up to DEAD SLOW AHEAD. As the rudder indicator confirmed the rudder was amidships, Carlos confirmed the point of helm. RPM indicator confirmed fifteen turns forward and Ian responded, "DEAD SLOW AHEAD."

The ship built up momentum and responded to the rudder, the pilot asked the captain to let go the tugs. "Start forward and work aft." he commanded. The captain called his deck mates and the task was accomplished. Tugs away… another entry for the log.

Davis Island passed close by the starboard side and the Cement Plant to the left. The pilot brought the ship left to a new course down the "C" cut channel and asked for SLOW AHEAD. Ian complied and rang the engine telegraph. The vibration of the ship began to change as the engineers increased the engine and propeller RPMs.  The ship moved along at seven knots. Several minutes later, the pilot asked for HALF AHEAD. The same routine and the ship moved along at nine to ten knots. Ian paced between the compasses and chart marking their position as they continued south down the shipping channel. It was a nice day and few ships competed for the narrow channel.

The pilot called for right rudder and settled the ship on a new southwesterly course within the "A" cut channel and the passage out to the Sunshine Skyway Bridge and the sea buoy. The sun was dead ahead and Carlos squinted and put on his sunglasses that were missing a lens. Ian stifled a laugh and handed Carlos his glasses.

"Here you go; you look ridiculous, Carlos."

The captain and pilot chatted and drank coffee. Ian was busy as he kept track of the ship's position and documented the transit, listened for engine orders and Carlos ... simple Carlos smiled and stood behind the wheel. He kept the ship on course. It was a simple symphony of movement with the chatter of the radios in the background and the vibration of the ship underfoot. *I love this life,* Ian thought.

They passed through "A" Cut, came right again into Gadsden Point Cut left on "F" Cut, then "E" Cut, "D" Cut, "C", "B", "A" passed under the Sunshine Skyway Bridge and then Mullet Key Cut to Egmont Channel and seaward bound. At the entrance to Egmont Channel, the ship was slowed and turned to the left to make a lee for the pilot to disembark. The pilot and captain exchanged pleasantries and farewells. Ian escorted the pilot to the main deck and the pilot ladder. The boat was already lying alongside under the ladder. The pilot waved to the bridge and hailed the boat. Then he stepped over the rail and down the boatswain's ladder to the pitching boat deck below. With the pilot aboard, the boat operator gunned his engines and sped away, heading back to the harbor for another assignment. The deck gang stowed the ladder while Ian returned to the bridge. He stopped briefly, to pull down the "H" flag.

On the bridge, the captain had put the engine AHEAD FULL and Carlos was steering a new course of two-two-three true. A moment after Ian got back, the captain went below and the watch was Ian's. He took a hastened look over the horizon, looked in at the radar and then to the chart; all was well. The sun was shining, the sea breeze was refreshing and they were moving through the water at sixteen knots. All was well; or so Ian thought.

The ship's clock approached 12:00 and Ian finished the log entries, put a position on the chart, checked the compass heading and again scanned the horizon. All was quiet. Neil stepped through the door at eleven fifty with his usual punctuality and they talked through the morning events, reviewed the ship's position, speed, and course and discussed the transit. "Continue south-west for Cristobal and then come left along this line."

Neil took the watch and Ian was relieved. He grabbed his jacket and headed down for the noon meal.

The Amore Islander was in deep water and made sixteen knots on a steady course. The ship took on a hypnotic sound, vibration, and her own gentle motion unique as she moved in the loving arms of the ocean.

Down the ladder Ian moved to the officer's deck and to his stateroom. He dropped his gear and washed his face. Ian looked in the mirror and could already see the change had started. Sun and wind has burned his face, his eyes were irritated and red and his face had two days of stubble that helped give him a rugged look. Ian wondered, *Did Bruce Banner have the same thoughts as he looked in the mirror, at the "Hulk" lurking beneath his skin?*

Down the ladder, Ian moved to the watch mess and ordered his lunch. He made it moments before the galley secured.

"A grilled cheese sandwich and fries would do," He told the steward. Without even enjoying the food, he shoved it down his throat and left. Ian was tired from the night before and was looking forward to an afternoon nap.

Inside the door of his stateroom he stripped off his clothes, left them in a pile on the floor and crawled into his freshly made bed. *It's nice to have steward service aboard. I rarely slept in a made bed at home. I'm just too lazy to make the bed.*

Ian drifted off into a numbing sleep as the motion and vibration of the ship coursed through his veins. He dreamt of Susan.

## The First Afternoon at Sea
### Caribbean Ocean

It was late in the afternoon when Ian awakened from his nap, feeling the vibration of the ship. The muffled humming of machinery below and the constant sound of forced air coming into the room through the overhead vent were constant reminders the heart and circulatory system of this living thing called the Amore Islander functioned properly.

Ian stretched, climbed out of bed, and made his way to the head where he leaned on the sink, braced himself with both hands, and studied the face in the faded mirror. Ian watched the slow transformation back into a Liberian Seaman. The change was gradual, but obvious just the same. With each contract, Ian observed the same thing. The first and most obvious change was the beard and the abuse the wind and sun had on his skin. Next was the growing length of his hair and his eyes becoming chronically blood shot; his teeth changed color from white to coffee stained and neglected. The final physical manifestation was he lost twenty-five pounds or so and his hygiene became nonexistent. His hair became oily and untended. His skin became dirty and he smelled of musk and sweat like an animal in the wild. He was not alone. This was a seaman's life and none more profound than those sailing under flags of convenience. They were an international brotherhood of mariners who for any number of reasons could not or chose not to work under their nation's flags.

Their stories all varied but they were all the same. It may be they were hiding from ex-wives, or in some cases, the law. They may have had their mariner documents revoked (for any number of reasons) and found refuge under Liberian documents. It may be they were drunks, druggies, or reprobates that fell below the low expectations other nations held for their seamen. In Ian's case, he was running away from the uncompromising demands of his tyrannical mother and the rigid plan she had in mind for him. She had told him, "I demand and expect nothing less. You will, with grace, honor, and if necessary, an iron fist rule and with Machiavellian cunning assume control of the dynasty your family has built for generations." He could hear the nagging and persistence in his mother's voice. Instead, he tried to find a sense of peace and distance to balance the pain and failure he felt for not meeting the lofty expectations set before him. Maybe with Susan's support and love it may be different.

Ian gathered his clothes from the floor, pulled them on, and laced up his boots. He reached for a cassette tape and loaded his Sony player. He pushed the play button and was surrounded by Journey's, "Lights." Ian drifted off to his home and his mother and the excitement and beauty of Amsterdam where cobblestone roads and canals ringed the city and boats transited the canals, painted in bright colors. All this was visible through the windows of his city home. *I miss my youth and how simple life used to be.* The walls seemed to close in on him.

There were still several hours of daylight before the evening meal and he needed the fresh air. Ian left his stateroom and walked around the ship to see any changes since he'd left five months ago.

He moved down to the main deck. The ship was empty and rode high in the water. Ian was nearly forty feet above the surface and had a commanding view of the horizon. There was nothing but water and a few fishing vessels working off in the distance. The warm sea breeze was invigorating and the bright sun warmed his forehead. He removed his shirt; his eyes were drawn to the deteriorated steel railings that lined the deck. Their purpose was to keep mariners safely aboard. Many of the secondary rails had rusted through and been discarded over the side. No apparent effort has been made to replace or repair the dilapidated sections. "Damn owners, damn captain," Ian grumbled under his breath.

The decks were rusted and plate welds pitted and neglected. The deck machinery, like the mooring winches, was heavily corroded. Their bearings longed for grease. The machinery wiring lay open and exposed to the elements.

Ian continued forward to the bow and climbed the ladder to the "eyes of the ship." The foredeck told a story of neglect and torture. Ian shook his head and said, "she's a good ship and deserves better. Like a beautiful woman married into an abusive relationship, the Amore Islander is dying at the hands of a violent and twisted partner."

Ian continued along the port side. It was more of the same. He accepted his share of the responsibility, for he had been a member of the crew for years and had done nothing to reverse the neglect.

By choice, Ian was only the third mate. He stood a bridge watch and oversaw cargo and ballast operations under the close oversight of the chief mate. It's easy work and allowed him time to reflect and hide with little responsibility. At one time, he wanted to be the captain and command a ship of his own. But time and his lack of commitment had stolen away those dreams.

Back on the stern Ian saw more decay. One of the mooring winches had broken free from its mounting. The deck was covered in orange rust scale. A large section of the railing was missing and replaced by rope that the bosun hastily made-up. "She has really gone down fast and the bottom of this trajectory must be close at hand," he mumbled.

Ian climbed down the aft deck hatch and through an open door to the steering engine room where he entered the bosun's locker. The locker was filthy, dark, and smelled of damp hemp. The steering room floor was covered in oil, from the leaking hydraulic steering system. In the dim light, he nearly fell as the ship moved underfoot. The space was loud and the vibration excessive from the propeller directly beneath the room. The throbbing sound reported the propeller's rotation as it thrashed angrily through the water. He thought, *This is, without a doubt, the worst place on the ship.* The machinery growled and hummed as the hydraulic rams moved the rudder back and forth. The steering engine, a large hydraulic system; worked twenty-four/seven when the ship was underway. Without it, the ship couldn't be steered and this system clearly needed a major overhaul. "No money for the engineers, either," Ian said under his breath. I've seen enough for now."

He walked out of the steering room and up on deck and with determinate strides moved forward to get away from the sound and vibration. He squinted his eyes and let the sun and salty air caress his face. He was out of the belly of the ship and saw the rolling waves and vast horizon around him, all seemed right with the world again.

The evening meal was just about ready and he could smell the food being prepared by the stewards below. Is anything better than this?   He thought of Susan and the softness of her touch.

*She's a hooker… what am I doing? No she's your soul mate.* He snapped out of his daydream. He knew, he was hopelessly in love.

**First Watch at Sea,**
**Gulf of Mexico**
**Heading: Southwest**

With the heavily seasoned meal of fatty pork and wilted vegetables grinding around in his belly, Ian remembered why he lost so much weight on this ship. He shoved down the food one bite at a time. The meal was one step short of disgusting. It was obvious the stewards prepared marginal, even expired food from the waterfront vendor. The Amore Islander bought what no other ship or restaurant would. The steward's imagination made the meals as close to "good" as anyone could, but the poor old man had just about run out of tricks.

With his stomach protesting the meal he'd just wolfed down, Ian got out of his seat, thanked the stewards and retired to the officer's lounge to relax before his watch. The lounge was quiet and an almost forgotten place on the ship. A carry-over from another time in the Amore Islander's history, the lounge was large and ornately paneled with comfortable furniture. The room was nearly half of the Senior Officer level along the starboard side, with an up-scale wooden bar, mirrors, and empty shelves behind the counter. Stools remained in front of the vacant bar now occupied by ghosts of the "good old days" as they killed time together. Only Ian saw them as they chat among themselves.

Years ago the Amore Islander reigned queen of the bulk carrier fleet. Her designer was a man of vision in an era when men of the sea, in proper surroundings, conducted themselves as gentlemen of refinement. Each stateroom provided its occupant unheard of amenities for the time. The officer's spaces were large, well-appointed, and comfortable. The Amore Islander was a maritime social experiment and a credit to the architects' vision and the original owner's commitment to his crew. Ian read the articles and awards posted under glass which reflected the ship's famous past. It must have been unbelievable. An equal amount of effort was spent to ensure the ship would be a profitable tool with a cutting edge cargo discharge system, too. Comfort and efficiency packed into a ship that was as pleasing to the eye as any liner of the time. A masterpiece for all times.

At least that was the way Ian had envisioned it. With much excitement she was christened in the builder's yard and entered the limelight, her original beauty and poise was now just a thing of a by-gone era.

Alone in the room Ian looked around the once elegant lounge where officers wore their uniforms and their wives enjoyed a drink and the companionship of others. The room was now dusty, neglected, and rarely used. It made him melancholy for the times gone by and the life that must have been wonderful. His imagination danced with visions of the officers conducting themselves as gentlemen, well-groomed, dressed, and accompanied by their wives, and occasionally their children. The ship must have had a calmer feel with women aboard with their husbands. Ian heard soft music in the background, the women's gentle laughter, the smell of cigars and the clinking glasses as a toast was offered. The beautiful women in their dresses alive with color and the warmth of friendship; secure their husbands were nearby. Ian leaned back in a dusty chair as he imagined new carpets and comfortable furniture inviting conversation and relaxation. Ian's attention was drawn to the vision of a steward in a white uniform standing behind the bar as he polished glasses and patiently waited to serve his clientele. *I found Camelot years too late,* Ian thought.

Then his mirage faded out to nothing. He was back to the tattered furniture and threadbare carpeting and moldy odor permeating the air. He liked the room better with the visions and ghosts. This was too much for him to share with his friends or family or they'd have him locked up. This was his secret and his alone. He turned and left the room, and closing the door behind him. He'd be back.

He looked at his watch and said, "Shit, it's that time." He made his way to the mess and looked in the refrigerator. He pulled out the night lunch and made an overstuffed sandwich. He kicked the refrigerator door closed with his foot, headed to his room, and grabbed his jacket. Two more flights of stairs and he was on the bridge. Ian stood for a moment in the lighted ladder-well then passed through the door into the dark bridge.

Standing in the dark Ian saw the dim lights in the chart room and the green glow coming from the radar screen as his eyes slowly adjusted. A seaman was standing in the corner and Dieter was scribbling his entries into the deck log. He looked up. "Hello, Ian."

"Hey there."

"I'll be with you in a minute … let me finish these entries first."

"Sure"

Ian walked forward and gazed out to the horizon. In the distance there were a number of lights from ships and boats.

Ian's watch partner, Carlos, came through the door. "Good evening, Mate." He said, walking over to his counterpart. In the corner they giggled for a moment in their language. Then the other man approached Dieter and requested permission to leave the bridge. Dieter waved his hand and bid him good night and the man disappeared out the bridge wing and down the stairs.

Dieter and Ian discussed the chart and the twenty-hundred (local) position on the chart. Dieter nodded towards the horizon. Dieter pointed to the light on the port bow, "That one is going to the east at twelve knots." Ian eyes glazed over as Dieter gave detailed information on each boat in the area. He would figure all that out for himself later.

"The weather seems to be holding and the visibility good." Dieter finished his turn-over and Ian assumed the watch. Dieter left and Ian and Carlos were alone on the bridge. One more look at the chart and Ian walked over to the coffee maker where Carlos had just made a fresh pot.

"The coffee smells good Carlos." Ian said as he stuck his nose in the warm cup and sipped the brew. Ian glanced at the radar and it confirmed what he saw on the horizon.

"It will be a slow watch, tonight, Carlos."

Carlos looked over with an impish smile and said, "We like them that way, right, Third?"

"Right!"

*Panama*
*Cristobal 9-21'N 79-54'W*
*Balboa 8-57'N 79-34'W*

The transit from Tampa to Cristobal, Panama was a pleasant eight day voyage. The Gulf of Mexico and the Caribbean were calm. The gentle sea breeze kept the temperature comfortable and time passed quickly.

After the Tampa departure, Captain Strauss retired to his cabin and wasn't seen again until the evening before arrival. It was out of character, but it was no secret he was a drunk.

Strauss was sprawled out on his mattress, the floor around his bed littered with liquor bottles. Some days he managed to get out of bed to splash cold water on his face and make a slow attempt at getting dressed. Ultimately, he just made it to the head to relieve himself and make another drink.

No matter, the officers and crew ran the ship with ease ... they'd been on this route before and there was no need for concern, in fact things ran better without the "old man" around anyway.

The Amore Islander was under a lucky star the day it arrived in Cristobal. The ship was given permission to move directly to the awaiting Gatun Locks. The canal pilot, a commissioner and an immigration officer boarded the ship at the sea buoy.

The pilot was an American and had all the attitude and confidence of a Texas cowboy. Tall and dressed in white, he walked onto the bridge and took command of the ship.

The other officials were Panamanian, wearing ridiculous uniforms with one hand out for themselves and the other out for their agency. Strauss was busy clearing the administrivia of canal passage. The captain must have been on his game because by the time the ship crossed the sill of the first lock, the commissioner had assessed the ship and levied the transit fee and immigration had cleared the ship. The Panama officials were very efficient. The commissioner and the immigration officer were off to the next ship, their employers paid and their "personal interests" handsomely compensated.

The pilot commanded the ship through the harbor to the first of three successive locks, sliding the one-hundred and six feet wide Amore Islander through the one-hundred and ten feet wide canal. It was a tight squeeze all the way around, as the ship was eight-hundred and fifty feet long and the lock was only nine-hundred feet long.

"The designer of this ship was a genius," Ian mumbled, "If the ship were any bigger they would have to make the long and dangerous passage around

Cape Horn." He gazed at the small Panamanian city of Cristobal, admiring the buildings favoring Spanish architecture with stucco walls and bright colors. Although he'd been through the canal many times, he'd never been ashore to explore the clean, quiet town … *maybe someday*, he thought.

The pilot maneuvered the ship to the entrance of the first lock. The crew stood in small groups forward, midships, and aft and received lines from the line handlers on the canal walls. The lines were made-up to tractors called "mules" and the mules, under the pilot's command, pull the ship into the lock. As the ship was nearly half way in the lock a second set of mules passed a line to the crew on deck and they helped pull the ship. The mules adjusted line tension to keep the ship within two feet of the lock sides.

A third pair of mules connected aft and the ship was gently positioned into the lock. The gate closed and the lock flooded. The ship gently rose and the mules adjusted the line tension to keep the ship in position. The Gatun Locks were three successive locks that raised ships eighty five feet above the Atlantic Ocean to Gatun Lake. The process became routine and the crew killed time basking in the tropical sun smoking cheap cigarettes. Gatun Lake was man-made and alleviated the need to excavate the entire forty-five mile length of the transit. In addition, it provided the source of water for the lock system on both the Atlantic and Pacific sides. Ian thought, *it's a strange site for an ocean going ship to be in a fresh water lake surrounded by jungle. Beautiful but strange.*

Ian and most seamen transiting the canal agreed the most spectacular part of the transit was Galland Cut. As the ship, eighty-five feet above sea level it passed through the Continental Divide and its stately cliffs, Ian had trouble keeping his mind on his job. The Amore Islander and her crew were grossly out of place in the face of so much beauty. *I'll have to remember to describe this to Susan,* he mused.

After Galland Cut the ship approached the Pedro Miguel Locks. Again the pilot, with help from the mechanical mules, moved the aging ship towards the lock. The identical procedure was followed. This time however, after the lock was closed, the water was removed and the Amore Islander gently settled thirty feet.

The lock opened and the pilot directed the ship to the Mira Flores Locks. Two more locks dropped the ship to the Pacific Ocean level. Thirty hours and fifteen minutes, total transit time. Ian noted the time in the logbook. Ahead was the vast expanse of Balboa Harbor and the Pacific Ocean beyond it.

Ian looked out at Balboa. It had none of the greatness of Cristobal; instead it possessed the seediness of most port cities. The buildings were dull and dirty. The people were less friendly. It was a necessary evil needed to support the canal, and the servicemen from the local U.S military bases. It was a thriving port haunt with ample bars and brothels.

The ship maneuvered to the duty-free anchorage. After twenty hours on his feet, Ian's back hurt and his eyes were getting heavy. He spent as much time as he could on the bridge wing with his face in the wind. No time for sleep now. The crew and I will sleep hard later.

Neil and his deck gang were on the forecastle and readied the port anchor. The pilot put the ship in a suitable location; the captain nodded and growled the order to release the port anchor into his radio. Neil acknowledged the command and released the anchor, the fact confirmed by a loud rattle of chain running out the chain locker, through the hawse pipe, and into the teal-colored Pacific. Its violence was controlled by the windless brake. Regardless, a cloud of dust, rust, mud and scale went up the nostrils of anyone in the vicinity. The pilot gave a slight backing bell to ensure the chain didn't pile up on the bottom. Strauss crooked into his radio again, "Six shots at the water's edge."

"Aye, Captain." Six shots, five-hundred and forty feet of chain measure from the water's edge to the anchor was ordered and carried out.

FINISHED WITH ENGINES... The pilot and captain went below and Ian took the opportunity to sit for ten minutes in the only seat in the wheelhouse; the captain's chair. No one sits in the captain's chair but the captain. "Fuck it. I'm exhausted," Ian grumbled.

The stay in the duty free anchorage would be short. The prearranged fuel barge came alongside and the weary deck gang tied it to the ship. The engineers, who were just as exhausted, lined up the fuel manifold and coordinated bunkering with the barge operator. Refueling was estimated to take ten hours.

Along the starboard side another smaller boat came alongside and the crew raced to meet it. The boat brought provisions, minimal spare parts, and the crew's orders for duty free alcohol. The owner's one concession was to allow crewmembers to consume booze aboard. Before leaving Tampa a list of individual orders for alcohol was compiled by the steward and sent ahead for delivery in Balboa. It would be a long time before the crew could get ashore, so Ian requested eight cases of Holstein beer.

The deck gang used a small boom and winch to bring the cases over the rail one at a time. "Don't drop my beer you devils" Ian yelled down from the bridge wing forty feet above them.

"No worry, Mate." The bosun responded, looking up at Ian. Both men were barely able to stand they were so exhausted.

"Hell, I hope so." Ian mumbled to himself and returned to the chair. Two more hours.

Later that evening, the steward knocked on Ian's door and delivered his beer.

"Great!" Ian, standing there with a towel wrapped around his waist, paid him on the spot and the steward left to deliver the rest of the crew's orders.

Duty free anchorages were two edged swords. Fuel and food were tax free and benefited the owners, but the crew was stuck aboard, captives kept within sight of land, ladies and booze. The Amore Islander crew was especially antsy because they knew the next port, San Nicolas, Peru had no town or facilities and the next leg of the voyage was thirty-one days to Japan. Two months with no liberty and no women. While the crew's restlessness and edginess would only manifest itself in trouble, their captain kept his secret.

### San Nicolas, Peru
### Ship Loading Facility
### 15-25.6'S 75-9.5'W

One in the morning and Ian was back on the bridge after a short and unsatisfying nap. The air was still and the sea flat. A small swell moved with no particular speed or direction. Bunkering was completed and the barge released. The rusty barge and its anemic tug made their way back into the harbor. The black smoke belching from the tug so dense it was visible even in the dead of night.

Neil was forward with a few deckhands, the captain and Ian were on the bridge. Preparations made; the engine room readied … the captain called, "DEAD SLOW AHEAD…Rudder midships"

Carlos centered the rudder and Ian rung up the engine order telegraph. The ship rumbled and came to life. After a moment the captain called, "ALL STOP" and the engine stopped. Ian heard the port windlass grind away as the anchor chain was pulled on deck and deposited into the chain locker. To bring six shots back aboard took twenty minutes. Ian and Strauss had time for a cup of coffee as they waited on the bridge, the activity on the forecastle continued. After what

308

seemed like an eternity, Neil reported the anchor was aweigh and the chain strained under the weight as the anchor swung under the ship. Ian marked the time in the log book then turned-off the deck lights and turned-on the running lights. This was routine for the men aboard. The radio crackled, "the anchor was clear of the water." The captain turned to Ian, "DEAD SLOW AHEAD." The engine coughed to life and the Amore Islander was under way and making way. *It's a good feeling to be moving again,* thought Ian. Neil called the bridge and reported, "Anchor, secured for sea. Captain, may we secure forward?"

"Yes"

"Aye, Captain. Good night."

A grunt back to the mate was Strauss' response. With that, Neil and the gang moved aft. They could be seen walking back along the darkened deck, their flashlights nervously moved back and forth in rhythm as they stepped. They made haste to their rooms and the beds that awaited them.

It was a dark night. The captain maneuvered the ship out of the anchorage and weaved around ships as they lay at anchor. Balboa was a busy anchorage full of vessels waiting their turn to go east through the canal. The captain turned to Ian and said, "San Nicolas ... set sea speed for one-hundred-three RPMs. The watch is yours." With that, the captain left the bridge.

Ian looked out at the vast and beautiful Pacific Ocean. *You're a lady tonight.* The ship, in ballast and at sea speed, cut through the water at fifteen point six knots. The Amore Islander was nearly motionless except the vibration of her machinery and the throbbing of the propeller as it chewed up the water and pushed it behind. The ocean gently rolled the ship as it cradled her exhausted crew through their first night on the Pacific. Ian and Carlos did everything they could to stay awake and alert until relieved.

Ian looked over the chart and called for course one-nine-two true and Carlos turned the helm to bring the ship on course. Visibility was unlimited and occasionally they saw ships in the distance ahead or on the starboard quarter heading to or from Balboa. All in all, it was a quiet watch. Ian looked up to see Neil waiting to relieve him. They chatted for a moment or two and turned over the watch. Ian staggered to his stateroom, his eyelids heavy.

Through the door he stripped off his clothes and dropped them in a pile on the floor. He crawled into his rack and was asleep before his head hit the pillow. The last two days had been hell.

The next port, San Nicolas, was located about one-hundred miles north of Lima, Peru. There was nothing there except an iron ore mining facility and a minimal port facility to load ships. It was in the middle of nowhere with no customs, immigration,

coast guard or government agents around.
Opportunity for the less scrupulous abounded. All the
crew knew was there were no restaurants, no bars and
no girls. Going ashore offered those poor souls
nothing but the opportunity to stretch their legs.

It was six days voyage south of Panama. The
Amore Islander coasted along Columbia and Ecuador;
the ship crossed the equator without ceremony. No
pollywogs in this crew. The Galapagos Islands were
barely visible to starboard, and then it coasted along
Peru until San Nicolas rose over the horizon to port.
*The Pacific was a lady the whole transit.*

Arrival was straight forward. At the right
moment, the port anchor was dropped under the ship
as it headed into the dock to stop the vessel before it
ran aground. Two grossly underpowered tugs helped
as much as they could. No pilot or authorities were
there in the wild frontier.

Before the ship was tied to the pier, the local
facilities' representative boarded the ship. He and
Strauss spoke in hushed tones and adjourned to the
captain's office. The door was closed and the details
ironed out.  The ship would receive a bill of lading for
approximately seventy-six thousand tons of high
grade iron ore. The ship would actually carry an
additional thirty thousand tons of undocumented
cargo that would go undocumented. For that
"miscalculation" the facilities rep had been

handsomely paid by a mysterious visitor the week before.

Everything went just as the visitor had explained to the captain back in Tampa. The ship would be severely overloaded with thousands of ocean miles ahead.

The captain blotted at the nervous sweat streaming down his temples while he and the rep drank Scotch before parting company.
"Oh by the way," said the rep as he passed out the door. "We have a labor issue going on and there are some snipers in the hills taking pot shots at the workers and ship's crew on deck …nothing to worry about. No one has been hit yet."

Cargo operations commenced, the iron pellets delivered by conveyor belt and dropped into the cavernous holds. The ore was heavy and dirty. In minutes the crew and the ship were covered in fine black dust.

Forty hours later, the ship would be full and on its way across the Pacific, heading to the Far East.

# WALKING THROUGH HELL

## *Over Laden … Storm Ahead*
## *San Nicolas*

The government nationalized the mining operation at San Nicolas in the early seventies. Like everything nationalized by governments, the equipment was neglected, the skilled labor lost and management became shackled. This facility had become the "poster child" to government inefficiency and business incompetence.

For some reason the bureaucratically installed management fired all of the local labor from the native villages in the region. These were simple men who slaved to provide a meager existence for their struggling families. As a group they had a reputation as honest and hard-working. Ian knew many of them from previous visits and he was left with the impression they depended on the mine and port for work, there was no other employment in the region. The decision replaced all of them with labor from the capital city. *Where was the wisdom in that?* Ian thought.

An ongoing feud ensued between the displaced workers and management. During the Amore Islander's port call the feud had notched-up to

313

a boiling point when one of the native women had
been run over by a company truck. The truck didn't
stop and there was no effort to investigate or
compensate the victim's family. The local paper
reported some of the locals had claimed the incident
was intentional and the accusation fueled up the
already angry men who took their weapons and
disappeared into the surrounding hills. From behind
trees or rocks they routinely took shots at the workers
at both the mining and loading facilities. Occasionally
they took shots at the crew on deck, too. Their rifles
were old and inaccurate and the shooters had neither
the skill or motivated to hit their targets, so it was an
acknowledged nuisance.

"Hell," Ian told Neil, "Here we are in this
third world shit hole on a third world shit hole ship
being shot at by third world assholes. We must have
our heads where the sun don't shine." They laughed
together, but their eyes were dull when they
exchanged knowing looks. The cargo operations
continued. The crew looked forward to clearing the
breakwater for the open sea.

Half way through the loading operations,
Strauss called Neil to his office. Neil came directly
from deck. His overalls, hands, and face black from
the ore dust. If everyone didn't look the same it
would have been comical. Neil stood in the doorway
with narrowed eyebrows and a toe-tapping boot. He

needed to be on deck managing cargo operations. "What's up, Captain?"

Strauss reached for the bottle of Scotch whiskey that he'd become too familiar with since Tampa. "Neil, come in and sit. Don't mind the mess. Here let me pour you a drink." Neil sat fidgeting on the settee as Strauss poured two drinks, handed one to his mate, closed the door to his office and returned to his desk.

"The Amore Islander has been sold and will be headed to the breaker yard after Oita." That much was true but the rest was a lie ..." The owner has washed his hands of the ship and the crew. I can't pay you or the rest of the crew. There will be no more provisions and the only money left, the ten-thousand dollars in the safe. The owners won't pay to fly us home. They've taken every penny. There's only one option ... but I need help." He paused and tugged at the collar of his dirty shirt, as if he was choking. "We're in a backwater port without authority over-site. The transit, thirty-one days and we'll be alone the whole way."

Neil listened, his jaw dropping to his chest. The glass of Scotch remained untouched. The captain continued, "If we load thirty thousand tons over our load limit, I've been guaranteed that the freight for the overage will be provided to the officers and crew to cover wages, expense, and travel and a little more for you and me ... Well?"

Neil's hand tightened around his glass until his knuckles turned white. "Captain, you know that I had been party to 'overing' several thousand tons knowing we would burn that in fuel before we arrived at the discharge port. But thirty thousand tons is nearly thirty-percent overage. That's dangerous and criminal. The ship may sink or break her back if we hit any bad weather. We'll be a long way from shelter in the event of a typhoon. How about the authorities in Japan? What happens if we get caught? It's jail time, Captain! I can't do that again!"

"I know" said the captain softly and he went on. "As for the authorities, we will discreetly meet a small bulk vessel south of Okinawa near an uninhabited island and discharge the thirty thousand tons and then proceed to Oita." Strauss looked into Neil's stormy eyes and flinched.

Neil stood up and set the untouched whiskey down on the desk and said, "No, Captain. I won't be party to this. I must resign immediately. I'll leave the ship at the end of this shift." Neil turned and left the office.

Captain Strauss said, "Shit," and reached into his desk pulled out a small piece of paper and dialed the number his visitor had left.

"Hello"

"He won't do it."

"I understand … I'll take care of it."

The phone was dead in Strauss' hand.

316

## WALKING THROUGH HELL

Neil walked out on deck and shook his head, his fists trembling. He heard a smattering of bullets from the natives on the hillside in the distance. Then a bullet pierced his temple. He slumped and fell forward, dead before his body hit the deck.

The crew was told it was a stray bullet from the native sharpshooters. "An accident, it was an unfortunate accident." Strauss assured the crew.

Neil's body was quietly removed from the ship with the assurance it would be sent back to the Isle of Man and properly buried.

"The owner's agent will tend to all the details," Strauss promised the concerned crewmembers.

Neil's body was carefully placed in the ambulance as the crew watched from the rail of the ship. The vehicle moved away in a cloud of dust on the winding road toward the distant gate. Later when the ambulance was out of site and long before cargo operations had resumed, the body was dumped alongside the road three miles outside the facility gate. The crew would be none the wiser.

Strauss called the mates together and told them he alone would take-over loading the ship. Dieter and Ian would stand six hour bridge watches in a six-on-six-off rotation until they arrived in Japan and another mate replaced Neil.

Ian's friend was gone. The captain's secret remained intact. The crew's fate sealed. None of them

317

were the wiser as the ship loaded deeper and deeper in to the sea.

*We must be alright* … Ian hoped but he knew there was more to Neil's death. *It was no accident*. He wrote a hurried note to his mother and another to Susan. In these notes he revealed his concern and suspicion in rushed thoughts. He mailed the letter to his mother but at the last minute tore up the letter to Susan. He didn't want to concern her.

The next day was calm and departure uneventful. The ship's course was set at two-nine-three true. The same monotonous course the Amore Islander maintained for the next month and the crew settled in for the long slow transit.

Typhoon Diana wasn't even on the weathermen's watch list yet. The captain stayed in his office as he falsified the ship's logs to protect the owner under the inclement weather provision in the charter to buy time to rendezvous with the smaller ship. If all went well, the Japanese steel maker would be none the wiser, the Amore Islander's owner richer, and the North Koreans would have something they desperately needed … high grade iron ore.

# WALKING THROUGH HELL

## *As the Demons of Hell Scream*
### *Approximate Position*
### *19-38.3'N 163-7.3'E*

Weeks later the skies were stormy and dark, sheets of heavy rain fell from the heavens and the winds howled. The Amore Islander groaned as it labored in Typhoon Diana's violence. The storm had unleashed the demons of hell upon the helpless ship. It mattered little that she was the size of a one-hundred story building and heavier than the combined weight of the automobiles stuck in a Cross Island Expressway traffic jam; the ship was tossed about like a beach ball at a rock concert.

Old and tired, the Amore Islander was laden with nearly thirty percent more cargo than the ship had been designed to carry. The cargo had been carelessly stowed and shifted in the holds due to Strauss' greed and lack of conscience. Now, caught in the jaws of a Pacific typhoon and no place to run, the ship and her crew were in dire straits. With no options left, Strauss quietly retired to his cabin like a cowardly fool. The fate of the ship and her crew had been carelessly cast before the merciful gods and unrelenting devils; whocver was hungrier for these wretched souls would win the prize. The dark and angry sea grew more confused and the winds howled like an ungodly beast. Lightening fractured the sky and thunder drove all hope from the men's hearts. Fast moving swells reached thirty feet in height and towered over the straining deck. Steeper and steeper the waves grew as the storm deepened. Violent winds tore off the wave tops and drove them horizontally against the hull with such force it could crush a man's skull like a melon.

The ship, like a person under duress, made guttural, raspy groans and quick, jerky movements. The Amore Islander moaned again as it labored under the tons of water crossing its decks and the heavy rolls that generated forces that tore at the weakened hull. Screeching mewls were heard by the crew, like Dante demons in Inferno. The violent movement made it all but impossible for the crew to move. Only the bravest dared; their movement slow, deliberate, and cautiously holding on each step of the way.

Normally, the crew gathered in common spaces to spend time together. Tonight the unnerving sounds and convulsive motion put an end to that. The crew inched their way to their rooms, crawled into their racks, and made peace with their God.

Thousands of miles from safety and squarely in the jaws of a monster storm; no one aboard was unaffected. The loud and confident became silent and withdrawn. The most timid of the crew were outwardly frightened and sobbing. The officers had long since retired to their staterooms, concerned with their own affairs … and Strauss had not been seen in twelve hours.

With laborious effort, Ian entered the bridge with a sandwich in one hand and the quart of milk in the other. Ian set the milk in the refrigerator inside the door to the left and then he walked into the chart room where he saw Dieter. His face had a greenish-yellow cast and he hugged a bucket to his chest. Ian took a step back when Dieter started gagging. "Whoa! Never seen you seasick before!" Ian said. *We're west of Hawaii by a thousand miles or so; no ships, islands or anything to hit, I'll fix our position for him as soon as I finish my sandwich,* Ian thought. He never guessed Dieter hadn't updated the chart in over four hours.

Ian swallowed the last bit of crust and went to check on his friend Carlos in the wheelhouse. It took him a while, the ship careened like nothing he had ever seen before. Stumbling and swaying worse than after a week-long bender, Ian held on to the rails. He squinted to see through the heavy rain. The ship rolled deeply and he found himself looking down into the sea and seconds later the ocean was replaced by the stormy sky.

Christ, this is worse than I thought! He was about to change course to reduce the battering the ship and her men were taking when he glanced into the corner.

Carlos was huddled there, clinging to the rail as if his life depended on it.

"Carlos, I need you at the helm. We will change course." It was hard to see forward. The rain pelted against the windows. Carlos' face was grey and his bulging eyes were blinking at an erratic pace. Ian feared he may be catatonic.

Outside the winds drove the water across the deck and the mountainous swells crashed over the bow, rolling down the deck; some as far back as the house seven-hundred feet away. Then all hell broke loose and Carlos screamed.

Ian looked over at him and then forward in time to see a sixty foot wall stand before the bow and engulf the forward third of the ship. The Amore Islander stopped in it tracks and pitched forward. The house shook violently and then, a terrible noise stopped their hearts. Steel groaned, twisted, and snapped. The deck cracked open near hold five and the bow twisted to the right and severed from the rest of the ship. Now unstable, the aft portion of the ship rolled to the left. Ian, still holding on, stood there helplessly. The Amore Islander's back was broken.

## *The Captain's Final Hours*

Strauss locked himself in his office with the one joy in life that never disappointed him – Scotch whiskey. The six empty bottles that rolled around on the office floor were testimonial to their one-sided love affair. They moved back and forth, thrown around by the sea's motion. The bottles clanked as they somersaulted along the deck; proof the ship was no longer under command. The only other person qualified to assume command had been ruthlessly murdered two weeks before.

The captain sobbed like a child as he sat in his chair. His hands shook, his clothes stained with sweat, tears, and urine as he drowned in cowardliness, greed, manipulation, and criminal disregard. His guilt from Neil's murder and the peril the ship faced drove him bat-shit crazy.

Like all weak men, he wouldn't accept responsibility for the mess he made, preferring to play the victim in his twisted mind. Everything seemed to close in around Strauss and he slowly suffocated in the shrinking room. He drank deeply and directly from his last bottle of Scotch. With the bottle in one hand, he slouched, leaning forward to brace against the violent motion of the ship. He lowered his face down near the sticky and stained surface. His greasy and balding head only inches from desk lamp, duct taped to the metal surface. In a nightmare of movement, filth, misery and hopelessness, he struggled to pull a pleasant memory from the recesses of his mind. Tears running down his cheeks and knees trembling, he thought back to his youth.

He closed his eyes and could smell the North Sea. The sounds and the familiar odors of his hometown Rostock, Germany fueled his feeble mind. He saw his father sitting in an easy chair, the consummate educator. He was a slight man with thick glasses perched on his large nose. Strauss remembered his father as a quiet man who avoid confrontation at all cost, preferring to put his nose in a book ... safely barricaded in his study. Strauss thought about the hours he and his father spent fishing in the harbor with a simple pole and pieces of sardines. They watched the ships in the harbor and the shipyards busy building Hitler's navy. His father told stories about faraway places only accessible by ship and Strauss remembered it was then that he became fascinated with ships and the adventures that lay over the horizon.

The Amore Islander dove into a sea and shook, Strauss grabbed the desk and whimpered and thought of his mother, Anna. She was a good Christian woman content with running a proper

German home in the Neinpreen district where she raised three children under both her's and God's guiding hands. Helmut remembered the color of her hair and the sound of her soothing voice as she called him out of a pleasant slumber each morning. She was a woman of faith and loyalty to her God, her husband and her family.

Strauss shook as he remembered wartime Germany. It didn't go well for the Nazis nor for the hundreds of thousands of families in Europe like the Strauss'. Helmut's safe and secure childhood was shattered as the war went from bad to worse. The sites, the hunger and pain changed him forever. He cringed.

By now, Strauss was bawling, he took a deep pull from the bottle and not knowing why, threw it against the bulkhead. It shattered into a thousand pieces and the alcohol dripped slowly down the wall.

Strauss, so far gone, opened memories he'd suppressed for years. Any hope of climbing out of his depression ended as he relived watching his father's murder at knife point by a retreating SS officer over a piece of stale bread and the nightmare of helplessly watching his mother and two sisters repeatedly raped by the Soviet hordes as they drove on Berlin. When the men were done, the women were murdered. Just as in nineteen forty five, Strauss' soul was void, he was alone and scared. He sobbed and trembled, a broken man.

At that moment, the killer wave boarded the ship, the end was upon them. The unbearable sound of the hull tearing itself in half startled him back to consciousness. The ship rolled to port and the blood curdling sounds of men screaming as they drowned was the last things he heard and felt. The captain grabbed his pistol and took the easy way out.

## *Her Back Broken, She Sinks in Two Minutes*
## *Position: Unknown*

Carlos was frozen as the aft section of the ship rolled over to the left. He began to pray through his tears. There was no time for the general alarm, call the captain, or even alert the poor souls in the engine room. The storm raged and the bow section began to sink from the back. Hold number five sunk first as the bow rose to the sky in defiance, the seas swirled around it and in an instant the whole bow section dropped below the boiling surface. A large bubble of air escaped, if to, temporarily mark the location and the sea momentarily opened up, then violently closed behind the bow as it dove quickly to the ocean bottom. Carlos and Ian were the only witnesses.

The stern section of the stricken vessel continued its roll over. Carlos and Ian looked at each other in panic. Not a word between them. The ship was in one slow death roll and soon lay on its side. The winds and sea continued to pound the ship without sympathy. Cold water rushed through the bridge port door and the windows around the wheelhouse began to break. The ocean came in from all sides. There was no use trying to get to the life

327

boats – they were either flooded or inaccessible. The two men stared at each other, but neither could speak. The other forty-one souls aboard dealt with their own destiny and there was nothing anyone could do to change it.

It may be best to die in the sinking ship than brave the extreme weather only to drown later. Only Carlos and Ian had the option, the others would drown in their bunks without a chance for survival.

The broken ship sank from the front first and in a moment it was vertical, the now stationary propeller poised in the air. Carlos and Ian were about eighty feet above the churning sea facing straight down into the cauldron of death. The ship held still for what seemed like an eternity. There was a series of loud explosions from inside the hull as the bulkheads began to collapse and water rushed into the holds, engine room, and the house where men's screams were being suffocated with gallons of water. Ian's eyes filled with tears. "We're done for. I'm sorry mother, I'm sorry Susan." His mouth formed the silent words.

Another tormented sound of steel letting go drove his stomach to his knees. The ship began her final plunge to the bottom. Ian looked at Carlos, his old friend. They whispered, "Goodbye," to one another.

The last of the Amore Islander dove into the boiling sea. The frigid water stole Ian's breath as it came rushing into the wheelhouse for the second time. Deeper the ship sped to the bottom and Ian could do nothing to resist. The frigid water grew darker and darker and the pressure crushed the remaining air from his lungs.

Numb and nearly unconscious, he saw a bright light shining. He reached out with his left hand and held onto Susan's memory and it seemed dream-like. *I love you Susan, forgive me.* Her image burned in his heart and soul. Then he reached out with his right hand to the image of his mother. *I love you mother. I am so sorry that I have failed you and the family. Please forgive me.*

Ian and his shipmates were committed to the deep for eternity.

Somewhere in his subconscious or the dream that carried Ian to his death, he focused on Susan. Her eyes burned into his soul, her hair reflected the light of the bright summer sunshine. She had always been the woman of Ian's dreams on the Rio de Janeiro beach. She was the one.

She had been there for him all along and it wasn't until death that it was so clear to him. She was his soul mate and he'd been given that opportunity, only to squander it.

Ian's final thought in this life … *Together we could have had a good life, raised a family, and grown old together. There were so many things I should have told you, so many promises I should have kept and so much life we should have experienced together.* As Ian left his body, he prayed she would somehow understand what he had discovered in death.

At that moment … thousands of miles away, Susan thought about Ian and she started to sob. She wondered, *What if* … and felt a cold chill pass through her. For some unknown reason, she knew she'd never see him again. Ian looked down at Susan and attempted to embrace and console her. Alas … he softly kissed her cheek and walked into the bright light. Ian van der Waterlaan was now only a memory.

Susan stood at the window with tears streaming down her rouged cheeks. Her young daughter clung to her waist. "Mommy, what's wrong?"

"I'm not sure, baby," Susan said, stroking the little one's hair. "There's just something not right."

Thousands of miles East in Amsterdam, a mother received news of the ship's disappearance and the same day a letter arrived from her son, postmarked from San Nicolas, Peru. She wouldn't open the letter until she knew whether her son Ian van der Waterlaan was alive or dead.

### *The Cycle Continues*
### *Hong Kong*

Two months later, Y.G. Yang Shipping Company; Hong Kong received notice their agreed value rider to the insurance policy would be honored by the underwriter. The authorities determined the ship was properly manned and properly loaded with seventy-six thousand tons of iron ore at San Nicolas. The ship was kept within classification and Liberian Maritime standards. The official report called the loss an "unfortunate accident."

The protection and indemnity insurance covered compensation for the families and any liability to creditors. The North Korean transaction remained invisible and carefully concealed by its government.

Records of the overage had long since been covered up in San Nicolas. So to the world, and any prying eyes, Super Typhoon Diana was blamed for the accident.

Y.G. Yang was a clever man who had all the angles covered. He sat behind his large desk with a drink of expensive Bourbon in his hand. He looked out the fifty-sixth floor window down onto the Hong

Kong Harbor. His slender young female assistant stood behind him and caressed his shoulders and nibbled on his ear. He chuckled at how well everything had worked out. He was just about to invite his assistant to lock the door when his receptionist rang, "Mr. Yang, you have a visitor." He looked into the eyes of the pretty woman next to him. *She'll have to wait.* He waved his hand and dismissed her. She slipped out the side door, smiling seductively as she pulled it closed behind her.

"Send him in," Yang spoke into the intercom.

In walked the Man in the Black Suit. He sat down in front of the desk, his calculating eyes assessed the owner.

The Yang was a heavy Asian man with skin pulled so tightly over his excessively round body that he looked like a balloon. The phone rang again. He lifted the phone and listened intently. A smile came over his fat face. I'm one-hundred million dollars richer today. Not a bad trade for a rusty old ship and forty-four seamen no one will miss anyway.

The insurance company had paid in full. He placed the phone back on the receiver and rubbed his belly as if he had just finished a delicious meal.

He looked across the desk and said, "Well the Amore Islander case is closed. Your timing is perfect. Your share will be wired to any account you choose. Let me know by tomorrow and I'll transfer the money myself."

The Man in the Black Suit nodded and half smiled. He got up and, without a word headed to the door. Before he reached the exit, the sound of gunfire echoed through the room as bullets tore a fist sized piece of flesh from his back. He spun around and faced Yang. Yang smiled, his pistol dangling from his finger.

"Nothing personal, its only business," was the last thing the fat man ever said. The Man in the Black Suit drew his pistol with lightning speed and fired three rounds, removing Yang's nose, eyes and forehead so Yang would enter Hell fifteen seconds ahead of his killer.

### *The End*
***

## *About the Author*

The author was raised in the rolling hills of Marin County, not far from the Golden Gate Bridge. He grew up on and around the San Francisco Bay and it was there he developed a keen passion for sailing, merchant ships, and the foreign ports they frequent. He pursued a career in the maritime industry where he spent 27 years between afloat and ashore assignments.

Most of these stories are the product of his imagination. Others were influenced by his personal experiences.

Today the author is semi-retired and living in New England where he spends time with his wife exploring the New England coastline, its harbors and inlets aboard their boat.

\*\*\*

## WALKING THROUGH HELL

If you enjoyed *Built to Walking Through Hell,* please consider my other books including: *Drawn to the Sea / Torn Between Destiny and Desire / Gentleman Pirate / Two Warriors Collide/ Bonnie Mae / The Cursed Seven / Leviathan and Death of a Liberian Seaman / Lobstah / Delivery Captain / Longboard Mike / Unlikely Mariner /Accidental Heir and You'll Never Get Out Alive.*

*Rex Inverness*

*Contact me at: rex.inverness@gmail.com*
*Check out: www.rex-inverness.com*

MV2

Maritime Fiction Novels
Bristol, Rhode Island
02809
www.rex-inverness.com

Made in the USA
Las Vegas, NV
09 March 2023